Southern Fried Intimacy

Joe R. McClain Jr.

Southern Fried Intimacy

Disclaimer: This book is a work of fiction, and any resemblance to actual persons, living or dead, or events is purely coincidental. Characters, places, and incidents are the product of the author's imagination and are used fictitiously. The intent is not to mirror reality but to explore the realms of possibility and the human experience through the lens of storytelling. While some inspiration may be drawn from real-world elements, the primary goal is to entertain, provoke thought, and evoke emotions. The story unfolds in a universe crafted by the author's artistic license. Readers are invited to interpret the story in their own way, drawing personal meanings and connections. The author's intent may not align with individual interpretations, and the beauty of fiction lies in its ability to be a mirror reflecting diverse perspectives. "Southern Fried Intimacy" may contain content that could be triggering for some readers, including but not limited to mature themes, or sensitive topics. Reader discretion is advised, and we encourage those who may be affected to approach the material with caution.

ISBN-13: 978-0-9996068-3-4

DEDICATION

In this heartfelt story, there is an important woman who holds significance in someone's life. She could easily be someone close to you - a sister, cousin, or a dear friend. Despite the fact that the person in question may not feel any strong negative emotions towards her, their indifference towards her existence is palpable. Nevertheless, deep down, a sense of love for her remains, albeit from a distance - as if standing on the opposite end of a vast expanse. Put it like this. On the perilous cliff of love, with her teetering on the edge and his grasp the only lifeline, he would relinquish her to certain death below. For he discovered that releasing the tendrils of love proves more facile than clinging to the corrosive embrace of toxicity.

Foreword By: The Artist Formerly Known as Commitment

What's the purpose of love if you don't find your purpose with the one you love? This question, at its core, encapsulates the essence of the profound journey we are about to embark upon in the pages of this book. The power of investments in intimate relationships, though often underestimated and overlooked, forms the cornerstone of our emotional and spiritual fulfillment. Love, as we know it, has been celebrated, romanticized, and mythologized throughout the ages. Countless sonnets, songs, and stories have been dedicated to it, and yet, for all its ubiquity, love often remains an elusive, mysterious force in our lives. Many of us seek it, yearn for it, and sometimes even despair over its complexities. But how often do we consider the fundamental role that investments, in various forms, play in nurturing and sustaining the love that is so central to our existence? In this exploration, we dive deep into the multifaceted aspects of investments in intimate relationships. Just as a financial investment can grow and flourish over time, so too can the investments we make in our relationships. These investments are not measured in dollars and cents, but rather in the currency of time, effort, understanding, and commitment. They are the bonds that tie us to our partners, the stocks that build trust, and the dividends that yield emotional wealth. At the heart of this book lies the belief that love is a dynamic and evolving entity. It is not a static, unchanging force but a living, breathing entity that requires nurturing and cultivation. Just as a garden needs care, attention, and effort to flourish, so do our relationships. The more we invest in our relationships, the greater the potential for love to bloom, deepen, and endure. In the chapters that follow, we will embark on a journey through the landscape of investments in intimate relationships. We will explore the various forms these investments can take, from the small, everyday gestures of kindness to the profound acts of vulnerability and selflessness. We will delve into the psychological and emotional principles that underlie these investments, discovering how they can shape the course of our love lives. Our journey will encompass the bonds of trust and communication, the investments in understanding and empathy, and the powerful dividends of shared dreams and growth. We will navigate the complexities of conflict resolution, forgiveness, and resilience in the face of life's challenges. We will examine the role of passion, intimacy, and the enduring power of human connection in the context of love and relationships. Throughout these pages, you will find stories of two people, their struggles, their triumphs, and the investments they have made in their intimate relationship. This writing is partially drawn upon the wisdom of psychologists, relationship experts, and timeless philosophical insights to shed light on the profound and often unexplored dimensions of love. The majority originates from the author's creative mind, intertwining with the intricate, everyday realities that we observe up close–a somber display of Black men versus Black women. It is the author's hope that, by the time you reach the final chapter, you will not only have gained a deeper understanding of the power of investments in intimate relationships but also a practical guide for nurturing and strengthening your own connections with the ones you love. The quest for lasting, fulfilling love is an endeavor that transcends cultural boundaries, age, and background, and in this book, Joe aims to provide you with the tools to embark on that quest with renewed vigor and insight, through creative and intrusive writing. So, as we embark on this exploration of love, investments, and the boundless potential of intimate relationships, let us keep in mind that love is not a destination but a journey–a journey of growth, discovery, and shared purpose. May the insights contained within these pages illuminate your path and inspire you to invest in love like never before, for it is in these investments that we discover the true purpose of love. This creative treasure transcends mere storytelling. It goes beyond being just a book. It surpasses the typical romance novel. This is love in its most exposed and raw form–the highs, the lows, and the conversations you'd rather avoid.

Contents

Contents

ACKNOWLEDGMENTS

In the face of slander, ridicule, lies, and demonization, let's take a moment to show gratitude to those extraordinary individuals who remained unwavering while loving someone who needed healing. Every story has three perspectives: your truth, their illusion, and your journey towards recovery. Remember, don't let one negative influence hinder your progress. Just like obstacles, toxic individuals shouldn't halt the show. Take heed when showering affection upon a mound of debilitated shit, for the buzzing horde of flies that envelops it whispers a grim tale of allure hidden within its repulsive facade.

THE LIGHT

*"And I be workin' out everyday thinkin' 'bout you, looking at my own
eyes in the rearview, catchin' flashbacks of our eye contact, wish I
could lay ya on your stomach and caress your back"*
–LL Cool J, Hey Lover

"Come inside."

Those words, right there, my people. When a woman drops that line, it takes a guy's mind to a whole different zone. You know, that twilight zone vibe. Honestly, I wasn't prepared. Everything leading up to this moment felt like something out of a storybook. But here's where the real world kicks in. Was I really about to make this happen? I mean, it was the first time, and it was more than just 'good.' It was an epic experience, a game-changer. When the morning sun peeked through my curtains, I was so amped that I nearly wiped out trying to get to the shower. My usual morning workout was gonna be a bit different on this lovely April Saturday. Normally, I'd save my intense 1000-watt CT Fletcher-style workout for like once every three months, and even then, I'd complete it on a mellow day. But today, I had to switch it up all for a date. Now, I know what some of you are thinking. "Dude, it's just a date, no big deal." Well, maybe for you, it's not a big deal, and that's cool. But maybe you've never had those three-hour conversations that go on for five days straight. I mean, these aren't just chit-chats;

1

they're deep, meaningful, and loaded with substance. Those kinds of convos tell you a lot about someone. My guy hit me up on a random Sunday night.

"Hey, fam. I got a friend who wants to chat with you about the whole book-writing process. She's pretty thorough, and she'll be hitting you up soon."

"Bet, that sounds good, fam."

I don't mind helping out. After all, I didn't construct multiple published works or speak professionally in cities across the country without some guidance and support. We all need a hand, whether it's with our passions, talents, or just navigating this crazy solo journey we call life. I was just chilling on my couch when a message popped up on my phone. "HEY! YOU ARE AMAZING" that's what I saw on the screen. I couldn't help but smile and even let out a little chuckle. I didn't know why this was so amazing, but getting such kind words from anyone, regardless of their background, meant a lot. That Sunday night, we chatted back and forth on messenger for about 20 minutes before she asked if she could give me a call. I had to work in the morning, but Mondays were my slow-moving days, so it worked out. What I thought would be a quick 20-30 minute chat turned into a three-hour conversation. The chat ended up being way less about books and more about us as people. I gotta admit, it was a breath of fresh air 'cause it's been ages since I had a convo like that. We gave each other just enough to keep the fire burning, kinda like an appetizer of our personalities and struggles, you feel me? I hit the sack that night, thinking about how life throws these moments at you that take you to a whole new level. I had some solid Z's, like, an incredibly good one. The next morning, it was time to hit my CrossFit class at a brutal 4:15 am start time. That's the early grind, as the young crowd likes to call it. It's like that "it's complicated" status on Facebook. Some days, I'm all in, and others, my life's on trial. Those 8-minute intervals felt like I was waiting for a jury to drop the verdict, and I was sweating it out. Post-workout, I chugged down the regular protein shake I picked up from the front desk. Man, I needed to get a grip on that habit. I was blowing at least a hundred bucks every month on those shakes when I could just head home and dig into the groceries I stacked up. My shower was extra invigorating that Monday morning, and so was my whole vibe. Baby girl had something going, and it felt damn good. Work was, well, work - the typical office stuff, trying to make life easier by bundling up my work into one file. Working for yourself is a game-changer. I could easily do it from home, but getting out of your comfort zone and into a new spot is how you test your limits. Renting an office space in an all-white neighborhood for a couple hundred a month? That was a whole challenge. First off, I was the only face of color I spotted in the whole building, and when security welcomed me at the entrance, it felt like my inner "out of place" alarm was activated. The fear of a "POSSIBLE DYING WHILE BLACK" alert crossed my mind. Then there were the random people coming up, peering over my shoulder, asking what I was up to. I wanted to drop the "Fuck around and find out" line, but I remembered where I was. One wrong move could get me kicked out or worse. So, I pulled out "The Look," the one that all Black grandmas and mamas gave us back in the day when we knew we'd crossed a line. They got the message. You leave me be, and I'll do the same. During that Monday in the office, baby girl hit me up on the messenger app again, firing more questions. I answered a few and let her know I'd holla when I got home. And that's exactly what went down. Another three-hour phone session, which ended up being the same on Tuesday and Wednesday. Finally, on Thursday, our marathon convo reached its peak.

"Whatcha got going on Saturday night?" she asked.

"Nothin. Down to meet up?"

"You think I'm asking you out on a date?"

"Nah, I know. Just drop the spot and time."

She laughed. She knew the deal, and we set it up. Saturday night was when Junior Mitchell and Paulette Jefferson were finally gonna link up.

"I'm in," I texted back.

Phew, man! Dang, she's here, and I'm here. We'd been having some epic week-long phone chats, and now we were at this upscale Mexican joint in the city. Honestly, I had my doubts. We all know the best Mexican grub (or any kind of grub, really) comes from those hidden gems run by local families. I mean, if the neighborhood doesn't have a dash of grit, with the scent of street life in the air, your tacos probably ain't hitting right. But here we were, in a fancy part of town. It's all clean and prestigious, where money flows like water. The restaurant looked bougie, and I had my reservations, but hey, it's what she wanted. Can't complain about grubbin' across from a beautiful queen, hoping she's got a great sense of humor, and yams included. I took a break from my phone and saw some balloons parading through the crowd. Now, that's some white people celebration type stuff right there. They go all out at these places. We, on the other hand, just shoot a text and say, "Meet me at the spot." I grabbed my shades and gave myself the once-over. Looking slick. Simple, yet stylish. A black sweater, sharp denim jeans, and some fresh kicks had me feeling on point. I know, some might clown the Under Armour choice, but I'm in my 30s now. Comfort's the wave, and I don't need to impress anyone but the bill collectors, so my credit score stays lit. My hair was looking right with some waves. Back in the day, I had a whole ocean up top, looking like the breeding ground of dolphins. Now, I'm just happy to still have a decent pond with some ripples. Could be worse, right? I could be all bald and barren. So, I steadily consume biotin like it's the secret sauce, because it is.

I hopped out of the truck and went around to the passenger side. I had a little something for my date tonight a snazzy white butterfly box. She's all about butterflies, and I wanted to bring some elegance to this game. Inside, there was a journal I copped for her, perfect for keeping track of her life's journey. The book was nestled on a bed of rose petals, and there's a card in there too. Trust me, I wasn't going for flowers those wilt way too fast. We're grown now. If you're bringing a first-date token, make it something useful. I'm all about words and art, so if a lady gifted me a golden pen with a killer quote, that's an A+ move right there. Thoughtful and deep. No more heart-shaped chocolate boxes, people. Time to step up the game. I grabbed the box and set it on my truck. Now, I had to decide cap or no cap? "C'mon, Junior," I said to myself. LJ blessed me with a sharp lineup, and I even scored a model chick from LA back in the day because of his clipper game. No need for the cap. Plus, the sun's blazing, and it's turning my waves into a glistening masterpiece, thanks to the wave butter. Cap went in the backseat, and I whipped out my trusty brush. Feeling pretty fly, gotta admit. At that moment, I was oozing confidence. It's only right I knew I was looking fresh. I could make simple things look classy. Not everyone's got that swag, but it's all good. Man, you gotta trust it, that top-notch confidence that is within you. It ain't about your size down there, your bank account, or the fancy labels you're rocking. Nah, it's something that's deep within you. Your character, swagger, the way you walk, it all gotta blend like a mouthwatering mix of collard greens, hot peppers, and ham hocks. That's just the real deal. Honestly, people of all backgrounds can pull it off. I was doing my thing, brushing my hair, and then I caught a glimpse out of the corner of my eye. Damn, there she is, right on the edge of the parking lot, staring my way. I won't lie, it kinda startled me, got me on the low. She's got that look, like those twins from 'The Shining,' you know, standing there in the hallway as the little dude rides his big wheel in the hotel. I tried to keep my cool, but I couldn't help but laugh. Caught red-handed, dripping swag juice all over the place, and she turns the faucet off. She laughs, flashing that beautiful smile that can light up a room, no matter who you are. I mean, who am I kidding? Her smile is like the Northern Lights in Alaska. It's a blessing to see she's got dental benefits you know some folks looking all fly on the outside but their smile's like they chew concrete cinder blocks for fun. I fixed my shades and kept it cool, even though I had made a complete fool of myself. I dusted myself off, grabbed her stuff from the roof of the car, and strutted up like I'm the man. But deep down, I'm just a kid with a crush. She leaned in for a side hug and said, 'Hey.' I'm not sure if it's because I'm holding a box or if she's checking that I'm not a weirdo.

"Sup," I respond.

Dang, I messed it up again. I was aiming for smoothness but ended up sounding more like Johnny Bravo than Johnny Gill. Strike two, man. We made our way to the restaurant. I didn't know what was on her mind, but I had those two little advisors on my shoulders that only I could see. The inner voices of good, and maliciousness.

"Isn't she beautiful? She looks even better in person," the voice of reason spoke.

But the mischievous one on the other side is like, "Dude, she's finer than fine! You better not fuck this up. I'd do some crazy stuff if I were bigger."

"Nah, it's not about getting into her drawers. It's about loving her for who she is," good boy tried to argue.

And the troublemaker just laughs and says, "Yeah, but we all know where it's headed. Chill with that corny shit, man."

I swear, these imaginary buddies, only I can see and hear, they're the best entertainment. And in person, the angel of the crew was right, she's even more amazing than all her social media pics. She's 5'2", with a toned, athletic body. No makeup, just natural beauty, and those unique braided locks. She's a Melanin Queen who doesn't need all that extra stuff European society pushes on our women. In my eyes, I'm already winning. We walked in, headed to a booth with balloons tied up. She's gone all out I thought it was some other person's celebration when I saw those balloons from the truck. Here I am, thinking I'm smooth with my butterfly box, and she's brought the balloons like it's a full-on celebration.

"Where do you wanna sit?" she asks.

"I was always taught to sit facing the door, see everything and everyone walking in. No man in their right mind sits with their back to the door that's some universal wisdom right there. You've gotta stay ready to dish out two to the body and take it to the head if necessary."

"And you gotta be ready to bolt, right?"

"Yeah, you've got it. No one's got time for pride when things get crazy. People from all walks of life know that when shit hits the fan, it's time to haul ass."

We shared a laugh as we took our seats, each on opposite ends of the booth. We exchanged those starry-eyed glances, making a minute feel like an eternity.

"Man, you're too cute," she said with a beaming smile.

"Paulette, why are you talking about yourself?"

We both chuckled. It was one of those moments where humor transcended any boundaries.

"So, I've got a little something for you. You know, you have to open this by six o'clock, like it's straight out of a suspense movie. But I'm not trying to meet any grim fate, so here."

I handed her the box, and a sly grin crossed her face. Earlier that day, we were chatting online, and I'd sent her a pic of the box, along with a cryptic message about opening it by six, or else. I was all about horror flicks, while she was more into sci-fi, which I never really understood. How could grown-ups watch Harry Potter or Star Wars for hours and love it? She shook the box, just to make sure there wasn't something explosive in there, while I sat there, maintaining my composure, wondering if she'd grasp the essence of the gift. As she opened it, an audible "aww" escaped her lips check, the gift hit the mark. She examined it from every angle with a smile, as if I didn't already know what it was.

"Alright, so I remember you talking about your journey to change things up. That's why I got you this journal it's for documenting every step, tracking your progress."

"Thanks," she said, still grinning.

She flipped through the pages.

"Turn back to the front," I suggested.

She turned to the front page, and there it was her favorite Bible verse, Romans 8:28, highlighted. "And we know that all things work together for good to those who love God, to those who are called according to His purpose." It's incredible how little tidbits from conversations can have such a big impact on someone's life.

"There's something else in there," I hinted. She looked up at me, then back in the box, where she found an envelope with a card. I thought she'd just grab it, give it a read, and call it a day. But no, she started tossing the petals into the air with abandon. The crazy part? They landed on the table perfectly, almost as if the universe wanted to make this moment even more magical. It was a joy to see a Black woman let loose, be free, and be themselves. After her delightful flower display, she finally opened the card and began to read.

You: Yo, what's up! You're seriously amazing, fam!

Me: Thanks. What's good with you?

You: Grinding on my book!

Me: Oh, word. Keep pushing. I'm hella proud of you.

You: I had some questions. You busy? Thank you. That put a smile on my face.

Me: Got my people here right now. I can hit you up soon.

You: Cool.

Me: Bet.

She went quiet for a minute. I glanced at her, wondering if I'd gone too hard for a first impression. I noticed her eyes getting kinda misty, and she started fanning herself.

"My bad, but you're getting me all in my feels. Wait, I'm not crying. I'm good."

Yeah, she was on the verge of tears, but she held it together. As for me, those two minions on my shoulders chimed in.

"You're so sweet. You really got her heart melting."

The other voice, though, didn't hold back.

"Man, don't listen to that soft talk. You probably got her panties drenched! Keep it going, man. Keep it going. She's probably got a pussy grip tighter than Melvin's chokehold on Jody."

I swear, my reality was all over the place. It wasn't just the pressure I was putting on myself, but it was also about soaking in this moment. I kept asking myself, how the heck did this happen? Our waiter came through, and his name was Julio. Funny 'cause I wasn't usually into drinking when I had to drive. But right then, I wanted a shot of Don Julio. The first impressions were done, it was time to grub. Paulette had insisted earlier that I try their filet mignon tacos,

8

and she ordered those and a mushroom taco. My greedy self went for a shrimp taco, a lobster taco, and the filet mignon joint. While we waited for our food, we were just goofing off, cracking jokes, and talking about all sorts of random stuff. Through it all, I kept thinking, she looks amazing. Black women, I swear. Damn. I mean, what was The Most High thinking when He created them? It's like He added a double scoop of chocolate, a couple of spoons of honey, a dash of cinnamon, agave nectar, a pinch of turmeric for that kick, and some onion powder. 'Cause no matter what, we're seasoning everything with onion powder, whether it's meat or veggies. Lawry's? Come on, we knew that was the secret sauce. Even The Most High knew it; I mean, He was in on the flavor game too. We used Lawry's on our ribs, chicken, pork chops, and every piece of meat imaginable. And it always turned out fire as fuck. So, I know He used it when creating Black women, especially her.

"Got the mushroom and filet mignon tacos."

"That's me," Paulette replied, throwing a hand up.

Julio's rookie waitress rolled up, moving as silent as a whisper and looking as jittery as a cat in a dog park. She had my plate of food, and I was worried sick.

I knew waiting tables wasn't a cakewalk, but I was praying she'd chill and not faint on us. I just didn't want her to fumble my tacos, 'cause then we'd have a real problem. Rule #08880: Never, ever drop Mexican grub, no matter what. And yeah, Tex-Mex doesn't even count–it's trash, just like every In-N-Out burger place on the planet.

"Hold up, peep this," I said.

Paulette took a bite of her mushroom dish. "What's up?"

"They loaded it with guacamole, then slid a whole avocado in there." I did a little happy dance, and she cracked up. Guac was my jam, like air to a bird. Tacos without guacamole? Nah, that's a no-go. I'd probably lose it if my guac was AWOL.

"So, you gotta try that filet mignon joint first. I'm telling you, it's gonna sweep you off your feet."

If the grub matched her fine looks and cool vibes, I might just fall in love. I scooped up that purple tortilla, dripping with flavor, and took a bite. I leaned back and felt my soul light up. That dish was straight fire.

"Yoooo." That's all I could manage. She was on point, with a great taste in food, and all-around fun. She was checking all the right boxes.

"Ughh. Gotta hit the bathroom. This lipstick's gotta be a mess. I'll be right back."

She stood up, and I watched her stroll to the bathroom. As soon as she disappeared around the corner, I grabbed my phone and messaged my boy who introduced us, also my unofficial hype man.

Me: "She stepped out for a sec. This is epic. Damn, she's bad as fuck! Ok, gotta chill before she returns, lol."

My guy: "lol, for real, she's bad. Glad it's going well!"

I saw her heading back, so I stashed my phone. Her lips were back to their natural beauty, and I wanted them to stay that way. No need for that lipstick. The next 45 minutes were all about good food, laughter, and me trying not to send an SOS to the bewildered rookie waitress every time she joined us with Julio.

"I'm thinking of dessert. You in?"

"Yeah, let me check out some ice cream spots, 'cause you know most of them around here close up early."

Honestly, I had a sweet tooth for her, but I had to keep it chill.

"Cool," she replied. "I don't want churro dessert either. I'd hit up Jack in the Box for that."

"Hey, there's a spot up the street called The Frozen Lick. They claim to have a ton of ice cream."

"I'm down."

"You look amazing."

"Quit bragging."

"Hold up, you're not gonna start with those boomerang comments on me, Ms. Paulette? That expired on Friday night during the call."

We both had a good laugh. She came around to my side, and we took selfie after selfie. It felt natural, like we'd been together for years instead of just meeting up as new acquaintances. One photo stood out from the rest. We both had genuine smiles, like we'd known each other for six years instead of six days. I wasn't even thinking about the bill at this point. It could've been $300 for all I cared. I could've stayed there all night talking to her, taking pictures, and I wouldn't have been bored. Our fun ended there, and we headed back to our cars, ready to meet at The Frozen Lick. I cruised down the road, playing Tevin Campbell's "Eye 2 Eye," taking me back to my childhood when Max hit the road with his dad to chase Roxanne. I even tried a perfect cast while driving. The sun was setting, and the sky looked beautiful, signaling that my already great adventure was about to get better. I pulled up to the traffic light before getting on the freeway. Windows down, I cranked up the music. "IF YOU'RE EVER LONELY... STOP!!! YOU DON'T HAVE TO BE!!!" A group of white women in the next car gave me funny looks, laughing their heads off. So, being the person I am, I looked right at them and sang, "IF WE LISTEN TO EACH OTHER'S HEART!!!" They weren't about to ruin my Tevin Campbell moment. Max set high standards for us. He traveled cross-country with his dad for some freshman yams. I was just going down the road for some ice cream with a woman. I wasn't on his level of daring, and I wasn't about to dance my way into her heart. My knees weren't what they used to be, and one wrong step could send me to the surgeon's table. The light turned green, I gave one last look to the folks in the other car, and merged onto the freeway smoother than a James Harden traveling stepback. Now, Eric Roberson's music was playing on my speakers, and I was grooving to the max. I didn't know what her car looked like or whether she'd already made it there or was behind me. I parked in the arts district, right across from the spot. Parking was just a dollar an hour here. Even though we weren't planning to stay long, it was still a bit annoying. The arts district wasn't downtown, but it was trying to step up its game. Parking used to be free everywhere around here. Now, it was a dollar. In some places, it was five dollars an hour. Oh well, I let it slide.

We were there for some ice cream. Cool it for a sec Junior, I told myself. This date is almost done, and you are about to bounce. I strolled over to the parking meter, tapping my card while hitting her up on the line.

"Where you at?"

"I see you."

I glanced around, quick as a flash. No sight of her.

"Why you messing with me?"

"What's up with those buttons you're pushing?"

I couldn't help but laugh. She pulled a move straight out of the Saw movies on me. Glancing around again as I waited for my parking ticket to print, it was clear she was messing with me big time.

"Look over."

I scanned in all directions, but still no sign of her.

"Girl, where are you hiding?"

"Right here in front," she said.

I looked once more. Oh man, seriously? Was I getting that blind? Apparently so. She was standing right in front of the ice cream spot. She got me, no doubt. I strolled across the street to join her, and we waited behind a few peeps to place our food orders. I squeezed between them, grabbed a menu, and started browsing with her.

"Aw, hell. I know what I'm getting."

"What's that?" she asked.

"Peanut butter lover."

Her eyes rolled harder than someone rolling dice on the block.

"What's that about?"

"I just had a feeling, you know? Like you're made of peanut butter."

"And how's that?"

"The way your eyes lit up at the menu. I saw your reaction. I had a gut instinct that you got excited when you came across anything with Reeses or peanut butter."

"Well, you're smooth like peanut butter, and I'm all in."

"I taste good, I know."

She smiled and laughed. I had to play it cool. We weren't close to that stage yet, but if we ever got there hold up, let me slow down. I was jumping ahead of myself. Let me get that "sucking the soul out of her body" thought out of my head. I ordered my grub while she grabbed a scoop of vanilla ice cream in a cup. This place was kinda corny; you couldn't grab a beer without an entrée. It didn't kill the vibe, though. Now, both of us had our ice cream fixes. There we were, posted up outside on this relaxed Saturday night, savoring this frozen goodness of heaven in a cup, and a bowl.

"Let me see those shades, girl."

She gave me a puzzled look, like, "Why this dude wanna peep my glasses?"

"They're just for style, you know."

"I know what's up. Hook me up with those shades."

She slid those stylish glasses off her face and passed them over to me. I grabbed those bold red-rimmed frames, pulled out my phone, and kicked off a selfie session. Just being my goofy self, you know. She shook her head, laughing, flashing that radiant smile that was brightening my world. I snapped a bunch of pics and handed her the shades back.

"HEY, FUCK YOU MAN!!! BRING IT ON???!!! WHAT!!!" We both turned our heads, and yeah, we stood up too. We're not about the drama we're street-smart. You know how some folks just dive headfirst into trouble? That's not Black folks style. It was a white dude making a ruckus. We thought he was yelling at someone, but he was just shouting into the night, head spinning like a top. I didn't want to stick around and see if he'd lock eyes with me.

"Yo," Paulette said, "I swear I was ready to bolt like Flo Jo."

"I'd have to hold on to you, though. My knees ain't great."

"Nah, man, I ran track. You'd be out of luck."

"Seriously, you'd leave me like that?"

"That wild white boy and potential chaos? Let me think... HELL YEAH!!!"

13

Can't blame her; it's a survival instinct. We bolt when we smell trouble. Like Cedric said on Kings of Comedy, "We see a bunch of people running, we take off!" The white boy disappeared into the night, and we carried on.

"So, I gotta check on my dogs at nine."

I glanced at my phone and saw that it was 8:45. So, there went my evening plans. Now I had to figure out what to do for the rest of the night. Maybe just head back home. Or take a quick spin downtown, see if there's some action going on. Saturday night in the city, anything's possible.

"You got a spot nearby where you can chill till I'm back? I'll only be about 15 minutes."

I thought, "There go my random plans."

"Yeah, I can find something," I replied.

"Great. Seriously. I'll hit you when I'm done, and I'll be back."

We hugged, and I watched her stroll to her car. Her backside might not have been the biggest, but it had its appeal. Scratch going home I was having too much fun, and I didn't want to cut it short. But finding something to do around here that didn't involve booze? That's a challenge. Then it hit me. I knew an arts center a few blocks away where they hosted poetry slams regularly. Maybe they're open, and there's something going on. I got in the car, managed not to wreck it while backing out of that tight lot, and turned the corner. As I reached the next stop sign, I saw the lights on at the arts center. Bet. Something's popping, at least giving me a spot to kick it until she calls back. I got lucky and snagged a parking spot right up front of the building, which was pretty unusual whenever there was an event happening. I strolled in, and there was a comedy show in full swing. It wasn't anything fancy, just some local comedians doing their thing. Ten minutes in, and after a few good laughs, my stomach started acting up. That last meal and that peanut butter was tearing through me like a freight train. Dang, the last thing I needed was to hit the restroom here; it was like doing it in the club, no thanks. But hey, desperate times call for desperate measures, right? I knew out of the three bathrooms in this place, the one with the busted door was always open. Sure enough, I headed to the back, and the first two were occupied. But that last one? It was wide open, like a prostitute on a Friday night in Houston, on Bissonnet Street. I couldn't resist. I walked in, and there it was, a massive dresser, of all things. Who keeps a dresser in a bathroom? Beats me, but in this case, it was a lifesaver. I slid it in front of that janky door and grabbed some two-ply TP, securing the throne. As soon as I dropped my pants, there was an explosion and an unpleasant sound, like a thunderclap. That meal had done a number on me, and it was trying to make a quick escape. As I enjoyed the heavenly relief, someone tried to barge in. "I'M IN HERE, MAN!!!" The door shut fast, and I knew the fool thought twice about barging in doors. After dropping off another payload of peanut butter meat filets, I shuffled back to the door, pants around my ankles, and barricaded it with the dresser. Close call avoided. Last thing I needed was another interruption in my sanctuary. Back in my comfort zone, my phone started ringing. Lucky for me, it was on the sink, and my left hand was free. "Hey there, what's good?" I had to multitask, phone in my left hand and a cleanup mission in my right. It was Paulette, and I was feeling hella embarrassed. I held back my grunts because chatting with your date while handling business is not the move.

"I'm about five minutes away."

"Alright, I'm on my way out."

I ended the call right on cue, right as the last turd splashed down. That sound was like Hiroshima all over again. I wiped up, washing my hands three times you can never be too cautious. The last thing you want is any lingering shit scents on your fingers; it can kill the mood, ya know? Feeling at least ten pounds lighter, I strutted back into the event area. I stepped out the door, and guess what? My phone rang again.

"Hello?"

"I'm right around the corner."

"I'm out front now."

I leaned against the back of my car, and there she was, rounding the corner. Damn, that was quick. You know when most Black folks say they're around the corner, it means they're a good three to five minutes away. Better than the infamous "I'm down the street," which usually means a 10-15 minute wait. She pulled up, rolled down the window, and there we were.

"Yo, hop on in."

"I thought we were rollin' in both cars."

"Nah, slide in. I got a dope spot I wanna show you."

Man, at that moment, I felt like less of a man. We linked up for the initial meetup, but I wasn't vibing with the idea of a lady behind the wheel. It's just how I was brought up. It felt like it would dent my pride. After a quick second of thought, I took a deep breath, said "alright," and hopped in. Life's taught me, sometimes you just gotta go with the flow. Not everything needs dissecting or some deep philosophical breakdown. We cruised through the arts district. I spotted some joints I didn't even know existed around here, and found some spots to hit up next time I'm in the area. We rolled past "The Field," a workout park I hit up every now and then when I ain't feelin' the gym crowds. The music was bumpin', and laughter was contagious. It was like poetry in motion, with no mics, or no audience. It felt like a slam dunk, and her smile, man, every time she cracked up, it was like the crowd going wild. We finally hit the downtown streets, watching the lights dancing on those skyscrapers like they had their own VIP club. It was lit downtown, thanks to the baseball rivalry game. We found a rare parking spot on the main strip for a Saturday night. The date was still on point.

"Where we going?"

"Trust me, you'll love it."

Stepping out of the car, the vibe was speaking to me. I swung around to open her door while she dug in her purse, hunting for some chapstick. She stepped out looking even finer than when the night started. We walked up to this spot, and as I held the door open, I knew right away she was getting date number two. The place was straight up amazing. It was like heaven, a hookah lounge, library, art gallery, and cafe all rolled into one. Dim lights, brick walls, it felt more like a basement than a lounge. I followed Paulette to the back. Plush leather seats along the walls, slick wooden tables in front of each section, added a swag to the upscale hookah stands. Books were everywhere. There were paintings. Not fancy museum-type paintings but a local vibe, like someone had painted 'em in their apartment and hung 'em here. We passed by the only other person there, a lady with her laptop, probably writing the story of us. We found a spot in the back corner, kicked back, and let our bones chill.

"You into hookah?" she asked.

"No doubt, this vibe is straight-up fire. I'm all in for this tonight."

The dude behind the bar slid us our hookah, stacked fresh coals on it, and our night in this unreal spot kept rolling. We passed it back and forth, chopping it up about everything, from art to relationships, the grind of life today, dreams, and whatnot. She didn't know it yet, but I'd already made my mind up that she wasn't going anywhere. You don't take a man to a spot like this and think he won't be sticking around. Her relationship status? Already marked "changed," even if she didn't realize it yet. For the next couple of hours, nobody else came through, except for a lady in dusty sandals who needed a pit stop at the bathroom. Time flew by, and when our boy came to us and said, "I gotta close you out," I peeped at my watch. Dang, it was 12:05 a.m. We both looked around; we were the last ones left in the joint. It's like the universe said, "I'm giving you both some space. This connection right here is that authentic shit." The universe even cursed, just for emphasis. Yup, in my mind, it dropped that S-bomb because it knew this was going to be epic. We stepped out into the downtown chaos, where folks were beefing and getting separated. Damn baseball fans, you know how they can be. As long as they didn't run into us, her, or the ride, we were all good. If they did, we'd handle it, quick and smooth. Fortunately, it was no drama, so we cruised off into the early Sunday morning darkness, bumping R&B jams as she sang along, while I sounded like a screeching cat. No worries, though. I didn't give a damn, and from the smile on her face, neither did she. We hit the streets along the ocean and parked. There, we kept the laughter, conversation, and close vibe going for what was now a six-hour moment.

17

"You down for hitting the beach?" she asked.

"You know I'm down," I replied.

Off we went, and as we hit the freeway, that Victoria Money F.U.C.K. track played. We locked eyes, sharing a loving grin. Simultaneously, we burst out laughing. For those living under a rock, the song's acronym stood for "Friend U Can Keep." In my head, I already knew that given the chance, I'd sweep this gorgeous woman off her feet, making her feel every line of this song, word for word. In another sense, after five days of connecting and finally meeting, she was shaping up to be the kind of friend worth keeping. The feminine energy was something else. There I was, a 36-year-old dude who had cut ties with all the toxic nonsense, not just from a messed-up ex I once called a spouse. I'd distanced myself from late-night drama, negativity, and anything that didn't contribute to my personal growth. My life was on the upswing, and unlike those who peaked in their teenage years, my prime wasn't defined by the clothes I wore or the points I scored in some game. Many of them ended up stuck in the same routine, living in the same hood, never broadening their horizons. It's that classic 50 Cent line, "Damn homey; in high school, you were the man homey; what the fuck happened to you?" Lucky me, I had no clue what that meant. I was still in the early stages of living life, focused on my creative magic, which was putting food on the table. Despite what the world might say, you can chase your dreams in the arts and make a decent living. Just like anything else, it takes dedication, hustle, and a willingness to grow. I wasn't even thinking about impressing a lady at this point. But then, a random Sunday night convo had me out here on a Saturday night, into the wee hours of Sunday morning. We cruised off the freeway, hitting the strip leading to the beach. The streets were alive, everyone was out and about, and the vibe was real. The best part? No drama to stress over. We found a spot by the ocean right in front of a 7-Eleven. Convenient because you could never catch me remembering where I parked, whether I was behind the wheel or not. We cut through an alley to get to the beach. On our right, we spotted a guy, looking like he had a rough night, face-first in a dumpster.

"Is he alright?"

"Girl, leave him be. He might be wildin' out."

Paulette laughed, but I was dead serious. When folks are messed up, I stay in my lane. Who knows, maybe he and that dumpster had a deep connection. I didn't care. We made it out of the alley, and the sounds of loud music and laughter filled the air.

"These people are wild, huh?"

"Well, what did you expect on a Saturday night at the beach?" she asked.

"Oh, I knew what to expect, no doubt. Still, it's crazy to see how folks get, or hear what they say when the liquor starts flowing."

We hit the boardwalk by the sand. Out there in the middle of the night, there were people around a bonfire under the pier, skaters doing their thing, and a couple off in the distance on the sand. Paulette strolled out onto the beach, and while I thought we were just taking a casual beach walk, she had other plans. I didn't want to kill the vibe, so I rolled with it. I followed her as she settled down on the sand, somewhere between the waves and the boardwalk.

"Man, this is something else," she said.

"For sure."

I looked up, and there it was, the Big Dipper shining bright. I glanced around some more, and there was the Scorpio constellation. You know Scorpios, they can be a handful, but I couldn't change the way the universe worked. Sitting there for a minute, watching her, I could care less, about anything else right now. She was too fine for me to stand; I had to join her on the sand, leaning in. My backside was freezing, colder than an ice cube, as soon as I took a seat. Man, I'm glad I wore this sweater. I knew it would be a bit chilly, but this beach was putting my toughness to the test. We kicked off the first 10 minutes just sitting side by side, not saying a word, just soaking in the sound of those waves crashing. When the water inched closer, it only made it about five to seven feet in front of us before retreating back into the deep. It was mind-blowing. The silent conversation we had, close and intimate, said more than words ever could.

19

Hold up. I ain't falling for this girl, am I? Nah, it's too early for that. This is just our first date, but this is wild. I've never spent over six hours with a woman and not made a move. The crazy thing is, I'm actually enjoying this without getting physical.

"So, what's your ultimate life goal?" she asked, her voice soothing. And just like that, we dove into a conversation that lasted well over an hour. Time became a blur out there. After a while, my rear end wasn't feeling the cold anymore; I'd completely brushed it off. I felt warm, both inside and out. She had this magnetic aura that was changing me in a single night. Her conversation alone was giving my mind a workout. Wait a minute. Am I slipping? Thinking about things other than just getting physical? I didn't know, but it sure felt good.

"Aww, look," I said to her.

"That's so sweet, she's sitting on him, kissing."

We both looked, but she seemed to spot something that my blind eyes couldn't see.

"Yo, they ain't just kissing. They're fucking."

I squinted my eyes. Sure enough, as my vision adjusted to the darkness, I could see the girl moving up and down. Worse yet, the homey backside was exposed to the sand. Now, I ain't judging a man for getting some action, but, damn, it was well past midnight, and I wasn't about to risk hypothermia for some cheeks. Yeah, I know the sand isn't that cold, but still, no woman was going to have me out there when the baby crabs are pinching ass cheeks. We might as well head home right then. I grabbed my phone from my pocket as we continued to witness this crazy scene.

"What time is it?" she asked.

"Dang, it's 1:45."

"Man, let's bounce. This was fun, but I ain't trying to be in for any more surprises tonight."

We got up, strolling back toward the concrete walkway. Some kids were chilling on the steps, probably chatting about some random stuff while holding their paddleboards. I just knew they weren't planning to go paddleboarding at this ungodly hour. But hey, these kids, man, nothing they do surprises me. We made it back to the car and drove toward the arts center where my ride was parked. As we re-entered the arts district, she made me think even more.

"Thanks for not being creepy," she said. I glanced at her.

"What do you mean?" I asked, with a concerned chuckle.

"I mean, I've been on dates with guys who, let's just say, pushed the boundaries just because we were hanging out."

"I didn't make you uncomfortable tonight, did I?"

"Nah, not at all. It was just refreshing not to have to worry about that stuff with a guy."

Honestly, I felt a sigh of relief that she didn't see me as some kind of weirdo, but the situation was just plain sad. It didn't sit right with me that any woman, particularly Black women, felt unprotected. See, most guys, no matter where they come from, take pride in looking out for the women in their lives, no questions asked. But here's the deal: in this day and age, a lot of women carry this "I don't need a man for anything" mindset. They're out to prove that they can do anything a man can. Some guys, not all, started thinking, "Alright, you do you," and stepped back. It's like we were balancing on a thin line, and it didn't need tipping. Men aren't built to do everything that women can, and vice versa. We have our strengths and weaknesses, and that's just the way it is. Men can't have babies or nurture like women can, and women can't impose themselves physically like men. That's what's messed up with the world today. You can call it feminism, delusion or whatever you want, but it's messed up. And it's appalling that some women have to feel this way. So, there we were, parked in front of the arts center, two in the morning. This is the part where most folks say, "Thanks for the great night, get home safe, and shoot me a text when you're in." But nah, not us. We just sat there, staring, talking, staring, and talking. It was like some sort of puppy love vibe, and love wasn't even on the table yet. We were so deep into this moment, that it took me a while to realize that we were holding hands the entire time.

21

"You're looking fly," she says.

"Why you talking about yourself ?"

I shot back, and those back-and-forth comments were back in play. She was definitely on the same wavelength as me. More importantly, she connected with my spirit.

"I know you've got to bounce, so yeah," she says.

She hopped out of the car, and I popped open my door. I thought we might end the night with a kiss because it felt right. But I wasn't going to push it. We ended up standing behind the car, in the middle of the street, hugging. A car could've shown up any second, but we didn't give a damn. This hug was speaking to my inner self. Her head was buried in my chest, and I bent down, giving her a gentle kiss on the forehead. She held me tighter, running her hands on my back, and it felt damn good. "Junior, keep it cool," I told myself. We eventually let go after about 15 minutes of hugging. Who hugs for 15 minutes, right? Apparently, we do. We just looked at each other, not saying a word, just grinning.

"One more?" she asks.

I opened my arms again, and she came back in for another embrace. It was probably three in the morning by now, but I didn't care at all. And then, those two little minions popped up on my shoulders again. The one on the right, the nice one, started talking.

"Junior, this is something special. You're connecting on a deeper level. It's going to let her rest easy and feel at peace. That forehead kiss was pure magic. I'm damn proud of you."

Then, there's this street-smart dude, whispering in my ear from my left side.

"I know damn well if you don't lay a kiss on this lady before you hit the road, I'll slap your ass repeatedly all the way home. All this laughing, joking, and her running her fingers on your back come on, bro, seize the moment! Forget about that sassy ass voice on your right side. Grab her face, plant one on her, and don't be shy about it."

I side-glanced to my right, where this more laid-back inner voice resided.

"Junior, just go with the flow. Let it happen naturally." Back to the left, the street-smart voice wasn't having any of it.

"I swear, if you listen to that soft-spoken moist ass ninja, I'll roast you all the way home. Take control, kiss her smoothly. I'll be a constant annoyance if you don't."

Message received. We parted again, but this time I gently caressed her face. One, two, three soft kisses on her lips. We both stepped back, grinning.

"Well, you have a great night," I said.

"Yeah, you too," she replied.

We locked eyes, both of us getting back into our cars. I couldn't take my eyes off her as she started her engine. She glanced back at me one last time before reversing. I waved. She waved back, disappearing into the night. I sat there for a moment, still processing the incredible experience.

"My man, you slicker than a can of oil and cooler than Freddie Jackson sipping a milkshake in a snowstorm," said the devil's assistant.

I glanced to my right.

"Junior, I'm a little disappointed. And then you think him quoting Outkast is supposed to validate your actions. Goodnight," he mumbled and vanished. I looked back to my left, where the confident, evil one was.

"Fuck him," we both said in unison.

I cranked up the truck and went to my playlist. Erykah Badu's voice filled the air, setting the mood. There was no better way to end this night than cruising to 'Love of my Life.' She might not be the love of my life, but it felt like a scene from a romantic movie. I hit the road, heading towards the freeway, and every traffic light was green. It was as if the universe was giving me a thumbs-up. Then, I looked down and, lo and behold, one traffic light remained red, and there was a car. I couldn't believe it. As I got closer to that car, I realized it was her car. Fate was definitely on my side. I restarted the Erykah Badu-Common track, pulled up next to her at the light, and she looked over, grinning. I lowered my window, and the music was bumping.

"You're really playing that?!" she asked.

"Of course!"

"Don't forget to hit me up when you get home!"

"I will!," I said, and we exchanged smiles.

I was on top of the world. I sped off into the night, entered the freeway, and let out a victorious shout. The whole ride back home, which took about 40 minutes, I was talking to myself, asking if all of this had actually happened. It was surreal. I'd never been so mentally engaged with a woman. My music faded into the background because my mind was still blown. Yet, the silence was a breath of fresh air. I pulled into my driveway at 3:27 a.m. Walking into my home, I tossed my clothes on the couch, and jumped into bed like a kid on Christmas morning. 'I made it back, baby girl. Thanks for a fantastic time,' I texted. She replied with a selfie, of the biggest grin I had ever seen. She was ecstatic, and so was I. Nine hours and some change later, I was finally ready to call it a night. Who goes out with a woman on a nine hour date? Me, that's who. Then, it hit me. I couldn't sleep just yet. I arose from my bed, grabbed my journal from my nightstand, and chronicled this night.

Journal Entry: A Magical First Date with Paulette

Tonight marked the beginning of something truly special, a magical first date with Paulette that I will cherish forever. The entire experience unfolded like a beautifully written novel, and I can't help but reflect on every moment with a heart full of gratitude and joy. Our day began with a meeting at a charming restaurant nestled in the heart of the city. We decided that tacos would be the perfect icebreaker, a delicious and informal way to start our date. Paulette arrived with a warm smile that instantly put me at ease. Over a shared table filled with various taco creations, we exchanged stories, dreams, and laughter. Her sense of humor and the way she lit up when talking about her passions were nothing short of captivating. What started as a simple dinner soon evolved into a shared adventure. We couldn't resist the allure of an ice cream parlor nearby, and our spontaneous decision led to another delightful chapter in our date. Sitting across from each other with scoops of our favorite flavors, we discovered more about each other's lives and uncovered numerous common interests. Our connection was growing stronger with each passing minute. The date took an exciting twist when Paulette shifted the night to hookah at a cozy lounge. It was a new experience for me, and I was grateful for her adventurous spirit. As we sat amidst the fragrant swirls of smoke, we delved into profound conversations, discussing everything from our past travels to our future aspirations. The dimly lit atmosphere of the lounge seemed to heighten the intimacy of the moment, making it feel like we'd known each other for much longer. The evening was still young, and we decided to extend our adventure by heading to the beach. The sound of the waves crashing on the shore welcomed us, providing the perfect backdrop for our continued connection. Hand in hand, we strolled along the moonlit shoreline, sharing stories, dreams, and our deepest thoughts. The moon hung in the sky like a radiant lantern, casting its glow on the glistening sand. Every moment felt like a painting, a snapshot of two souls connecting in the tranquil night. As we found a quiet spot to sit and gaze at the starry sky, the chemistry between us became undeniable. Our shared hopes for the future and the promise of what lay ahead hung in the air. Under the serene moonlight, at the end of our blissful adventure, our lips finally met in an invigorating, soul-stirring kiss. It was a moment that sent shivers down my spine, filled with the promise of something beautiful and enduring. As I write this journal entry, I can't help but feel a sense of wonder and gratitude for the enchanting first date with Paulette. It spanned nine hours, yet it felt like mere moments in each other's company. The world seemed to disappear as we got to know one another, and I eagerly await the chapters of our story that have yet to unfold.

This date will forever be etched in my memory as the day I embarked on a remarkable journey with someone extraordinary. At this moment, I can only think about powerful words LL Cool J once said on his timeless classic, Hey Lover:

"I touched you gently with my hands, we talked about traveling to distant lands, escaping all the madness out here in the world, becoming my wife, no longer my girl, Then, you let your dress fall down to the floor, I kissed you softly and you yearned for more, We experienced pleasure unparalleled, into an ocean of love we both fell, Swimming in the timeless currents of pure bliss, fantasies interchanging with each kiss, Undying passion unites our souls, together we swim until the point of no control"

Goodnight Junior. Sleep well, so she can awaken you in your dreams, until reality comes back.

2

PUT IT ON ME

*"If you were worried 'bout where, I been or who I saw, what club I
went to with my homies, baby don't worry, you know that you got me."*
– The Roots ft. Erykah Badu, You Got Me.

The text hit me outta nowhere. I was having one of those epic office days, you
know? My personal projects were on fire, moving at warp speed. But life's got that
twist, right? One moment can flip your vibe real quick. I was hustlin', trying to
wrap everything up before my regular two o'clock escape. Then, right after lunch,
a mountain of requests flooded my inbox. Man, you wouldn't believe it. This
ain't supposed to be a Thursday thing. My regular requests and writing demands
usually pour in on Mondays and Tuesdays. This was some next-level chaos, like,
I'm talking extinction level event territory. Now, I had no issue working through
my self mandated lunch break, but nah, that wasn't happening. See, what bugs
me about American work culture is those folks who give up their chill time just
to make someone else richer. I was determined to take every precious hour I
carved out for myself. It was my escape from the grind, you feel me? For those
60 minutes, I could just be Junior, the man, not Junior, the creator. I'm not the
grilled ham and cheese with tomato soup type. Nope. Lunchtime is lunchtime,
and I'm all about that mostly plant-based vibe. Health is wealth, and that's at
the top of my list. We all have our issues when it comes to eating right. Grease,
grease, and more grease? It's like an old love affair we refuse to break up with.

Remember the chicken sandwich madness? Even The Boondocks warned us about it. We just survived a crazy pandemic, too. Personally, I wasn't exactly thrilled about getting that shot, but I had to make a choice. It was my values vs. my livelihood. I aim to join the league of the great creatives, and I held out for as long as I could. But it ain't just about me. I mentor some seriously talented peeps, so they can do what I've been doing for two decades. I've rocked stages at weddings, retirements, anniversaries–everything. I ain't about putting anyone at risk, you know? I talked to some other folks who also had their own hustle spots, and they got the shot. I asked about the side effects, and it was the same story across the board. That second dose hit 'em harder than Mike Tyson in the '90s. I got that first shot, and it was a cakewalk. No biggie at all. But for the second dose, I prepped like it was the big showdown. The day before, I went all out with my workout, pushing myself to the limit. I made sure my blood was pumping, my body was on point, and my immune system was ready to handle business, like street hustlers slangin' their goods. When that second dose came, I waited. And waited. Two days, three days, even four days went by, and nothing outta the ordinary went down. So, what's the story? It told me my immune system's rock-solid. It was like Jay-Z's first Blueprint album–straight CLASSIC! This really got under my skin, 'cause I felt like I'd willingly swallowed some toxic stuff. Believe me, any shot where they're dishing out cash, trips, or gift cards to take it screams "suspicious" from a mile away. The hilarious part? All these social media "experts" hollering about the vaccine, pushing the science angle. What they didn't catch on to is that Uncle Sam's the puppeteer pulling the strings behind the scenes, and they ain't losing sleep over us. Of course, they're gonna sing praises 'cause their paychecks depend on it. The real deal, though, is that the remedies we need are right here, courtesy of Mother Nature. I tried to keep my diet mostly plant-based, but I'd sneak in some meat a couple of times a week. The issue with the grub stateside is it's all processed junk. I've been to places like Seychelles in East Africa, and let me tell you, I saw elders living off chicken, goat, and other critters who looked younger than folks half their age.

Nah, I didn't follow the so-called Facebook "experts." It's just funny how the same people pushing the vaccine live the unhealthiest lives. You're quick to get jabbed, but you're turning a blind eye to diabetes, high blood pressure, heart disease, cancer, and all that bad stuff. You're masking up but acting like condoms don't exist. Now, that's some next-level "brilliance." So, before anyone starts dropping science, they ought to do some homework on the Tuskegee experiments. After my lunch an egg-white, lean turkey, and vegan cheese sandwich I whipped up at home I decided to catch a quick nap at my desk. Just as my alarm was about to jolt me awake, my phone buzzed, and a grin the size of Texas took over my face. Paulette wanted to swing by and kick it. This would be our first link-up since our epic nine-hour date. When I asked her what time she was thinking, she said four. That left me with a solid two hours to whip up a mouthwatering feast for her. Now, the big decision was what culinary magic I was gonna conjure. We'd already done the takeout scene, but now it was my turn to put on a show in the kitchen. I wrapped everything up around 1:30, declaring it an early day. The perk of being your own boss is that you can set your own schedule. I dipped out of the office and power-walked to the parking lot. "Chill, bro," I reminded myself. Anxiety was running through me like a freight train. Seriously, I was jittery as hell and needed to dial it back. I was stoked, but I didn't wanna go into full-blown panic mode. What felt like an eternity turned out to be just a 15-minute drive from the office to my crib. I parked, hopped out, and threw down a beastly stretch. Right off the bat, I caught a whiff of barbecue in the air and the sweet sounds of Latin music drifting from next door. I knew it was my man, C.J., no doubt. This dude never played around when it came to living life to the fullest. I swear he's got the grill fired up every other day. I once stepped out at 5:30 a.m., heading to the gym, and this guy had the music blasting and the grill sizzling. He gives zero fucks, and I respect that. We've got a tight-knit crew in this neighborhood. On my right, it's C.J. and the older Mexican dude who only says "hola" when we cross paths. Him and his wife always put in work on their garden. To my left, I had my dude, David, and his lady, followed by Marshall and his fam. We had two Mexican neighbors on one side and two cool Black folks on the other. No matter which way you sliced it, we all had each other's backs, and nothing was gonna mess with our vibe. And if it did, best believe everyone was strapped, and the party was gonna get real. But what mattered most was seeing folks who looked like us owning their homes, even if we were technically paying rent to the bank. I stepped inside the crib, dropped my gear, and headed straight for the kitchen. But I had to make a pit stop in the bathroom first and drop a bomb that felt like nuclear fusion. One of those that smacks you as soon as you cross the threshold. I'm just glad I made it home without any issues. As soon as I put the key in the door, a knot in my gut reminded me I had some business to handle. Thank the heavens it hit when it did. I dropped my pants and let it rip, and man, it was like Snoops '95 murder trial, and I was found not guilty, with a side of relief. I would've done the prayer hands, but I just wiped and wasn't about to go there. A thorough hand wash, and I made my way to the kitchen to see what I had in the fridge. Let's be real, even a mouse would've peeked in there and asked, 'Why bother, man?' It was clear I needed a trip to the store. A quick freezer check revealed some meat and frozen veggies, but I didn't have time for thawing. You don't serve bagged veggies to a lady on her first visit. You gotta impress, so I channeled my inner grandmother. I swapped out my office attire for shorts and a T-shirt. Lucky for me, the farmers market was right down the block, and it was a healthy move. I bounced from the crib; time was of the essence. In the garage, my big boy Benz truck was waiting, and today was a special occasion. I'd spent nine hours with this woman, so I had to show some love with a meal that said, 'Thanks for your time, I appreciate you.' If it were a casual thing, I might've snagged some Chinese takeout, but I wanted round two with Junior to be on another level. I rolled out and drove two blocks down the street. But as I turned into the plaza, I had to slam on the brakes.

"YO, MOVE THAT OLD ASS OUT THE WAY!!!"

I hollered at this lady, yelling at herself in the middle of the plaza, acting all wild. It was a real heart-wrenching scene, man. I ain't trying to be a jerk, but cars don't care who you are. You step out in front of one, sober or not, you're in for a bad time. And the sad part? It's just where I'm at. My block, it's all harmony, with nice houses and fancy condos. It's a chill middle-class neighborhood where everyone feels safe. But two blocks in the other direction, it's like the underbelly of society. I wish folks with mental health issues could get the help they need, you know? Seeing people sleeping on the concrete, talking to themselves, living out of their cars, it's rough. There's this clinic near the farmers market, but all they do is dish out meds. It's the wrong approach, man. No real help. It's like, "Here, take these pills and good luck." We sometimes take what we have for granted, even just being decent human beings. I ain't saying some folks didn't end up where they are from making bad choices, but ignoring those who want help and just giving them pills? That's messed up. Big Pharma is a real deal, and those doctors and nurses? They're like the dealers. Our country's got some serious issues. She finally moved, and I cruised to the store. It was Thursday, not too crowded, and parking was wide open. I had my game plan. When guys shop, we keep it efficient, no running around. Women, though, they turn it into a puzzle. They'll hit aisles in a random order and take forever. I don't get it, but hey, I love all y'all, especially the gold mine called Black women. I grabbed a cart and got down to business. Organic fruits at the entrance, but I passed on raspberries. Blueberries were cool, but not for $4.99 a pop. I'll wait for that $2.00 sale. Then I spotted those $2.00 a pound apples. I didn't need 'em, but they make the kitchen look fresh. I bagged 'em up and kept moving. Next up, granola, deli meats, and all that jazz. I said bye to that, too. My fosho stop was the salad and veggie aisle. I took a quick look. Canned stuff? You can chef that up, reheat, and make it look gourmet. Nah, that wasn't my vibe. I kept it real. No fakin' it, not even in the kitchen. I strolled over to the meat aisle, checking out the chicken, turkey, and the rest. Pork wasn't even on my radar, but those organic chicken breasts caught my eye. Grabbed a pack for $10.39, then thought, "Why not?" and snagged another one. Why, you ask? It's simple. Saving cash was my game. And when the $8.32 pack looked just as good, it was a no-brainer. That's just how

Black folks roll, and it's in our DNA. That's what being an adult meant saving money at any cost. As I was about to bounce from the aisle, my left eye spied my guilty pleasure: pickles. These were the bomb big, organic spears. I didn't really need 'em, but at $2.50, I had to cop a jar. I kept it moving, leaving all that red meat behind. I'd been trying to cut back on it, only indulging when it was in a carne asada burrito or when I was out in Wyoming or someplace where folks hunted their own grub. I circled back to the first frozen section. It was cool how this spot had two of 'em. I took a quick look. Shrimp nah. Pig ears maybe for a random day when I wanted some country flavor. But not today. Last thing I wanted was to freak someone out with a plate of pig ears. Duck, rabbit bypassed 'em all. On the other side, I spotted those beyond sausage joints. Tempting, but not at $8.59 a pack. I'd wait for a sale, like under six bucks, before I copped some. At the end of the first frozen section, I couldn't resist. They had organic frozen blueberries on sale at $2.50 a pop. I said, "Give me ten of those." As I walked away, something caught my eye apricot stuffing. That was intriguing, and I had never seen it before. Then, my grandma's voice popped into my head, "Stuff those chicken breasts with this. She might let you stuff her." Game on granny. I tossed 'em in the cart and kept it moving. I skipped the plant-based milk, eggs, all that, and headed straight for the veggies. Bananas for me, check. Mushrooms for her, major check. Bell peppers? I wasn't sure if I needed 'em, but when my brain started cooking up ideas, I knew a master plan was brewing. Those minions on my shoulder were now back at it.

"Keep it simple," said the laid-back angel.

Then the wild one chimed in.

"Nah, forget that soft stuff. Go exotic. Chop up some portabellas and stuff 'em with that goodness."

Whoever says the voice of mischief can't help you out sometimes, they lied. By the end of my shopping trip, I had it all set. Apricot-stuffed chicken breasts, stuffed portabella mushrooms, topped with vegan cheese and organic tomato paste. Homemade chicken fettuccine alfredo, with a little extra flair from the leftover mushrooms. That's what's cooking for dinner. I had some fettuccine noodles at home, so I was all set on the pasta front. As I hit the checkout, I noticed Jordan was on the register today, looking fine as ever. She always flashed a grin my way whenever our paths crossed. She was cool, but she's a bit on the young side for my taste. The only thing I'd do with a young lady is belch her after I took her to clap cheek city. Still, she was holding up well for someone in her late 20s. If tonight didn't pan out, I was thinking about testing if age is just a number. She seemed like the kind of girl you could impress with some chicken wings and fries, for reasons I can't explain.

"Dang, who's the lucky one you're cooking for tonight?"

"This is actually for Saturday night. My brother's coming to town, and he's got a healthy appetite."

"Got it. What's his name?" She inquired as she kept scanning.

"Darrell."

"Darrell, huh? Sounds like a big-eater's name."

"What are your plans for the weekend?"

"I'm heading up north with some friends, going to a party, you know, just chilling for a bit. $71.68, please."

I swiped my card.

"Alright, don't get too wild," I chuckled.

"You mean like you and your 'brother?' I know how 'guys' get after a good meal; they try to burn it off."

"And you're an expert in that, too?"

She shrugged and flashed a smile. Deep down, she knew no guy was putting together all this parsley, sauce, and colorful stuff just for another guy. Folks visiting their homies typically don't get a five-course meal; we'd grab some wings, maybe some fast food, cruise past all the In-N-Out joints with a middle finger, and call it a day. She sensed that someone was coming to see me, and she might just throw in another meal if things didn't work out. I walked off, chuckling, fully aware that I'd leave a lasting impression better than any surgeon ever could, given the chance. I hopped into the car, linked my bluetooth, and even though the house was just a minute away, I needed my vibe music. UGK it was. Pimp and Bun might not be your typical choice for a date night playlist, but the date hadn't started yet, so I was down. "EVERY LADY AIN'T NO HOE AND EVERY HOE AIN'T MY BITCH."

Dang, I missed the Pimp C vibe. I rolled home and embraced an old-school tradition that folks from all walks of life can dig. I had four bags, and I wasn't about to make multiple trips back to the car. You thought getting your strength on was all about hitting the gym? Nah, we've been building muscles by hauling mad bags from the whip since we were knee-high to a grasshopper. Our parents didn't do the heavy lifting; that was kid territory. We could have an armload of 30 grocery bags, and somehow, someway, we'd make it a one-shot deal. I somehow managed to balance it all while fumbling for the key. Once I got that door open, I hustled to the kitchen and dropped the bags on the counter. It was time to get busy in the kitchen, a real culinary operation. My man Alonzo was surgical with the shotgun, and I was surgical with the spices. I cranked up the oven to 400, which was a solid 50 degrees hotter than the usual temp some old heads said was gospel. Don't ask me who made 350 degrees the magic number for all things baked; that's just how it was in the Black community. And before I touched anything, I did the handwash shuffle, not 'cause of COVID, but 'cause that's how you do it when food's involved. It's wild that some folks don't get that. I dashed over to the couch to grab the remote.

"YOUTUBE!!!"

"Opening YouTube," the TV replied.

Crazy how tech was running the show nowadays. No need to push a button, just say the word, and it's served up. Won't be surprised if AI takes over everything in a decade. I cued up some smooth R&B, setting the mood for a chill vibe. I wasn't in a romantic mood, no siree. I was a grown man in his thirties; it wasn't like my twenties when a lady's visit meant instant action. If it happened, it happened. Case and Foxy Brown 'Touch Me, Tease Me' was the perfect soundtrack for my kitchen adventure, kicking off a playlist full of '90s hits. First up, the chicken. No doubt, I gave it a good wash. Who knows who started that "don't wash your meat" nonsense? Probably the same crew that skips washing their legs in the shower. I treated those chicken breasts like they were newborns, showing 'em the kind of love they deserved. I trimmed off most of that fat but left a bit to do its natural basting thing, keeping that meat juicy. I gave 'em all a light coating of avocado oil before slicin' 'em up just right, so they looked like some slick duck lips. Then, I took that apricot stuffing, which was semi-thawed, and stuffed a good amount in each slice. It was like playing surgeon, pulling out those wooden picks, snappin' 'em in half, and sealing up those gaps to make sure none of the good stuff spilled out in the oven. Let me drop some knowledge never, ever use olive oil for cooking. Olive oil ain't built for that. Go with avocado or coconut oil instead. Now, with those chicken breasts on their way to culinary heaven, I turned my focus to those portobello mushrooms. Trinidad James was blastin' on the stereo, throwin' down on All Gold Everything remix. How did he even land on a '90s R&B playlist? Beats me, but I didn't care. I was in the zone. It didn't matter if he was a one-hit wonder or a party animal that song was fire. I gave those portobellos a gentle wash and chopped off their stems. Quick check on the clock it was quarter past three. "Alright," I told myself. "I've got enough time. I'll be done at least five minutes before four." I handled those bell peppers like a kitchen ninja. Red, yellow, and orange they turned it into a food art show. People, regardless of where they're from, appreciate some color on their plates. Young ones, you better be taking notes from your favorite, world-wise uncle. After choppin' 'em up, I stuffed 'em in those portobellos, sprinkled on vegan mozzarella and tomato paste, and into the oven they went. Twenty minutes later, we'd have ourselves a winner. Now, onto that fettuccine alfredo. But let me tell you, this ain't your run-of-the-mill fettuccine alfredo. It's that pure, unadulterated, as close to Italy as you can get without a plane ticket kind of dish. I was gonna whip this up so good that even Olive Garden would want to hire me to fix their Italian food mess. I mean, I like their breadsticks and a couple of their soups, but the rest is trash. Now, young bloods, pay attention back in the '90s, Olive Garden and Red Lobster were the places to be. Taking a date there was like taking 'em to a Benihana's today you knew it was gonna be a good night. Especially at Red Lobster, those cheddar biscuits were a promise of a fantastic evening. Now, we know better the food back then was just straight-up garbage. "Exiting now." My heart was pounding like a three-ring circus in my chest when that text came through. I needed to catch my breath. Strolling over to the front door, I opened it and leaned against the frame, playing with my phone. You know that cool lean, like you're trying to play it off, even though your nerves are doing the Cha-Cha in a room full of wobbly chairs. I wanted her to spot me when she rolls up, no confusion about where the crib is. But as I'm trying to be smooth, I started giving myself a mental beatdown. I forgot to chop up one of those chicken breasts and toss it in the pasta. Oh well, too late now. I'm just gonna roll with it.

"ELSA!!!"

I stepped out, and one of my neighbors from up the block was hollering down the street.

"ELSA!!!," she calls again.

Just as she yells the second time, I see Elsa darting up the block. I dashed away from my front door, only to find she'd vanished. This dog's off the rails.

"I'll find her, Marsha. ELSA!!!," I shouted.

Then it hit me. I know exactly where she's at. Two doors down from me, there's another neighbor with a dog named KeKe. Elsa and KeKe are like Forrest and Jenny, minus the low IQ and bust it open nature. She's either hanging out by the side of the house, peeping through a window, or she's jumped the back gate to go look for her. I jogged down to that house and there's Elsa, barking at the window. She looked at me, flipping her head like, "Nah, I'm good, man."

"Come on, girl," I say, grabbing her by the collar.

I led her back up front. Shewas still trying to bark and look back. Guess it's playtime in her eyes.

"Thanks a lot," Marsha said.

"No problem. This girl's a handful." As Marsha headed back with Elsa, the dog turned around and growled at me. Well, fuck you too, dog. Next time, I might just let you run into the street and play chicken with an old-school Crown Vic on those 22s. Dogs, man, they can be more human than us sometimes. Just then, my phone rang.

"Hello?"

"YASSS!!! I SEE YOU!!!"

I looked toward the street and saw her pulling up in her gray car.

"Park in the driveway."

"You sure?"

Why did ladies do this kind of thing? You gave them a direct instruction, and they always had to second-guess it. It was wild to me, but that's just how it goes sometimes. She pulled up right behind my ride. I could tell she had a solid taste in tunes, vibing to Kelly Rowland. I strolled up to her door as she popped it open, which was probably the only time I didn't play the chivalry card. You didn't want to rush the door on the first visit. You had to keep it smooth, you know? But after that, it's all about opening doors for any classy lady, no matter where she's from. I seriously can't stand folks who skip out on that. Some dudes would say, "These ladies these days don't even say 'thank you,' man." Sure, there might be a few who forget their manners, but does that mean you quit being the respectful gent you know you should be? If you had one bad date, do you swear off dating for good? Nah, you don't. You bounce back, 'cause every person is unique. You can't judge the whole game off one fumble; that's how you miss out on all the wins. We've all been rookies at some point, right?

"Hey."

Her greeting came with a contagious smile. Damn, she was gorgeous.

"What's going on beautiful?"

I gave her a hug, like a throwback to the one we shared on the street after our first date. We both stepped back, grinning at each other.

"You bring a bag or anything?" I asked.

37

"Yeah, got a little somethin'. Brought some wine. Cool with that?"

It was more than cool; it was exactly what I was hoping for.

"Fosho. Let me grab that for you."

She handed me the bag, and I led her inside. I hoped the aroma did something special for her. I'd closed all the windows on purpose, setting the mood. It was warm outside, but not hot enough to make it stuffy indoors, even with all the food I'd whipped up.

"Oh, man. Smells incredible. YASSS!!!"

She said that as soon as she crossed the threshold.

"You're killin' it. You're in there like swimwear," that little devil on my shoulder whispered. I was ready for that response.

"Make yourself at home. The remote's right there. I gotta hit the bathroom real quick."

"Alright," she said, in that sexy voice of hers.

I didn't even need to hit the bathroom; I had to make sure everything in there was on point. I take pride in my cleaning skills, but I couldn't have a single speck of dirt. So, I closed the door, lifted the toilet seat, and thanked the heavens I did. That shit I dropped when I first got home had left a few marks in the bowl. No way, that won't fly. I reached for the toilet cleaner, but ain't nobody got time to wait around for five minutes. I poured some in and scrubbed that bowl like a pro. By the time I flushed, you could practically see your reflection in there. As I hit the sink to wash up, I noticed one last thing I had to take care of. I stashed away my body wash, you know, for the fresh-smelling hand soap. It's one of my secret weapons to keep the skin on point. I came out, headed to the kitchen, and threw a question her way.

"How was your drive?" I asked while setting out the plates.

"It was a cool ride. Took a bit longer thanks to traffic, but not too bad."

"Alright, no worries. Kick back and relax while I prepare our plates."

This was test #1. Could I make the meal look five-star even though I'm all about keeping it simple? They say simple is the way to go, and they're right. But

38

today, I had to go the extra mile. I plated everything just right; I knew those flavors would blend, especially when I drizzled the natural basting juice over that chicken, making it gleam. I grabbed the fancy dishes I keep for special occasions. My regular ceramic plates are for everyday stuff. I swung open the fridge and poured some mango nectar, giving it a healthy, fruity vibe. Gotta hit all five food groups, right? As I poured and slid the drink back into the fridge, I did a quick scan to make sure I hadn't missed anything. Then, I glanced back at the stove and had a moment of realization. Why the heck did I cook corn? I even forgot I had it in the freezer for ages. But, no biggie. I reached for the seasoning cabinet and gave the plate one last sprinkle of parsley, just like the salt meme you've seen. I may not be the meme, but I could put any restaurant out of business right now.

"Yo, my bad, sweetheart. Ain't got no trays, but check it, I'm pullin' this table right up for you."

Hold up, did I just say sweetheart? Nah, I ain't mean it like that, but you know, some folks, no matter their background, get spooked when they hear that word. They bounce like they'll never come back.

"No worries," she replied. I set the grub on the table and slid it over to her.

"Thanks."

"No problem."

"Damn, this looks fire. Look at this chicken breast, it's massive!"

"I feel you, my bad. It's all-natural, straight from the farmer's market. A hearty portion, you know."

She chuckled, and I headed back to the kitchen to fix my plate.

"YASSS!!!" I heard from the living room.

"You good?"

"BOY, YOU'RE KILLING IT!!!"

I hit a little dance move when I heard that. Mission one accomplished - whip up some banging grub and make her dig it. I rolled back into the living room, my plate in hand, and some mango nectar for myself.

"So, what you wanna watch?"

39

"Well, you know," she said between bites. "I'm down for some sci-fi."

That's what I'm talking about. AT&T better not let me down. Sure, it's just 50 bucks a month for cable and internet, but I needed them to bring their A-game. As I browsed through the options, the stars aligned. "I, Robot" had just started. I didn't care about any drama or what folks said about the lead actor, Will Smith. He was still golden in my book. It's wild how this dude saved the world from aliens, fought his own clone, dropped "Summertime" on us, played the Fresh Prince, Hitch the love guru, and a Miami cop, and still got played. Life's no cakewalk for any man, no matter where he's from. We kicked back, watched the flick, and got into some deep convo over that top-notch meal. We even got so wrapped up in it that the movie seemed to be watching us. Even after we'd cleared our plates and I'd tidied up, the conversation kept flowing. We connected on a level I wasn't expecting. I opened up about my past divorce and how I bought into the idea that a man's gotta do it all. In some ways, that's true - be a protector and provider, you know? I had no issue with that. The issue became when my ex wife thought all she had to do was show up. It got draining just to enter my home and feel like I was greeting a roommate. I mean, I am surprised that I didn't cheat in that relationship. I had plenty of good reasons too. I was getting more action from my hand than my wife. When we were intimate, it was always the same ol' shit. It was rarely let's try this, let's try that, or let's go here with it. It was always nice and gentle. Outside the bedroom, I couldn't even be a man. Some dude had smarted off at her one day, and being her husband, me and homey immediately had issues. Could you believe that she was upset at me? I knew we were living in a world where everyone was overly sensitive, and offended by the smallest shit, but you seriously got mad at your husband for defending your honor? After that, things went on a downward spiral. Luckily, for me, I won in court. I kept everything that was in my name. She didn't get a piece of anything. I forked over some bread in alimony for about few months, but paying for my peace was worth it. I learned a valuable lesson with that marriage. All that I have a good heart and good soul bullshit was for the birds. You gotta actually be a woman who has something going for herself, and not be coddled by a mother whose baby daddy didn't want her, and whose ex-husband was smart enough to bounce. The fruit didn't fall too far from the tree, and I learned that. Hey, I mean, it could've been worse, right? I could've been a dog ass nigga, cheated, impregnated her, given my wife an STD, and threatened her life and my unborn child's. But, that's another story that I won't get into. Just know some niggas ain't 100 as they portray themselves to be. Paulette began to delve into her story. She was divorced once as well, and on the verge of another. I was gonna immediately send up the red flag, but her current story was far, far more dramatic. One, she showed me the picture. This negro defined the word ugly. I mean, if you opened up Webster's Dictionary, this nigga's picture would be right next to the word. Second, he was shorter than her, so you know a sister had to love you if you were a human troll. I'm talking 5'1 short. She really fell for his heart, cause looks damn sure didn't cut it. I mean, you had to be attracted to someone in some form, but I guess he had a mouthpiece. Then, I found out he didn't. She disclosed they fell for each other after three months on the road together, doing photography. I get people connecting because of their passions, but what could make any woman love a nigga this ugly and short, boggled me. Anywho, long story short. He cheated, and it wasn't any ordinary type of cheating. He pulled some complete fuck shit. A preteen, his son's girlfriend, in the back seat of her car. Now, what in the good hell would make a grown ass man, with a fine ass wife at home, go sleep with a minor? Sickness. That's what it was. I don't like to use the word hate. As a youngin, I did hate a lot of things. My home life and my body took a hit 'cause my mom labeled me as a fat kid and gave me an earful sometimes. I dreaded those long suit shopping sessions with my old man 'cause he could spend hours in the store. Now, as a grown-up, there are only two things I truly despise in this world: child molesters and rapists. I'm dead certain both should get the death penalty pronto. It's tough to listen to these stories. Tears would sneak out sometimes, and having to console a near stranger just added to my baggage. Sickening stuff. I was still perplexed on how they jumped into marriage after just three months of knowing each other. This kinda thing is happening a lot these days falling for someone you hardly know. Sure, you hear stories about folks marrying after just a few weeks and it working out forever. That's all well and good, but that ain't how it rolls for most. You gotta be certain about who you're laying down with for life. Sadly, many end up going to bed with someone's front and waking up next to a total stranger. "Wait up," I said, about an hour into our convo. I hit the kitchen to fetch my whiteboard from the fridge. 'I, Robot' was ancient history, with Sonny and Will saving the world from those red-light metal villains. I'm just a regular guy not perfect, but real. I sensed this could be a friendship that's got some longevity. Back on the couch, I continued.

"Alright, first and foremost, I'm sorry for what you had to go through, hell, what we both went through. I know we've been through some tough times. None of us are perfect, but all we've been through they're lessons and opportunities to grow. So, let's jot down ten things we wanna achieve as friends to build on this. Cool?"

She looked at me for a moment.

"Cool."

"Alright, I'll kick it off. One, stay connected to something higher. Two, keep communication open. Three, my bad for not letting you speak."

She chuckled.

"No worries, I'm digging this." I got right back to brainstorming.

"Three, whether we're listening to respond or not. We have to make that clear."

People out there just didn't seem to get it, you know? Chris Rock once dropped some wisdom in one of his stand-up specials. He said, sometimes when a lady's talking, you gotta just chill and let her speak her piece, and not in those words. Same goes for life, really. Sometimes, folks just want to vent, be heard, and that's all right. Other times, they're looking for your two cents. That's why it's essential to kick off a conversation with this question: "You want me to listen and understand, or are we going for the exchange of ideas?" You gotta know the difference. Now, my fourth goal in any friendship? Fun. Enjoy the heck out of it. It's kind of an underrated deal. Fun can mean different things to different folks. You've got to tune into your friend, partner, or whoever you roll with. Maybe it's video games, maybe it's something else. Whatever floats your boat. Number five, and this is major. Space. Sometimes, people just need to be left alone, no biggie. It doesn't mean you messed up; it's just how it is. I know when I get back from a hard day at the office, I spend the first 15 minutes on my couch, just relaxing and letting go of the day's madness. Stressful coworkers, boring requests, or even that dreaded check engine light. Let it all go. Six, it's vital in my book for any friendship. Make every moment count. We often take stuff for granted in this day and age, thinking we can do it tomorrow or next week. Not me, though. Health scares, unexpected loss, and more have taught me that every moment matters. You never know when it might be your last. Seven, mental therapy. Make sure you're in a good place, so you can be a good friend. If whipping up dishes soothes your soul, go for it. If she finds peace in a good run, respect that. We can't knock how someone chooses to keep their sanity. I rounded out the last three with simplicity, diversity, and time. Keep things straightforward, avoid making stuff too complicated. Mix it up, don't get stuck in the same old routine. And time? If I have to explain that, we might not need this friendship.

"Sorry for rambling so much."

"Nah, you're all good," she replied, feeling more relaxed.

"You down for a little prayer?" I asked her. Man, why did I bring this up? Didn't want her thinking I'm some religious nut.

"Wow," she said.

I was half-expecting her to think I'm off my rocker. It did feel a little crazy to ask.

"Sure thing. No problem."

Her tone shifted when she said that.

"All right, let's hold hands."

I set the board down next to us and we locked hands. No way was I diving into those deep, back-road preacher prayers that take 40 days and nights. I kept it simple, straight to the point, and just tried to manifest these words into our lives.

"Amen," she said. You know, I peeped all your tattoos on your Facebook. Yep, I did a little online stalking."

Her words drew a chuckle out of me.

"That back ink of yours, how long did that masterpiece take?"

Everyone dug my back piece. I had my whole back inked in a four part, marathon 30-hour session, a real statement for civil rights, Black pride, and everything for my people. I moved to the end of the couch, peeled off my shirt, and began talking about the piece. She came up behind me, touching me, running her fingers down my back as I explained the meaning of every detail. While I kept on talking, I felt a warm tongue glide across my upper back. The look on my face was like, "Whoa, didn't see this coming." Then again, when you're a genuine dude, your mind isn't in the bedroom. She licked across the other way this time, adding a few kisses. Her hands roamed up around my shoulders and down to my chest. Her tongue played a tune in my ear, accompanied by nibbles that said, "Make me your personal project." Her fingertips begged my tattoos to spill their stories to her personally.

"Come on," she whispered.

I got up and watched her with a grin as she headed to my bedroom. I walked back to the living room, chuckled to myself, and thought, "Man, writing down goals done led to writing a novel in some cooch."

As I flipped off the light switch, that inner devil on my left shoulder showed up.

"Boy, you better turn that pussy into poetry and make it drop some bars." I cracked a sly grin. Then, that angelic voice on my right side chimed in, probably with a counterpoint.

"Show no mercy. That pussy needs some proper attention."

"That what?," I whispered.

"THAT PUSSY, MAN!!! MAKE THAT SHIT SING A TUNE!!!" the inner devil shouted.

Well, damn, I thought. These two opposing forces actually agreed. Time to get to work. I walked into my bedroom. The blinds were open, letting the backyard lights filter in, setting a cool ambiance.

"Hey, turn on the lights and see what you got."

I reached up, pulled the cord for the light, and damn. She had to be one of the most beautiful creations I'd ever seen. Not to mention, everything was on point.

"Drop them shorts?," she said.

I moved quickly, shedding my shorts. She smiled.

"Nice. Now, get on over here."

Yes, ma'am, I thought. I cut the lights back off, and without Teddy Pendergrass's instructions, I slid on top of her. Our tongues started a smooth dance inside each other's mouths. I touched her body in a way that conveyed safety. This was a moment for exploring and comfort. No fear in sight. I was chill as ice at that moment, no fronting. I'm a fit dude, but I've always side-eyed those stubborn love handles around my waist. Her words, her touch, made it clear that she was all about this body, and that acceptance was top of mind. I moved down, slow and steady, kissing every inch of her. Her breasts? Man, they were perky and a guy like me, I'm all about them nips. Besides the tummy, the twins were my absolute favorite. But then, I ventured down to her midsection. My smooches and licks revealed a C-section scar. And guess what? That didn't phase me, it elevated me. Many women feel self-conscious about C-section scars, but not this one. We were embracing it, just like the rest of her unique self. I got down on my knees, slowly guiding her hips over. It was time for one of my favorite pastimes. Skipping out on going down? Not an option, especially with a stunning lady like her. My first taste sent shivers down her spine, and it was like my taste buds hit the jackpot. She was wetter than the Pacific Ocean, and her flavor? It was life itself. I know what you're thinking how can you say someone tastes like life? Well, life is beautiful, it's what we all desire, what we live and breathe. Life is all things good, great, and amazing. Her lady parts? They were all of that and then some. I lost myself completely in her goodness. She was a whole experience, and her natural sweetness? Nutritious was an understatement. I kept writing love poems with my tongue, and her heavy breathing was the background music. That scream she let out, followed by a burst of liquid pleasure, caught me off guard. I didn't flinch on the outside, but inside, I was ecstatic. This girl was a squirter. That part was overflowing. I'd been around for over 30 years and never experienced anything like this. It turned me on so much that I stayed down there, eager for more. In total, she hit about six more times. My manhood was rock-hard, and I was determined to make her forget every other dude. I came up, and she grabbed my head, kissing me with her unique taste. This girl was adventurous, and I was all for it. Suddenly, she flipped me onto my back. It surprised the heck out of me. Here I was, over six feet tall and solid, and she handled me like a pro.

"Scoot up," she said, and I obliged. My head flopped back on the mattress. She didn't waste time, no teasing or playing around. She went full throttle, showing off her skills. I was so blown away that I cocked my leg up. No woman had ever made me do that, let alone have me contemplating like that. I couldn't help but think, "What's her secret? Nobody should be giving head like this." This wasn't your average act. This was a full-on journey. Giving head was a special art, and many folks do it just to do it. But her? Nah. She was saying, "Thank you for treating me like a queen. Thank you for real talk, for spending time, for listening to my vulnerabilities without being a creep. Thank you for those nine-plus hours. Thank you for simply being a stand-up man." That's what she was saying to me. She finished and hopped right on it. There's something about a woman taking control that makes you want to spoil her, whether you're buying her a house, a yacht, or something else. As she took me in, I leaned back and enjoyed the ride. Every time I tried to take the wheel, she sped up, running the show. As her curves danced, the atmosphere buzzed with chatter. All I could think was, 'I ain't supposed to be on the receiving end like this. I should be the one taking charge.' She was completely in the moment, and so was I. I let her have her fun until I decided it was my turn. It was time to show her what I've got. I flipped her over, and our lips locked in a passionate embrace. This wasn't your standard position; this was about exploring uncharted territory, igniting a new spark. Our hands clung together like they were meant to be, as if our souls whispered, 'You're the one.' I was working up a sweat, but this was a workout I couldn't wait to do again. It wasn't just about the act itself; it was everything leading up to it. We rolled and tumbled, and then she climbed back on top, taking control. Damn, I thought. Cardinal rule #1: never finish inside the first time. But at that moment, I was seriously contemplating breaking that rule. As I tried to pull out, a voice in my head said 'Remember, pull out.'

You know who that voice was. Then, that evil demon surfaced:

"NUT IN HER AND ESTABLISH DOMINANCE!!! DON'T BE NO BITCH!!!"

Game, demon, and with a few more powerful moves from her, I erupted like a volcano. I'd been intimate before, but this was something else entirely. She leaned in for a kiss, a kiss that expressed sheer exhaustion. My body was still trembling, and I couldn't help but think, 'Man, what did you just do, Junior? Did you really nut in her on the first night?' I tried to withdraw because I was hypersensitive, but she pushed me back down.

"Leave it in," she said. "Let it marinate."

Marinate? I thought I was the one who cooked up the heat tonight, but she turned into the Master of Seduction, marinating my desires. You know what? I know they say you can't get too hooked after just one night, but let me tell you, she had me spellbound. Eventually, I had to pull out. She rolled over, gazing at me with a sly grin. Me? I tried to muster a smile, but honestly, I was drained, thinking, 'What the heck did she just do to me?'

"Yo, you good?" she asked, sporting a massive grin.

"Yeah, yeah, I'm chillin."

I was trying to keep it cool, but she had me all messed up. She strolled over to the bathroom, turning on the shower.

"You got towels, right?"

"In that cabinet in the hallway, right across from the bathroom door."

The hallway light let me peep her choosing the perfect cotton stuff. She grabbed a towel and a washcloth, checked me out, smiled, and stepped into the shower. I sat up in bed. Slapped myself twice. Nah, fam, you ain't just get embarrassed in your own spot. Man, what's gotten into you? I knew exactly what had me feeling some type of way. As far as I could see, we were together. This ain't some hit-it-and-quit-it deal; it's not about repeating the process until it feels right. Nah, after a nine-hour date, me cooking for you, and then you bringin' that A-game, you were mine. I had to get up and go to the bathroom.

"Ayo," I told her as she was looking all fine in that shower glow. "You know we're a thing, right?"

She cracked up.

"Oh, that's all it took, huh?"

"Nah, that was just the icing. After that nine-hour marathon, I knew you were it. But this right here? This sealed the deal."

Once again, she laughed.

"Slide on in. Let me wash you up." I shook my head as I hopped in the shower with her. No need for any romantic stuff in there; we were still tired from our activities. This woman fucked around and got commitment from the jump. Man, how do you even plan for something like this? We washed up, dried off, and threw on our clothes. Me in my bedtime gear, her in what she came in.

"Well, it's past 10, and I gotta bounce."

"You sure you don't wanna crash here?"

She bit her lip.

"Yeah, but we gotta save some excitement for the next time. Thanks for dinner."

"You're welcome. Let me walk you to your ride."

"You don't have to."

"Hold up. Two things. One, there's no 'sorry' dude over here. Maybe these new-school cats ain't about opening doors or walking ladies to their car, but I'm not about that. If I do anything, I'm making sure you're straight."

I wanted her to feel safe. Forget all the other stuff; this was necessary. I don't know why folks let TV and stereotypes change who they are. I mean, if you eat a bad batch of broccoli, do you stop eating vegetables? If your car's check engine light comes on, do you stop driving altogether? Nah, you don't. I don't get why people let one bad experience change them. Trust me, ten women might not say a word when I hold the door open for them, but I'll still hold it for number eleven. Sheesh. I hated sounding like a broken record. We hugged by the car, said our goodbyes, and sealed it with a kiss.

"Text me when you're back home."

"I got you."

She started up the whip and peeled off. I stood in that empty driveway spot for a good 30 seconds after she took off. I was feeling some type of way, in a good way. Damn, that was some top-notch cooch. I walked back into the crib, shut the door, and knocked out. The next day, I rolled into the office space around nine, just like my usual. But being a Friday, I switched lanes and headed across town to a buzzing coworking spot, where all of the Black creatives hung out.

"What's crackin', fam?" I dapped up these wild folks, with most of them being ladies.

"Big Sur. How it's going?"

"Black men don't cheat."

"No doubt, we don't stray," I nodded back.

"Don't even think about bringing that drama in here today. Y'all got some tricks up your sleeves."

Torri was on that tip. We dubbed her the space's auntie, even though her vibe was more grandma than anything.

"Listen up. We don't got cheat codes in our DNA; we're Black men."

"Boy, you better cut that shit out."

That was Ree Ree, my girl and the coding game's undisputed boss. She might be pint-sized, but she could drop bombs without hesitation.

"Aye, my man said it like it is. We don't cheat. It's not in our blood."

"Sur, respect, fam. These girls don't know the deal."

I snagged an open desk and the debates raged on.

"Come on, now. Stop your bullshit," Torri said.

"Torri, you gotta school your own wild sisters. Talking 'bout entanglements."

"She entangled! Not cheating."

"BULLSHIT!!!" Sur and I shouted in harmony.

"They were on a break!"

"Oh, so 'cause I'm on a break from my crib right now, it ain't mine?"

Man, I lucked out being in the hood with this office, 'cause back on my side of the city, the others might've banned us.

"Shut the hell up. Y'all cheat more than ever. None of y'all keep it 100."

"Then name me some guys who've stepped out."

"OFFSET!!!"

"Nah, hold up. We said Black. Migos means 'friends' in Spanish, so they're Mexican. You can't deny that 'cause some Mexicans got that darker shade. NEXT!!!"

I got 'em heated with that one.

"I know for a fact. Kevin Hart."

"Forget that, you gotta hit a certain height to be a certified Black man. Anything below 5'10" is a boy's club."

Oh, they went in on me. Sur was cracking up, and I was just riding the wave. I knew these girls were itching to whoop on me any minute.

"TIGER!!!" Torri screamed.

"Girl, that dude's Asian. Move on."

I pushed their buttons even more. At this point, they were ready to throw down.

"So with all that said," Sur hollered, "it's a done deal, BLACK MEN DON'T CHEAT!!!"

We kept spitting facts for a good minute, and then Torri hit me with a curveball.

"Hold up, you way too jolly this morning. What's up?"

The room went dead silent. I kicked back, grinning.

"What, I'm always on the up and up."

Torri lowered her shades and locked eyes on me.

"You got some cutty last night, didn't you?"

I started grooving at my desk.

"Hoe," Ree Ree dropped.

"Dang, why I gotta be all that?"

"Cause you're a hoe."

Man, they were ruthless here. The day was on fire as we hustled hard, using our unique skills to make a living. No doubt, it was inspiring to see talented women crushing it in tech, coding, web development, and accounting, all with their own businesses. That's some real impressive stuff deserving of mad props. Lunchtime rolled around, and I was deep into texting with Paulette when I headed back to the office. I grabbed a Jersey Mike's sub, while Torri went all out with a soul food feast.

"Dang, you didn't ask if anyone else wanted in on that."

"You're not my man," she shot back.

"Torri, you know the deal. Anyone looking to date my sister has to go through me."

"She's a grown woman, nigga. Shut the fuck up."

"Ree, why you gotta be so intense?"

"Because none of y'all are worth a damn. You're not worth a damn. My husband ain't worth shit either. None of y'all are worth shit."

"So you don't cook for your husband?"

"Fuck him. He better cook for me. I pushed out two kids for his lazy ass. All he had to do was grab a leg."

"I mean, the guy's the reason those babies came into this world. The gardener plants the seed."

I saw that stapler flying towards me and pulled a slick dodge, just like George W. Bush dodging those shoes in Iraq.

"Why'd you throw that at me?"

"'Cause I was trying to kill yo' triflin' ass."

The office erupted in laughter, and I knew we were in for another one of these hilarious conversations.

"Listen, don't put me in the same category as those sorry Florida dudes. If they can't keep it up, there's gotta be some murky swamp water down there." Ducking again, this time, she aimed a hole punch at me.

"You mad?"

"Whatever, nigga. Y'all ain't worth shit. You ain't shit. Sur ain't shit. Just be thankful we ain't resorting to violence. Hell, she probably fucked you, then bounced."

"Oh, come on, please."

"See, Torri," she pointed out. "That's the reaction of a guy who got fucked. She's probably just coming back tonight 'cause she's bored."

"Ladies don't come back 'cause they're bored."

"Nah, we don't come at all."

Man, that was a low blow right there.

"Listen up," Sur chimed in. "Ain't nobody trying to mess around all night. I'm young, but I've got things to do. Like Bernie Mac once said, 'Stop all that hollering, bust a nut, so we can go to sleep.'"

"We're already asleep by the time y'all finish the job!"

"And judging by your face, you could use all the sleep you can get."

Why the heck did I say that? I found myself sprinting as she grabbed the rolling chair and hurled it. I barely dodged it. I glanced back at her.

"Damn, Ree. Why are you trying to take me out?"

"One less useless fucker in the world. Again, y'all ain't worth shit."

I felt like I was in the middle of some wild drama. This was unlike anything I'd ever experienced. I wouldn't trade it for all the money in the world. We shot the breeze for a bit longer before I left. It was cool that Paulette had a real passion for writing and wanted to have a session tonight. This time, though, I'd be ready if she wanted me to write a chapter with her. I had time today, and I was feeling great. I peeled out of the parking lot and headed straight to the dollar store. I had to get my Lifesavers gummies, so I picked up two bags. I wasn't cooking tonight, as I still had leftovers from last night. I got home, indulged in my 15-minute relaxation exercise, and I'd recommend it to everyone. After dedicating hours to others, or even yourself, take some time to gather your thoughts. Get familiar with your home, whether you rent or own it. And speaking of that, let's stop the endless debate about renting versus owning. There's someone out there with nothing but the clothes on their back, sleeping on a sidewalk, who'd gladly trade places with you and give you a piece of their mind for arguing over minor stuff. In this day and age, having four walls and a roof is something to be grateful for. I sent a text to Paulette asking what time she was coming over. She replied, saying 5:30. Great, this gave me time to relax, work out, and freshen up before she arrived. I switched out of chill mode, and took a quick seven to ten-minute shower. I made a rule not to hit the gym smelling like a sweaty mess. I couldn't believe how many folks strolled into that place reeking like a swamp. Nah, I couldn't do it. I had too much self-respect for that. I wrapped up at the gym, smashing a solid hour-long workout, and hit the sauna. When I got home, it was 4:30. That left me a solid hour to clean up and set the mood for the night. She took me by surprise last night. If it was going down tonight, I was ready for round two. No way shorty was gonna catch me slipping again. After a quick shower, I spent the time waiting for her watching Hallmark movies. It wasn't just any girl coming over; I had to brainstorm some romantic ideas. This was all on me, and I was loving it. Yo, if y'all haven't seen "Chance at Romance," you gotta check it out. Quick rundown: an eight-year-old dude pretends to be his dad on an online dating site. He connects with a woman who decides to visit. She's bummed when she finds out it's a kid but can't bounce back to her town due to a weekend storm shutting down the train. When his pops pushes him to say why he did it, he drops the wisdom "Mom's gone, and you need some cooch." Long story short, it's cool to move on after a loss. I got a message on my phone, "Exiting now. Gonna pull up in the driveway" I pulled out my laptop, gearing up to write. She knew I was into reading and writing, so my living room library wasn't just for show. I'd read every book on those shelves, and this was my life. We might end up getting intimate, but writing was gonna happen tonight. I heard her car pull up and quickly put on a T-shirt and shorts. Opening the door, I saw she'd already propped it open.

"Man, you know I dig opening car doors."

She gave me a sly smile and shut it.

I opened her car door and asked how she was doing.

"I'm good. Consistency is your middle name, huh?"

"Absolutely," I replied, shutting her door.

"If that's the case, then...nevermind."

Looks like she had jokes. Well, it seemed I had to bring my A-game tonight. We got settled in the house, opened our laptops, and muted the TV to really focus. Talking about her dream to write a book on the phone was one thing, but seeing her do it in person was something else. An intellectual woman was hot, and an intellectual woman who could turn heads was damn sexy. I had to be able to look at you. You didn't have to be a model, but if I couldn't stand to look at you, it wasn't gonna work. A while back, my sister told me to lower my standards, claiming I only dated glamor chicks. So, when this woman, who wasn't a stunner, asked to meet, I reluctantly agreed. After two dates and my sister's friend rating her a 3 out of 10 with makeup, I was done. A good heart and personality counted, but I couldn't deal with disgust. About 30 minutes in, I saw her struggling with writer's block. I felt her frustration in those grunts. I was in the zone, but I was low-key waiting for her to say, "This is hard."

"Ugh, this is annoying."

"What's going on?"

"I'm really trying to do this. I've got so much I want to share with the world. This is tough." I shook my head. "Nah, don't look at it like that. What's hard is the choice you made to write. This is the easy part. You know your story better than anyone else because it's yours."

I went back to typing. Out of the corner of my eye, I saw her giving me that look. If you want to get a woman in the mood, tell her what she needs to hear in a firm yet reassuring voice, and act like it ain't no big deal.

"You know what? I'm not even in the mood to write anymore. You want some wine?"

"Yeah, give me a small glass. I don't need much. I'm in my zone."

Checkmate. I saw the look she gave me out of the corner of my eye. Yo, peep how I played it, fam. I stayed sharp, answered her query, and hinted that my game extended beyond this screen. Shorty strolled to the kitchen to pour up some glasses. In my mind, I was lowkey smirking. I knew payback was gonna be sweet. I wasn't about to lay down that young gun action, that was the 25-year-old me when all I cared about was smashing. I'm pushing past 35 now, I'm in my prime, and I know how to lay it down. She was about to get that unforgettable lovin', you feel me? Forget about realigning her spine; I was gonna scramble her brain cells. She brought over the wine, and finally, I put the brakes on.

"Appreciate it, sweetheart."

"Oh, now I'm a sweetheart?"

"You cool."

We both chuckled as she playfully tapped my arm. I had her wrapped around my finger. The mood was probably off the charts. I moved the laptop and switched to the music app on the TV. Neo Soul was just right for the vibe. I didn't want that super sensual R&B; Neo Soul hits that perfect balance between wanting to get down and wanting to chill, all at once. As I was about to shut the laptop, she laid her hand on it.

"Hold up, run through what you wrote real quick."

"You sure, though?"

She gave me a look, got up, and turned off the living room lights. The glow from the stove light, combined with the TV and the music, set the mood just right. She came back to the couch, sippin' her wine slow. I glanced at her and chuckled.

"Alright, let's dive in. And you want that emphasis, right?"

She nodded in agreement. Here goes nothing:

As he smiled, hanging up the phone, he said his prayers. A talk earlier with a friend, who had a heavy spirituality, revealed something he never knew. When Moses went to the mountain, asking God what He should be called, God responded, "I AM. I AM THE ALPHA, AND THE OMEGA. THE BEGINNING, AND THE END." There was no name. He was just "I AM" because you can't put a name on an all-powerful entity. He doesn't know if she noticed, but all night, he referred to The One as The Almighty because he felt slighted in saying "God" this whole time. As he prayed over her, his home, and other things, he immediately thought back to the conversation. She ended it with "Goodnight Love." He remembers the look on his face when he asked her what she said. She repeated it. He responded with "Goodnight Love." He thought, "Bruh, are you falling in love? Nah. Can't be. You've only known her for less than two weeks. You've only been with her one time. But it was an amazing time. The most exciting time in your entire life. You've talked about family, wants, and needs. Hell, you even spoke of a dream honeymoon scenario with her. Marriage. All that. Are you in love?" he asked. The answer was simply scary. He wanted to say it, but he knew love consisted of a whole lot more. As he began to lay on his back, he began to think about her upcoming arrival. OMG, he shouldn't be thinking about sex, but he is. He is conflicted. He knows the situation. Hers and his. What if life split them permanently? What if regret would set in? He does not want to mess this up either? For so long in his life, he was conflicted about his body, his mental, just being him. Lies he used to tell to mask his pain. Now, here was a broken woman, who was still a woman. He knew her foundation. She knew him. He was conflicted. He prayed for self-control as she asked for, and also for himself. They were building brick by brick, but concrete can overflow, and that was fear and joy wrapped into one. Phewww. Man, he wanted to say he loved her, and he did to end the call. But, he couldn't mean it FULLY until THE ALMIGHTY signified it from above. That was the forever type of love, where the sight of her next to him daily made him a better man. He wanted her being, her mind, her heart, and soul. He knew what it was like to hurt and to be hurt. He wanted to be past that. He wasn't even looking for this. He just wanted to handle everything else, and then hope someone came along to love and cherish. He was definitely going to try his darndest tomorrow to hold back because they both know The Almighty honors obedience, even though the flesh is weak. He slept well. He woke up at 3:15, heading to the kitchen for a sea moss shake, followed by a shower. As he arrived at the gym, his mind became focused on his body. He worked out legs as usual. His toughest day. Then, he went into the dark room with the red lights. He and her had a virtual gym date last night. She saw his body and it appealed to her. At that moment, he took his shirt off, as everyone else was outside, doing a boot camp-style CrossFit. She made him feel comfortable. So, shirtless and sweaty, he did medicine ball push-ups. He was comfortable, for once. The insecurity was gone. Tired after an hour and a half, he left to go back home and shower. As he prepared to take shake #2, he opened his phone. It was a letter from her. Her fears began with her daughter. It pained him to see this, as he knew this situation all too well. This, he has never shared, and it's part of the reason why he feels God cursed him for his father's sins. She feared getting her heart broken. He feared breaking it because of career, or just not being good enough. He fears him not labeling himself as a Christian will steer her away. The church was a refuge to him but also hurt him. He didn't want a label. Religion had destroyed his life in so many areas. He valued a relationship with THE ALMIGHTY more than anything. Now, he was concerned that would drive her away. As he drank, he only hoped that today he could fill her with peace. Not in the physical, but everything else. Lord, brick by brick. He then walked into the shower.

"That's that piece."

I looked over at her. Her head went down, and then came back up. I saw a tear fall from her left eye, reminding me of the same tears I dropped from my left eye, when Left Eye died.

"Didn't think I'd write that did you?" She just cried some more.

"What was the thing that haunted you the most about all that? Outside of the fear for your daughter's safety, and the obvious."

The waterworks kept coming. I wrote based on our conversations in quiet times, where my four walls became my biggest audience. I got up and got some tissue, handing it to her. As she wiped her tears, the broken spirit came out.

"You would think, as a woman, that if your husband created a situation of infidelity, it would be with another grown woman. No. You sleep with a minor. In the back of our car of all places. We are supposed to be a connected unit. And the crazy shit is, as much as I am upset at the foul act that he displayed as a bitch. Not a man. Two things hurt me. One, the people who lie and try to take up for him. Making lies about him being in the hospital fighting cancer, when he's in prison, fighting men, who hopefully are beating the dog shit out of him. The second thing is the trauma that young lady will have to endure for the rest of her life. I mean. A grown man that manipulates a teenager into thinking, this is what life is about. I've been through that. It's not something you ever forget. I'm still trying to ask myself, as a grown woman, why I even still associate with my rapist when I see him. I was 14 and he was 22. I tell myself it's cool, knowing, it's not."

I remember the day she told me the whole story surrounding her divorce. I was on the phone, dead silent. I had no words, even if she did ask me to listen to respond. Some stuff was so off the meter that you couldn't respond to it. I was fuming. There were a lot of things that I didn't agree with in life. Child molesters and rapists dying, that was a no brainer. With all the breath in my body, if they all died, I would go to their funerals and volunteer to be their gravediggers. Dirt was not worthy of being put on their bodies. Hell, their bodies weren't even worth being put inside of a casket. If I had it my way, I would simply throw their dead carcasses into the ground, have a cement truck pour liquid concrete over them, and let it harden. Even so, Mother Earth may be so ashamed of them, that she may spit them up. Truthfully, I didn't blame her. Why would you want to swallow something that was so disgusting? I held her as she cried in my arms. I don't know if this was trauma bonding or not. In this moment, however, I started to think about the young women in my life, whether family or friends who had at one point been molested, raped or manipulated by a grown adult. I saw that shit in prevalence during my high school years. As a teen, we were conscious of the decisions we made. However, we weren't fully aware of the consequences of our choices. I remember girls not wanting to talk to the 'school dudes,' just so they could roll with a 23 year old, or older nigga, who would pull up during their lunch periods, in a Box Chevy. It was a sad sight to see. In their eyes, they were getting clout. The truth was that they were willingly opening themselves up to rape and trauma. A lot of those women ended up pregnant before ever thinking about taking the SAT exam. I commend the ones that grew up, seeked help and raised their kids despite that trauma. However, babies shouldn't be raising babies. Trust me, there was nothing cool or dope about making a baby while in high school, especially with a grown ass man who knew better, yet still manipulated an undeveloped mind into thinking that shit was cool. I spent the next twenty or odd something minutes just trying to be a friend, and nothing more. As the time elapsed and we drank some glasses of wine, two simple words brought ease over this whole situation.

"Thank you."

"Just doing what a man is supposed to do."

"I'M SORRY I'M SO BROKEN!!!," she yelled, as tears swelled up in her eyes again, and she buried her face in her hands.

"Yo," I said, giving her a sly grin as I gently cupped her face. "I'm your pottery artist, here to mend, shape, and vibe."

"Are you sure you want this? I'm not healthy. I want this, but I'm scared to care for you. Just be there if you decide to ride this out with me."

"I got you."

She leaned in for a kiss, and after that, it was all systems go. Our clothes came off, each piece telling a story of its own. I couldn't help but remember the wild night we had before, where she left me reeling in the best way. Tonight, I was about to deliver a show-stopping encore. However, it was not merely sex. It was a therapeutic session. I flipped her onto her stomach, pressing up close, my lips trailing down her neck and back. Amidst her sweet moans, I made a quick pit stop to grab a bag of gummy bears. You know what was about to happen next. I popped one in my mouth while my tongue embarked on an exhilarating journey. No shame in my game; she was mine, and what's mine gets taken care of. From the roota to the toota. This wasn't just about the physical; it was about finding solace, wiping away any doubts, and healing old wounds. Tonight, it wasn't Paulette Jefferson meeting Junior Mitchell; it was about her meeting a man, something she hadn't experienced in a long while.

Journal Entry: The Decision to Love Past Hurt

Today was a turning point in my relationship with Paulette, a day when I made the decision to love her through all her hurt, trauma, and pain. We're together now, and I know that Paulette carries a heavy burden from her past. She's been through so much, and she often carries the weight of her trauma like invisible armor. It has taken time for her to open up to me, to trust me with her pain, and today, that trust reached a new level. We were sitting on the couch at my home, writing our lives on a laptop, casting a warm, golden hue on everything around us. Paulette had always been a woman of few words, but today she finally found the courage to share some of her deepest scars with me. The pain in her eyes was raw and vulnerable, and as she spoke, I could feel my heart aching for her. She talked about the childhood she lost, the wounds that never quite healed, and the nightmares that haunted her every night. Listening to her, I realized that loving someone means loving every part of them, even the broken parts. It's not just about cherishing their strengths and joys but also being there during their darkest moments. In that moment, I knew that Paulette was more than just the woman I wanted; she was a survivor, a warrior who had faced battles I couldn't even begin to comprehend. She had been hurt and scarred, but she had also shown immense resilience and strength. She was so much more than her pain. I held her hand as she spoke, offering silent support. I didn't need to say much; I just needed to be there, to listen, and to let her know that I loved her unconditionally, even without saying it. I made a silent promise to myself that I would be the constant in her life, the safe harbor where she could find solace when the storms of her past threatened to overwhelm her. Paulette and I have a long journey ahead, navigating the complex terrain of her past and the scars that it has left. But today, I took the first step towards loving her through it all, because I know that love has the power to heal, to mend, and to help her find peace. It's not always easy, and it might not always be perfect, but our love is worth every moment of pain, healing, and growth. Today, I chose to love her not in spite of her pain but because of it. But, there is always that what if. As E40 once said. Everybody got choices. I had to live with mine.

3

DA ART OF STORYTELLING

"They say you can't turn a bad girl good, but once a good girl's gone
bad, she's gone forever"
–Jay Z, Song Cry

We had been in this fly groove for a month, almost two months now. From all the stuff I've been through since I was a kid, right into my grown-up years, it's just in my blood to have that healing vibe when there's a cut that needs more than just a band-aid. I'm talking about being there for anyone, not just the ladies, but for anyone in need. Men like me ain't in it for the rewards or with some shady motives. We're just cut from a different cloth. It's like we've been raised around people who've been through some heavy stuff, and they need someone to lean on. Trust me, I've been around that struggle my whole life, thanks to my folks. They were basically roomies with a marriage certificate. I grew up in the midst of all that pain, but somehow, I found my rebirth. Don't ask me how; it's like divine intervention. Now, could this all blow up in my face? Hell yeah, I'm no stranger to that "don't save 'em" rule or trying to fix a busted clock that can't even tell time. Life's a gamble, from new relationships to business moves. We're all about taking risks. I'm not trying to be some savior for this woman sinking in her troubles, but her story had me hooked. There are a million reasons why guys walk out on their families, but you'd never guess it's because they're feeding some messed-up, unethical obsession, destroying minds and bodies of people who ain't even got a taste of life yet. Violating innocence, that's what gets to me. I want to handle him myself, honestly. I'm praying someone inside the prison's dealing with it for me. Not every situation calls for life sentences; sometimes, we gotta handle things our way, right then and there. Hearing his name, Cliff, man, it's like nails on a chalkboard. That's how I feel about dudes like him. They need to get thrown in the deep ocean with a juicy steak around their neck and let the sharks do their thing. Paulette, in the short time I've known her, she earned my trust, my love, and my heart. Yeah, it might seem like things are moving quickly, but it feels right to me. I ain't one to mess with the natural flow. In my mind, everything's falling into place. We talked midweek about hanging out on the weekend, but this weekend, I wanted it to be something more. I wanted it to be the start of a journey for her spirit, her soul, and her mind. Our conversations, man, they're like a shot of energy. Man, our nights together were off the charts. I was all about unlocking those deep, hidden desires. Instead of asking her, I straight-up told her to drop whatever weekend plans she had. I had some epic plans in mind, you know, to treat her right, make her vibe with me so hard she'd catch a buzz just from my presence. She hit me with the classic question, wanting to know what I had up my sleeve. But this time, I couldn't spill the beans; it was all hush-hush. I just told her to clear her schedule for three days straight. It all kicked off that Wednesday when I went on a mad search for the perfect spot. This city was stacked with choices for setting the mood right. Oceanfront? Nah, too typical. I didn't want to be basic like everyone else, especially considering how our first date went down. I wanted her to step out of her comfort zone. I scoured the web for a good half-hour, and Google wasn't much help, until, out of nowhere, it hit me like a lightning bolt. I locked in reservations at this low-key downtown hotel, in the heart of where all the nighttime madness took place. It was a hidden gem, so discreet you could miss it driving by. The place was called Serendipity, a name that just oozes romance. According to Merriam-Webster, serendipity means things falling into place in a happy and unexpected way. That's exactly how things were playing out between us, kind of random, but oh so rewarding. I was in the business of helping her rebuild herself, and the transformation of both of us was in the works, whether we admitted it or not. I dove deep into researching the hotel. I always wanted nothing but the best. You see, fellas, especially young guns, remember this: always aim for the top-notch stuff, just in case things don't go as planned. If you take a lady to a fancy restaurant and her mood sours, at least you can savor a fantastic meal. Even a high-maintenance lady can't mess up the taste of some killer lemon pepper wings. The hotel, though, was the real deal, with a rooftop bar and pool that served up epic views of downtown skyscrapers. It was like a plate of shrimp and grits, loaded with bacon bits, cheese, and topped with green onions, and the experience? Man, it was something else. Then came the tough part–choosing the right room. It was kinda nerve-wracking because every time I thought I'd found the perfect suite, another one came along that was even more lit. The place was all about high-end vibes. No matter what I picked, it was gonna be good, but you know, choices come with consequences, even when they're all good. After weighing all the options, I went with the corner suite. It had everything: a chill living room, a master bedroom with sliding doors, and a hot tub right there in the room. It rang up to over 700 bucks, but I didn't even blink. It was gonna be worth every penny. No amount of cash could ever put a price on fixing a woman's heart, her spirit, and her mind–especially if she's genuinely one of the good ones. Friday came quicker than a navy sailor losing his virginity in The Philippines. I lived about 30-35 minutes north of downtown, so it was a must to dip out from the 9-to-5 early and get things prepped. Who was I fooling, though? I was about to sweep this woman off her feet, get her on cloud nine, and make her heart skip a beat. I took the whole day off from work. Fridays were usually chill for me, so skipping one wouldn't hurt, even if it took a chunk out of my wallet. First stop: the local flower joint. You know, the spot for setting up that romantic vibe just right. I needed rose petals on a budget, because, you know, decorating the carpet and the bed was on the agenda. Things were about to get steamy, and I wanted to melt her heart before we turned up the heat. As I strolled in, the wise sister was at the counter.

"You're back. How'd the night go?"

"It went real smooth. Like, incredibly smooth. I need more rose petals." She gave me that look.

"What's up?" I asked.

"Rose petals on the bed, huh?"

"How'd you know?"

"Child, your face tells the whole story. That woman left her mark on you. I bet you went all out."

"WHAT!!!???"

"Oh, I can tell. I've been there, done that, and let me tell you, Cecil knows how to keep me happy."

I couldn't believe it. I didn't know how she knew, but she did. I guess the older generation gets it, you know? As she packed the rose petals and handed them over, she dropped a piece of wisdom on me.

"I'm not saying it's not real, but make sure you've met her true self, not just the public persona."

"I think I have."

"Feelings and reality don't always align. You'll know who you're dealing with when you have your first disagreement. Until then, make her feel special."

"That's one hell of an advice piece."

"Nah, baby. When you die, you find peace. Be her peace, while you give her a piece of yourself. If she goes, let her go in your arms."

"Are you the love guru now?"

"Nah, I'm Heather. Now, go do your thing."

It was an interesting way to break down life. I finished my task and made a quick stop at the taco spot. I needed a surf-n-turf burrito. I know, it was barely past 10 in the morning, but there's never a bad time for a burrito. But I had a second thought. I made a detour to the health spot down the street. There, I grabbed a pineapple, mango, dragon fruit, and sea moss smoothie, just in case she wanted to swallow some kids tonight. It was all about that fruity goodness, and making the experience pleasurable for her as well. Trust me, it makes a difference. Always be prepared. I texted Paulette, letting her know I'd scoop her up at four, so I had ample time to get everything set. She replied with an "ok," and I continued my day. With my stomach happy, I hit up Dollar Tree. I know what you might be thinking: why go cheap after dropping over 700 bucks on a room? But trust, there's a method to the madness. This was for the little things: cards, envelopes, balloons, and everything to make the moment special. She loved the color orange, so every card would be in an orange envelope. It's the little details that people often think we ignore. Well, I paid attention, because those little things can lead to big results. As I wandered the aisles, I stumbled upon a pack of orange and blue balloons. "BINGO!!!" I tossed those in my basket, and I had cards, balloons, and envelopes. Anything else I was missing? A lady nearby gave me a look like I was wildin' out. I probably was wild for shouting bingo out loud, but she needed to worry about her own issues instead of mine. I hustled to the candy aisle, snagged a pack of her favorite chocolates, just for kicks. I figured she might need some sweet stuff after I left her breathless and her spine realigned. I paid for my stuff, left Dollar Tree, and noticed it wasn't even 11 yet. Why does time always pass by slowly when you are awaiting a special moment? Paulette: Morning, yo!

Me: What's good, beautiful? Hope you're ready for a weekend that's gonna stick in your memory forever.

Paulette: For real?

Me: No doubt. I'll catch you at 4.

Paulette: You really gonna be on time at 4?

Me: Nah. 3:58, to be exact. Peace.

That quick text convo set the vibe for the day. I was chilling at home, plotting this move with precision. I wasn't trying to make her fall for me; the mission was to uplift her spirit enough so she could heal from her past pain. The first envelope, I had "TRAUMA" written on it in bold black letters with a permanent marker. The card inside talked about surviving tough times meant to break us. I

67

can't even fathom what it'd be like if I got a call about someone hurting my nieces, little cousins, or any close friend's daughter, regardless of their background. The same rules apply to my nephews because it ain't cool when older folks prey on young boys. It's a crime. Saying stuff like "one day you're gonna be my boyfriend" to a five-year-old ain't right. It's pedophilia. I'd probably be locked up with two life sentences if I ever got that news. I had to pause for a sec, 'cause the itch for words hit me. Thinking about all those young guys out there who've suffered. I'm one of 'em. It's crazy how some of us met darkness before puberty hit, and didn't even realize it 'til we got older. Boys can be hurt, manipulated, and preyed upon. What some thought was cute turned out to be nothing but mind games, making you think your body's worth more than your mind. This shit ain't talked about enough. I had to pause real quick and go to my journal, to expel my thoughts.

Journal entry: The Miseducation of Black boys.

Today, I find myself reflecting on a deeply troubling and often overlooked issue in our society - the victimization of Black boys by sexual predator adult women. This issue is shrouded in silence and seldom receives the attention it deserves. The damage wrought by the harmful narrative perpetuated by grown men, who encourage young Black boys to be reckless with their private parts, is a disturbing and pressing concern. As a society, we must first acknowledge that sexual victimization is not limited by gender. Just as young girls are vulnerable to sexual predators, so are young boys. It is heart-wrenching to realize that Black boys are victims of this form of abuse, and the silence surrounding this issue compounds the suffering they endure. The stereotypes and stigmas attached to masculinity often overshadow the traumatic experiences these young boys face, leaving them without a safe space to express their pain and seek help. One aspect of this issue that is particularly disconcerting is the societal failure to discuss it openly. The lack of dialogue surrounding the sexual abuse of Black boys by adult women perpetuates a culture of secrecy and denial. Such silence deprives these young victims of the support, empathy, and understanding they so desperately need. It's high time that we break through the barriers of shame and silence to give a voice to these young survivors. The role of grown men in reinforcing reckless behavior among young Black boys cannot be underestimated. Their misguided advice and toxic masculinity play a significant part in perpetuating the cycle of abuse. They encourage boys to be sexually active without promoting the importance of consent, safety, or emotional well-being. This fosters an environment where predatory adult women can exploit the vulnerabilities of these young boys, leaving them deeply scarred and confused. The consequences of this abuse, which often linger for a lifetime, include emotional trauma, shattered self-esteem, and trust issues. It is crucial that we, as a society, recognize the harm in perpetuating toxic notions of masculinity and actively work to create a safer space for young Black boys to express themselves and seek help when they have been victimized. In addressing this issue, we must take steps to break the silence and raise awareness about the sexual victimization of Black boys. We need more support systems, both within the community and through professional counseling, to help these young survivors heal and rebuild their lives. Additionally, it is essential to challenge and transform the harmful narratives that continue to put these boys at risk. This journal entry is a call to action, a plea to acknowledge the suffering of Black boys who have been victims of sexual abuse, and an appeal to our collective conscience to work towards a society that empowers and protects them rather than perpetuating harmful stereotypes and narratives. We must confront this issue head-on, as it is only through open conversation, empathy, and advocacy that we can hope to bring about lasting change. Lastly, I write this as a once victim, and perpetuator of this twisted narrative. I had to learn what to unlearn to become healthy.

After using my writing as a vent session, I sat in silence for a few minutes. My journal often talked back to me. Here, at this moment, it was mute. Paper comes to life when we add words. As I learned at this moment, it chose death. Eventually, I took my mind off the disturbing experience and refocused on Paulette. I began to write inside the first card:

'Paulette. As you see this word, TRAUMA, I know what reflects inside your head. This is not meant for you to relive what you have gone through. This is indeed a moment for you to break down those bricks around your heart and know that it is not your fault. Whether brick by brick or with a wrecking ball, do not let the trauma define you.'

The second envelope was marked with the words THANK YOU. The card was simple, just telling someone thank you for being there. I didn't find one that explained the value of coming into my life, so I went with the next best thing and wrote my own personal message inside:

'Paulette. There aren't enough words in the dictionary to explain what you have meant to me since you sent me a random message on a random April night. It was simply a question about writing a book. Since that moment, we have been writing our own story. This is only the beginning, and the best thing someone can say sometimes is simply...thank you.'

That's how I honestly felt. I was riding with my heart on this one, not my mind, because the mind can deceive you in so many ways, especially with worry and fear. Hip hop's favorite smoker and Pittsburgh native, Wiz Khalifa once said, "Worrying is stupid. it's like walking around with an umbrella waiting for it to rain." James Baldwin, arguably the greatest writer ever, once said, "To defend oneself against a fear is simply to ensure that one will, one day, be conquered by it. Fears must be faced." You will start doubting yourself and all of your abilities once those two attributes creep in. For me, the fear of love not working has always been a constant thought in my mind. However, each time I faced it, I showed my ability to be vulnerable. As for worry, well, after you've put your hands in the life of surgeons, you pretty much don't worry about anything. More so, I looked at who said these quotes. We live in a world where different choices and lifestyles will make others despise you, when they don't know you. Many people aren't upset at the message. Only the messenger. I wonder who would refute wise words about worry and fear because they came from a tattooed rapper and an openly gay man? It was a very intriguing thought to have. The third envelope was labeled with the word RESTORE. I knew for a fact that this one was going on the bed. Restoration is defined as the action of returning something to a former owner, place, or condition. It was the last step in any process. The bedroom is where we would not fix the issue, but celebrate the fixing of the issue. Tonight, I wasn't trying to make love to her. I was attempting to erase every negative experience she ever encountered before me. There was passion, love making, realignment, and soul connection. After I was finished with this whole experience, her body, mind, and spirit would experience a full eclipse that wouldn't be encountered for another 2,500 years. In short, I was the only man that would hold her heart from this point on. That was the goal. Additionally, even if this situation went south and we faltered, I would be the most unforgettable thing she ever encountered. She wouldn't be able to look at another man without envisioning me. The taste of me would forever linger in her mouth, even without my presence. She wouldn't be able to breathe without exhaling and inhaling me. Even kissing another man would bring pain, instead of bliss, because it wasn't me. The standards were high, and I liked to reside in high elevation settings. She would never recover mentally from what I was about to do to her. The words that flowed on this next card were ones of trust:

> 'Paulette. This is about trust. The bed, with these flowers, isn't symbolic of sex. This is a symbol that you can trust me with all aspects of your being. This is not just about physical intimacy; it's about emotional security. If I never make you feel anything else, know that I will always ensure that you are safe and secure, both physically and mentally.'

The word to go on the last envelope was simply LOVE. Why, Junior, why? Why are you writing this? I asked myself that as I stared into the air after writing that on the envelope. That word gets tossed around too many times nowadays. I started to become confused about how I was really feeling. On one hand, I knew what I wanted it to mean. On the other hand, I knew how she could interpret it and the emotions it could evoke, especially with all the efforts I was making to make her feel special. This was going to be tough because the last thing I wanted to do with a broken woman was to trigger her emotions from what she thought she had in her previous relationship. I muted the music coming from my television and just sat in silence, pondering whether this move was worth it. Then, like the Bulls in '91 and '92, those two little minions ran it back, right on my shoulders. The angel of the bunch started with his advice.

"Junior, you have to be transparent and risk losing if you want to win." Then, OG Demon Brown chimed in.

"You know what? I don't usually agree with this soft, moist ass nigga, but let it all hang out, my man. The presentation is already going to have that bitch juicy. You know she's going to cherish this moment and your connection. Tell her you love her and get it over with."

"She ain't a bitch man."

"Alright, alright, my bad. But, you're going the extra mile, so go all in. Just do me a favor and make her feel the intensity of your passion. Make her scream so loud that the walls start shaking. Give her that nigga dick experience she'll never forget."

"Okay, both of you, calm down. You're both right. I just need to figure out how to finesse this."

"Junior, I am so proud of you."

I looked down at OG again, who had a puzzled look on his face.

"Yeah, anyway. Forget this emotional nigga, my man. But, you're putting in the work, so go all the way. Just let her know how you feel and enjoy the moment."

"Alright, let's do this."

They both disappeared into whatever realms they came from, and I was back to square one. What would my decision be? I quickly made it with the final words that I had to write:

'Paulette. This is Love. Restoration. This is Love. Acceptance of flaws. This is Love. Going all out. This is Love. Being authentically us, in this space, in this time. Let me be the first step in showing you what Love is again. Not just the actions, but the person behind the actions. Me!'

–Junior.

I made sure my signature was at the bottom of that card wanted her to feel the authenticity. As I sealed the last envelope, I couldn't help but feel like I was either about to be the genius of the century or the biggest fool on the planet. Either way, it was game on. That knot in my stomach, man, it was something else. Partly jitters, partly an urgent call from nature. Have you ever found yourself needing to hit the bathroom while you're deep in the middle of an intimate moment? Yeah, I'd never been there before, and tonight wasn't gonna be that night. You're in the heat of the moment, giving it your all, holding in more than just your breath. Thank the heavens, I had the bathroom situation covered. After that liberating trip to the throne, I caught a quick nap and woke up right on schedule at 1:30 p.m. I know, it might not seem like much time for a refresh, but sometimes, less is more. A 20-minute shower session with that seaweed body wash in the sleek black bottle was a game-changer. It had bladderwrack, olive oil, coconut oil, and a whole bunch of vitamins and minerals that made you feel like a new person. And after the shower, when you hit your body with the detox lotion with green tea extract, it's like your swagger gets a dose of superhero vibes a mix of Venom, Superman, and Wolverine, all rolled into one. Okay, I get it, Marvel and DC don't usually mix, but this stuff ? It's a league of its own. Before I was ready to roll, there was one last mission on my checklist. Grooming time, my friend. Yep, you heard me right. Gotta keep the intimate area nice and smooth. It's not just for the intimate action; it's self-care, man. You've gotta look at yourself in the mirror and think, "Yep, looking good down there." Plus, it gave you an extra inch of dick down there, and women were all about the visual. I had everything packed from the night before, so I was good to go. A fresh stick of AXE Chocolate Dark Temptation deodorant, a fresh white tee, black jeans, and I was good to roll. I packed everything meticulously into the truck no room for mistakes. I didn't want anything getting messed up, even though it's pretty hard to wreck some envelopes and rose petals. Before hitting the road for good, I did one last sweep around the house. To ensure everything was turned off and in check, but also, I needed my secret weapon. I mixed up some almond milk, beetroot powder, added apple cider vinegar, green tea extract, and organic berry blast protein. And don't forget the L-Arginine supplement. You might wonder why I'm doing this, right? It's not just about getting some nutrients in me. That beetroot, ACV, and green tea mix? It's all about nitric oxide for max blood flow. L-arginine? It's like a natural power-up. Long story short, I never needed any blue pills, but this was as close as it gets. It's like an energy and mood booster that'll keep you going all night. I rinsed out the shaker, stepped out the door, and hit the road. Traffic was the usual mix sometimes smooth, sometimes not so much. I kept my eye on the clock, hoping everything would align perfectly. I hated being late or having to mess with the schedule. And while I was stuck in traffic, I shot her a quick text.

Me: Catch you at 4:00, maybe 4:05 max.

Paulette: What's up with 3:58?

Me: I know folks tend to run a little late, so I left a 2-7 minute window open for you. You're a woman. Late is what y'all do.

Paulette: (middle finger emoji)

I had to keep it playful, even if I wasn't kidding. But if I were any later than I should be, I'd be giving myself a hard time. The road was a rollercoaster, full of stops and starts. My playlist was hitting its stride by 2:40. From my calculations, it'd be another 15 minutes before I hit the hotel. And just as Migos' 'Handsome and Wealthy' bumped in, I felt like a million bucks, even if I wasn't rolling in dough. My weekend companion was as gorgeous as ever. Takeoff's verse came in strong, and I was in the zone. That verse couldn't have dropped at a better time. I had to give props to him because I was on the brink of an unforgettable night. But I had to remind myself, this was about more than just a good time; it was about rejuvenation. Still, a genuine guy can't help but want a little action. I'd already had a taste, and it was amazing. I pulled up to the hotel at 2:59 p.m., beating the GPS's prediction of 3:04. Valet parking was a godsend. I handed over my stuff to the valet, telling him to be ready in 30 minutes. I had two bags: one with my clothes and the other with everything for her, including the wine she'd left behind. The girl at the front desk, though not my usual type, meaning not a Black woman, was looking A-1 if I do say so myself. I usually stayed away from certain things, like snow bunnies, but there was no denying she was thick as grits.

"Room 410, sir. Enjoy your stay."

"Thanks."

I grabbed the key card and headed for the elevators, where I spotted a friendly Black couple waiting.

"Ayo, we're from Jersey. Where's the good grub around here?"

"What's on your mind? We've got the classics, some solid spots, and a few hidden gems. Even though we're a bit short on folks like us around here."

"Man, we can see that. We heard you've got a banging Creole spot."

"True that. If you've got a ride, cruise five minutes down by the waterfront to this spot called 'The Village.' Look for my man's place, 'Southern Chucks'–they say it takes a family of real Southern folk to run it. It's a real spot, with some crazy good gator."

"Is it a tourist trap or a local gem?"

"In this city, it's all ours, my man. The folks from other cities let outsiders claim their territory. We keep it real."

The doors swung open. I dapped up fam, who introduced himself as Jeff, and strolled out to the fourth floor. The room was right across from the elevator, so Paulette wouldn't have a long trek to her place of ultimate bliss. As soon as I slid the card in front of the sensor, the door clicked, and my first step inside revealed everything I needed to know. This night was gearing up to be epic. The bathroom was massive, oversized, to say the least. Even in the dim light, it was clear. I dropped my bags and wandered through, flicking on the bathroom light. A huge hot tub beckoned me, whispering, "Let her soak in here after you've taken her soul." Check. I emerged and entered the living area. It was pure awesomeness. A massive, plush sectional against one wall, a sleek 55-inch flat-screen TV for entertainment, and a slick oak wood office desk gave this room a bachelor pad vibe rather than your standard luxury suite. Finally, I reached the sliding glass doors, opening them up. It led to a breathtaking bedroom with a king-sized bed, another TV, and oversized windows. I cracked one open, and the downtown scent of fun and excitement flooded in. The baseball team had a game tonight, and the park lights were a perfect view from here. With the way I planned to make her feel, she might just announce her presence to the entire downtown. I snapped back to the task at hand and switched into decorating mode. I rifled through the gift bag and pulled out the balloons. Man, it had been ages since I blew up balloons the old-school way. I remember doing that as a kid, feeling like one breath away from passing out. I inflated 10 of them, all the orange ones except for three. I taped a few around the room, and the rest I just let them land where they may. It gave an innocent touch to this adult playground. Now, onto the letters. I had to be strategic with these. I knew right away that the "THANK YOU" card belonged in the glove compartment of my ride. She could pull it out on her way here and feel her heart warm up. It would show her that someone was willing to go through hell and high water to make her whole again. "TRAUMA," that was a tough one. Nobody wants to dive into that. So, I taped it right above the bathroom door. It'd be the first thing she'd see when she walked in. She'd be blown away by the ambiance, then realize that the journey to healing sometimes begins by confronting the past, even if it's just mentally. It was risky, because you can't predict someone's reaction, but it was a risk I was willing to take. The third envelope, labeled "RESTORE," I placed on the sliding doors to the bedroom. With the pane glass doors, it looked awesome, but more importantly, it told her that the ultimate place of peace for most people, the bedroom, would be her sanctuary. There's nothing like returning home and sleeping in your own bed, in your own space, in your own comfort. For the next two days, this would be our home, and I wanted it to feel like that. Lastly, the one labeled "LOVE" was going right on the bed, along with three long-stemmed roses. This was where we'd solidify it all. I'd already decided she wouldn't have a worry in the world. You don't go on a nine-hour date for nothing. That's the stuff of fairy tales, even Hallmark movies. I was a fan of their films, but I never expected to star in one in real life. I scattered the rose petals from the bedroom to the room's entrance. Everything looked set, and I checked the clock. It read 3:36 p.m. Perfect, I thought. Just enough time to roll out and pick up my queen. Then, the phone rang.

"What's up, my lady?"

"My lady?"

"You heard me right. I'll see you in about 20 minutes. Hold me to it; if I'm not there by 4:05, call me out."

"I sure will. But, umm, I'm hungry."

"Well, damn. Where do you want to grab a bite?"

"I don't know."

"Alright, we'll figure it out. See you in a bit."

"Okay. Bye."

"Goodbye, love."

Just like women worldwide, they often make the dining decision a real head-scratcher. I mean, it's like some folks turn into foodie anonymous, acting like they never ate a bite in their lives, you know what I'm saying? If you've got a moment, hit up YouTube and search for 'Guy Moments.' Look for the one called 'Turkey Burger.' Trust me, you'll be thanking me for the accuracy and the good laughs. I swung by the valet stand to pick up my ride, and I couldn't help but wonder - do these valet guys ever take our cars for a joyride when we're not looking? Honestly, I didn't want to find out, as long as my baby was scratch-free, I was good to go. Like Eddie Murphy said in 'The Nutty Professor,' if it's a scratch on the car, it's a scratch on your ass. My ride rolled up, I jumped in, and I was off. My bluetooth was always locked and loaded, so when I hit the first red light, Eric Roberson's 'Leave It In' came booming through the speakers. Yeah, I damn sure wasn't pulling out tonight. When you're going all out for someone, you've got to fill up that love tank, regardless of how you feel about it. Truth be told, I didn't need to put the pedal to the metal since I'd be at her exit in about 10 minutes and still on time. But as I got closer, the nerves kicked in. I've done some grand gestures for the ladies before, but this one? This would make my grandma up in heaven raise her eyebrows. At each stoplight, I couldn't help but glance at the glove compartment. That envelope labeled 'THANK YOU' was still sitting there, you see. It's a habit of mine, like triple-checking if all the lights are off at home. Something hardwired in me that's tough to break. As I pulled up to the last light before her place, those minions on my shoulder chimed in.

"Aye, you such a romantic ass nigga."

You probably recognize that one.

"I've never seen a dude who's street-smart, tough, and still a sappy ass romantic like you."

"What do you mean, bro?"

"Don't listen to him, Junior," the JC of the group said. "What you're doing is admirable. You've put together something special for this lady, and it's amazing to see."

I shot a glance over my shoulder as he grinned. Deep down, I wished that light would turn green so I could jet without hearing more of their chatter. I turned to my left, and the other voice had a smirk.

"Did your mama raise you to be all moist and shit, man? Nah, I don't think your daddy even had a set of nuts. Look, Junior, forget all that. Since you're going all lovey-dovey, you better make sure that stroke game is unforgettable. It's gotta be like Game six of the Finals, you know? When Ray Allen hit that three in Miami and saved LeBron's ass."

"Man, I'm not trying to be anyone's savior. I'm just being me. And don't talk about that man's parents again."

"That's right. He's a man who appreciates women for who they are."

"Test tube baby. Shut the fuck up."

The light turned green, they disappeared, and I was back on my way. I made that right turn and handled it like I was Snoop rolling in the 'lac back in '92. I reached the middle of the street and pulled a U-turn 'cause, honestly, I was too lazy to drive down the block and hit one. With a clear path ahead, I whipped it perfectly and landed right in front of her crib. I said a quick prayer to the OG, hoping things would go smoothly. A final mirror check before stepping out city drivers get wild around here, and I didn't want to be the one getting side-swiped by a truck. With the coast clear, I made my exit and walked up to her front door. As I climbed the steps, she was already waiting outside.

"Fast and furious, huh?"

"Nah, just some smooth driving skills."

"Whatever. It's 3:57. You're early."

"Nah, I'm right on time. I don't come early."

The look on her face? Priceless. I had her completely shook with that one. I made it to the top of the stairs, gave her a hug and a kiss. Those lips? They were like music to my soul. I mean, both pairs were, but her kisses had me humming melodies that would make The Temptations jealous. We headed inside for a minute, her dog jumping all over me. It's moments like these when I know I'm where I'm supposed to be. Even her dog, Quiche (yeah, she's got a fancy name), vibed with me. Animals can sense good vibes, no matter who you are. I remember this one time when my sister was messing with a dude, and her dog decided to mark his territory right on the guy's shoe and then walked away like it was no big deal. She couldn't believe the dog's audacity, but I could. You see, Oreo, my sister's four-legged friend, was all about showing love by jumping all over you and giving out smooches. He never held back, no matter who you were. But little did my sister know, Oreo had some street smarts. That guy was bad news, and Oreo's impromptu puddle proved it.

"What are you doing?"

"Making me a PB and J," I replied, as I casually rummaged through her kitchen cabinets. After what I'd just done, I knew she wouldn't be mad for long.

"Are we not stopping somewhere to grab a bite?" she said.

"Yeah, and this sandwich will hold me over until we get there. Have you figured out what you want to eat?"

"I dunno," she replied.

Women, right? I can now see why Adam might've had his moments with Eve. In a whole garden filled with delicious fruit, she took 40 days and nights to munch on an apple from the wrong tree.

"What are you going to do with the dog?"

"You see that spacious cage, stocked with food and everything? She'll be good. Got her own space to do her business, food bowls, the works. We'll check up on her tomorrow. Wait a sec. QUICHE!!! CAGE!!!"

Quiche zipped into that cage like she'd done it a hundred times before. I grabbed her bag, and we headed for the car.

"Yo, what are you doing?" I inquired as I opened her car door.

"Oh, my bad," she replied.

I had to remind her that no woman with me was going to carry her bag, open doors, or feel less like a queen. I opened the door for her, and she hopped in, grinning. I placed her bag in the backseat, got in the driver's seat, and off we went. The tunes were bumping low, and we started up some random chatter. In my head, I was figuring out when to ask her to pop open the glove compartment. The right moment came as we waited at a red light across from what I called the "rival strip" two competing stores side by side, like Bobby Gore and Larry Hoover living next door to each other in the Chicago '70s.

"Hey, can you open the glove compartment for me and hand me my Butterfinger?"

In all honesty, I did have a Butterfinger stashed in there as my secret energy booster. The envelope was supposed to slip out first. I watched her dig around, but I played it cool.

"Here."

I glanced over as we waited for the light to change, and the envelope was still sitting there.

"Thanks, but grab that envelope too."

Darn it. I thought it would be the first thing to fall out. She looked at me, flashed a smile, and reached for it.

"Aww," she said as she pulled it out.

I acted like my whole focus was on driving.

"Open it."

I pretended like I wasn't the one who placed it there, and our journey continued. We had about ten minutes before we'd reach the hotel. The music was mellow, and the vibe in the car had shifted. I saw her slip the card back into the envelope out of the corner of my eye.

"You're sweet," she said, reaching down to grab my dick.

"Oh, you really like it, huh," I teased, trying not to let on how much it turned me on.

"I've already had it, and I definitely approve," she replied.

"I was talking about the letter."

"Me too."

We both laughed. It was clear that our night was going to be quite the adventure, and it had already gone from PG to Rated R. By the time it was over, it might just hit NC-17. We ended up stopping at a smoothie joint on the outskirts of downtown. She ordered a turkey sandwich with avocado, and I grabbed a grilled cheese with ham and fresh tomatoes. We left, chowing down as we strolled through the streets, and eventually, we pulled up at the hotel. The valet opened her door, and I got out, snagging her bag. We made our way to the elevator, and even the receptionist gave me a sly smile. Either she was feeling me, or she knew that Room 410 was about to become a "do not disturb" zone. We kept the convo flowing until we hit the fourth-floor. When the elevator doors popped open,

I swear, my nerves went through the roof. As I played tour guide, I spotted a lone rose petal chillin' outside the door. Damn, talk about bad timing. No way I was letting her peep that before the big reveal. I hustled to distract her, staying ahead, diggin' in my wallet, doing anything to keep her from seeing the surprise. I reached the door with my key card and casually stepped on that petal, slid my foot back as I cracked it open.

"After you, my lady," I smoothly threw out.

She sauntered in, and suddenly, she was in a trance. I mean, it was like she'd stepped into another dimension. That's when my nerves started taking a breather. I trailed behind her, tossed her bag in the living room, and claimed a spot on the couch, actin' like it was just another Friday. She was still standing there, by the door, takin' it all in, lost in the moment, not knowing what to think. Then, she spotted the RESTORE card and sauntered up to it.

"Oh my God. You're a sweetheart. This is, like, incredible."

She hit pause. Tears were already making their way down her cheeks.

"You missed one. It's above the bathroom."

She turned around, went back to the bathroom door, and her hand shot straight to her mouth. That's when I stood up.

"Paulette, before you open it, I ain't tryna make you relive all that stuff. I get it, we gotta confront the things we'd rather avoid to get where we need to be. I just want you to know I'm down for all of it, the ups and the downs, until you're whole again. If I'm overdoing it, I apologize. But for you, there's no such thing as 'too much.' I really love you."

She just stood there, tears flowing. I walked over, wrapped her up in a hug, and let her bury her face in my chest. Everybody needs a rock at their lowest, and I didn't mind being that for her. I'd been there when I needed someone, and no one was around. As she took her time, she finally took down the envelope, and I grabbed her hand.

"You've got one more," I said.

I pointed to the doors, and the look in her eyes told the whole story. She glided over to the doors, pushed them open, and her reaction?

"Oh my God."

Her breath practically left her body. I knew then that I'd melted her heart and taken layers of hurt off her. Being genuine didn't require much a good heart, a positive vibe, and, of course, the occasional acts of love and words of appreciation. She strolled back to me, kissed me, and gave me a hug. Truth be told, I didn't wanna start anything too early. I wanted to save the heat for later when the night sky took over. We had all night for that. Right now, I just wanted her to feel amazing.

"Let's hit up the rooftop. Chill, have a few drinks, and soak up each other's company. This place is gonna be here. It's your weekend to unwind. I got you. This is all for you. I'm all in, so you can shine."

She looked a bit lost for words. The look in her eyes said she wanted to fuck me, fuck me again, and disappear in bliss, all at once. But deep down, she probably wasn't sure how to fully embrace this.

"Alright. Let me freshen up in the bathroom."

She disappeared inside and shut the door. Once that bathroom door clicked shut, I let out a sigh of relief. Then, those two conflicting voices came back, chilling on my shoulders.

"I've never seen a love display like that in my life. You've made me proud." I looked to my left, expecting some wild comments. Then, I heard a loud smack. I turned to my right shoulder. Evil minion there was slappin' the nonsense out of cupid's little brother. He was laying on my shoulder, feeling the pain.

"Man, you know I don't do this soft stuff. Dude sounds like he graduated from Simp A&M University. But, bro, you better fuck the corns off her feet tonight. I'm takin' this guy away, so you won't be bothered by the leader of the simps. Go ahead, you affectionate ass nigga with tattoos."

"Fuck you," I whispered to him.

"Nah, man. Fuck her, and do it right."

Both of them disappeared when she came out of the bathroom, face dry and ready to roll. She changed into some comfy clothes, and we hit the rooftop lounge, on the fourth floor. It was a dope spot, with a mini heated pool. It was only four feet deep, meant for kickin' back and sipping on drinks, not serious swimming. From the looks of it, people had been having a blast. Neo-soul music was playing, and Erykah Badu was taking over. It was deja vu from our first date. There were plenty of folks of all backgrounds, so it wasn't an odd scene. It had a great mix. We made it to the bar, and the fun began. I had no clue what a peanut butter fireball was until she put me on. After that first shot, it was clear I was in for a wild night. They also had some grub, and honestly, that sandwich from earlier wasn't gonna cut it.

"Yo babe, they got that coochie board."

"Nigga, what?"

"The coochie board, with the meat and cheese. You know what I'm sayin'?"

"You mean a charcuterie board?"

"Yeah, that's the one. The 'coochie' stuff. Let's get that."

"Can you say it right? Char-coot-ter-ree."

"Nah, coo-chee board sounds better."

"I can't deal with you."

"Are you sure?"

We both grinned and laughed, and she just shook her head, half amazed, half amused. I ordered up that board at the bar. No matter how you say it, those little slices of bread, cheese, and meat could hit the spot. After a few more shots and some more quality time, our food rolled in. Our conversation went from deep and thoughtful to... honestly, I didn't even know what the hell we were talking about. We were too busy laughing, jokin', and soaking up each other's vibes. Plus, the food was hittin'. People, especially Black folks, focus intently on what's on the plate. After a solid hour, a bunch of fireball shots, and two Crown and Cokes down, we were both way past tipsy. She looked more gone than me, but at least the food had been a buffer. We headed over to the rooftop's edge. We cuddled, feeling complete, taking in the sounds of a lively crowd adding to this epic Friday night. The energy was on fire, thanks to a baseball game. It was pure joy to see her back in the groove, carefree. As we watched the sun dip behind the buildings, we headed back to our room. When we walked in, she stretched like there was no tomorrow. As she turned to face me, she dropped the L-bomb.

"I love you."

"I love you too, Paulette."

The way we said those words, it was like we were possessed by something beyond ourselves. Amidst the booze and the vibe, we both knew we meant every word. The clothes came off, and the energy was electric. This wasn't just your typical night of intimacy; it was like we were going for an Olympic gold medal in pleasure. Even in my thirties, my body was still rockin'. I lifted her onto my shoulders near the window. My strength might have aged, but it hadn't faded. I went all out, giving her everything she could handle, and then some. She was gasping, trying to catch her breath, but I wasn't holding back it was an all-in performance of my tongue and jaw muscles.

"Put me down," she managed to say through heavy breaths.

I obliged, and we locked lips, our tongues dancing like it was a main event WWE match. I took a firm hold of her, and we changed positions.

"Open the window," I said.

"What?" she asked, trying to regain her composure.

"Never mind," I replied.

I cracked the window, letting the sounds of a nearby baseball game and passing cars mix with our own symphony of pleasure. But I was determined to make our soundtrack stand out. Returning to her, bent over, head damn near outside, I slid in and took her on a wild ride. These weren't just 'beat it up' strokes; they were the kind that had her thinking about life, credit scores, and real estate deals. I don't brag often, but if this was the last time I rocked someone's world, I knew it'd be a hall of fame performance. She tried to hold back her screams, but it was a lost cause. Her high notes were ringing out for the whole downtown neighborhood to hear. Once I saw the lights from the ballpark, I kicked it up a notch. No one could see us from there, but I was putting on a show. After what felt like an eternity of bliss for her, I tossed her to the edge of the bed. I pulled her legs back, gazing into her eyes with each deep thrust. I let her know that nothing before me mattered. As her face tightened, and she bit her lip, she pushed back against me, unleashing a powerful climax. I'd never seen anything like it, and I even had to pause and appreciate the moment. It was a once-in-a-blue-moon experience, and I was impressed with myself. She squirted and hit me with a blast, directly center chest. She was exhausted, but I wasn't ready to finish. It was only right that I continued to show her what I was made of. I laid her down on her stomach and unleashed a relentless rhythm while whispering sweet nothings in her ear. Feeling a woman climax on your shaft is a unique sensation, and I knew her mind was racing with a thousand thoughts. I knew that everything leading up to this moment was racing through her head. With one final climax, she put her hand back, and I knew it was time to stop. She was crying in the sheets as I rolled off and sat on the edge of the bed. I glanced at the mirror near the television and smiled at my reflection. "Good job," I told myself. Turning back to her, I noticed she was still struggling in a good way. I got up, stretched, and settled on the couch, casually flipping on the TV. As I browsed through the channels, still hearing her moans, I saw that familiar demon on the screen. I knew I was the only one who could see him, but it still startled me a little. He grinned and pointed at me.

"GAVE THAT BITCH THAT YOU DON'T KNOW WHO YOU'RE FUCK-ING WITH DICK!!!"

"Don't call her that" I whispered to him.

"My bad," he mouthed back, clearly aware that he didn't want to ruin the moment.

I switched the TV to ESPN and saw her on the floor by the bedroom doors, still screaming and shaking. Now, I was genuinely concerned. I didn't know if it was the aftermath of our passionate encounter or if something was wrong. Once she was all settled, I strolled over to the fridge, snagged a water bottle, and handed it to her - she definitely needed it. I'll never forget what Bernie Mac once dropped, saying that some good pussy and an ice-cold glass of H2O can be lethal. Lucky for me, I wasn't the one in dire need of hydration at that point.

"Thanks."

"No problem."

I kicked back, watching some sports highlights, acting like I hadn't just worked some magic on her body, fixing up all her kinks and aches.

"Why'd you do that to me?"

I glanced over at her.

"I didn't do anything except deliver what you should've been getting all along. There's a world of difference between getting fucked and forging that deep emotional connection, you feel me?"

I don't know what made me say it, but I meant every word. It wasn't just about the physical; it was about making her feel safe and secure. I was apologizing for another guy's blunders. It was wild, but it was real. I wasn't trying to put myself on a pedestal; I was the pedestal, because I knew how to treat a woman right. As I continued to chill, she rose up, ending with her head between my legs. She took care of business slowly and with precision. It was one of those "thank you for treating me right" kind of moments. I tried to keep my cool, but when someone's working their mouth magic and you're on the receiving end, keeping it together isn't easy. All of a sudden, my breathing got deeper, and now, I was the one who couldn't handle it. After what felt like an eternity but not long enough, she had me shooting like John Wick, you know, after he went rogue. Did she move her mouth? Nah, she held her ground. She was a trooper because I know it was no small feat. She took it like a champ, swallowing every drop. I don't know what was more amazing: her skills, her head game, or the fact that I was now sober after all the booze. She came up and just laid on me. This was refreshing. I loved this part, man. I was at that age where if there wasn't a real connection or meaningful conversation after, I didn't want it. I could handle business by myself by just firing up some adult content online. Many people my age were still stuck on surface-level interactions. Sure, we had our go-to options for emergencies, but for the most part, it was about a genuine connection or personal growth. No substance, no satisfaction. We got into a chill zone, she put on my Tom and Jerry hat, got goofy, sat on top of me, and made a video. She looked genuinely happy. I was feeling good, a bit worn out, but still content, especially with her assets right in front of me. I understood what Bernie Mac meant in Kings of Comedy. As you get older, your physical drive might decrease. In my case, it hadn't, but my joints weren't what they used to be. With age comes the wisdom to enhance the experience, multitasking - doing some stretches, controlling your breathing to last longer, and throwing in some teasing moves to either delay or refresh the session. Getting older and wiser is a blessing. Some folks just age, but I was learning to finesse things. Eventually, we went for round two, pushing the boundaries of what was safe. We somehow ended up in one of those rolling chairs from the office table. I had to take a break after a few minutes; we were in the zone, just one clap away from a serious accident. So, I did the logical thing - I picked her up and placed her on the nearest surface, in this case, the office desk. I was doing my thing, but her positioning on the desk was a bit off. I pushed her back and kept the momentum going. She grabbed the lamp, and in her enthusiasm, she yanked the plug out of the wall. Her movements forced me to make a quick save to prevent her from taking a spill. After that near-death experience, I had to put her back on the bed, where I gave her the final knockout stroke. No pulling out this time. If she got pregnant, fuck it, that's what I honestly thought. Now, the wild ride was over, and we were both more exhausted than a scale bearing one of those folks on "My 600-lb Life." Ain't no talking, no hugging, none of that. When I finally blinked my eyes open, it was two in the morning, and the room had that sweet mix of satisfaction and weariness in the air. I had to get up, hit the bathroom, but ended up slamming my toe into a damn table. I kept my scream in check 'cause I didn't want to wake her up, but inside my head, I cussed like 500 times. Ouch, that hurt like a motherfucker. I managed to find my way to the bathroom, pretty much turning into a vampire when I flipped on the light. I looked at myself in the mirror, deep in thought. Was this it for real, or just a front? Did she genuinely care for me, or was our intimate connection just a band-aid for her still-open wounds? I mean, she was technically still married to that messed-up dude, that predator. He was doing time, and she was in the middle of a divorce. I had to stop overthinking things. I had this habit of overanalyzing everything. I put my head down, then looked back up. The devil came back to taunt me.

"Not now, my man. Not now. I'm pondering some heavy stuff."

"Listen, just remember, even a dude like me who sees evil as a joy knows right from wrong. Right now, you have a choice to make. Remember, even I roam the earth; I ain't stuck in hell all day. Think about it, bro. Think about it."

"What you talkin' 'bout, man?"

Just like that, he vanished. I was waiting for the angel to pop up on my right side, but he stayed put wherever he was. Damn, that was deep, what the devil said. If even the devil ain't cozy in his own crib, then I shouldn't be mad about feeling uncomfortable at times. Growth doesn't happen in your comfort zone; it's when you're pushed out of it. It might sound crazy, but even God uses the dark side to teach us some lessons. Even when they're hella harsh. The weekend rolled into Saturday, still packed with excitement. We swung by her place to let the dog out, give it some fresh air, and clean up the mess it made in the cage. That dog must've had a feast because I'd never seen such a small pup drop bricks that size. We kept the good times going, driving up north about 20 minutes from the city to a low-key public beach. It was tucked away in a quiet neighborhood, not a tourist hotspot. That's why it stayed off most people's radars. We kicked it there, by the cliffs, leaning on the rocks, talking about everything under the sun. I felt free to open up, and so did she. I can't even count how many times we went from the water back to the sand, but even our connection with the waves felt like a whole different level of communication. Holding a woman close with the ocean crashing around you, man, that was something else. We rolled back to the hotel later that night, grabbed some grub, took showers, and once more, we broke each other off. Mission accomplished. I made her feel complete, even if just for a while. It felt like love on a whole new level, at least from where I stood. Another month flew by, and we were still good. Paulette wanted to visit for a weekend and crash at the crib. The drama with her ex was winding down, as she'd sent the divorce papers off to the prison for his signature. I didn't know how that whole prison paperwork thing went, but I knew she was making progress, so I was cool with it. I was still wondering, though, what that dude had said or done to win her over. She's 5'2, he's 5'1, as dark as night, and not exactly a looker. But hey, sometimes even the most unlikely folks catch a break. Photography couldn't have been that damn good. One relaxing Friday towards the end of June, she brought over a bottle of wine, and we kicked it in the living room, flipping through the TV channels. I sipped one glass, but she downed like four or five. I wasn't tripping, though; she wasn't going anywhere, and neither was I. It's always better to get lit at home than being out in public, wondering how the hell you're getting back.

"So, what's your body count?"

"Huh?" I couldn't believe she dropped that question. I tried to play it off like a joke.

"Junior, tell me what your body count was."

"Seriously. Like, why are you asking, though?"

"I'm just trying to have a conversation, come on."

"Yeah, but that's not really important. You ain't a virgin, and I wasn't one before I met you. We're together, loving each other, just you and me. I rock with you. You rock with me. I don't care about what was before me. I'm good."

She gave me a strange look.

"I think. No, I know I'm well over 100."

Now, I was shocked, a bit annoyed, and wondering why in the world she'd tell me that. I didn't need to know, and if liquor was making her spill the beans like this, maybe she should chill on the drinks.

"Are you in the same ballpark as me?"

"I don't know, maybe around 30," I said with a smirk.

"Man, I thought you'd have way more stories than that. For real, you're good."

To be honest, on my people's grave, I straight up lied. I just threw out the number thirty like it was the universal "shut up and let's keep this vibe" digit. I was nowhere near that. Most of my sexual acts were done in committed relationships. I learned from my brother and pops, who had multiple kids by multiple women, that your dick ain't meant to unlock every pink door. That was probably the first buzzkill with her. It's the kind of stuff you don't spill to someone you love or chop it up about.

"Yeah, I was a huge thotty back in the day. Do you know Memphis Tone? I think y'all on facebook. I slept with him."

"YO, PAULETTE!!! STOP WITH THIS OVERSHARING SHIT!!! I DON'T NEED TO KNOW ABOUT ALL THAT!!! IT'S ABOUT US, IT'S ABOUT YOU AND ME!!! WHY'D YOU EVEN THINK IT WAS COOL TO DROP THE BOMB THAT YOU'VE FUCKED OVER 100 NIGGAS!!! FUCK!!! WHAT WOMEN PROUD OF THAT SHIT???!!! I didn't want to lose it like that, but she wasn't catching the hint, and she was pushing my last button.

"You know what," she said, getting up from the couch. "My ex used to talk to me like that, and I'm not taking it anymore. You just played me into thinking you cared. I'm out."

She said "played." Now, I knew she was seriously messed up in the head.

"No, you're in no condition to drive. Please, leave those keys."

"My baby daddy didn't tell me what to do. My ex-husband didn't tell me what to do. And neither will you. I'm out."

I was left in disbelief. Now, caring for someone's well-being was suddenly a bad thing. She was way more self-absorbed than I'd thought. Even after revealing that I was basically Captain Save-a-hoe, a literal hoe, I still treated her as the woman I needed. I walked up to her, asking her to reconsider.

"Yo, give me some space? You gonna go all in on me and throw a punch? You gone punch me?"

"Look, I'm not gonna hurt you, but I really don't want you hurting yourself. You've been drinking, and you ain't fit to drive. Please don't get behind the wheel. My bad for raising my voice. Let's sit down, talk this out in a calm way. Please."

"Fuck you, Junior."

I stepped back as she grabbed her stuff and headed out the door. I followed at a safe distance.

"Quit following me, man."

"Paulette, I just don't want you to hurt yourself. If you want to crash in my place while I take the couch, I'm good with that. Just don't drive, please."

"Fuck you."

Right then and there, I stopped following. I didn't want the neighbors thinking it was some domestic mess. Where I lived, if someone called the cops on you for a domestic disturbance, you, as the guy, were in hot water. I watched her toss her bag in the car, rev it up, and peel out. All I could do was hope she stayed safe. I went back inside and pondered the evening. I knew she'd been through some heavy stuff, but this body count topic was messing with me. Why was it such a big deal to her? Regret, or something deeper I couldn't grasp? I had no clue, but it weighed on me big time. I figured it was just part of her dark journey. She didn't know her ex was messed up. Maybe she needed to spill everything about herself before someone else did to me. It was confusing, 'cause I'd realized I'd fallen for not just a woman with trauma but a real-life hoe. Who, at 32, has fucked over a hundred partners? That, right there, was pure sexual irresponsibility. Heather, the flower lady was right. You find out the real person you are with after your first disagreement. I shook it off and chilled out the rest of the night. Eventually, I texted her, asking if she got home safe. No response. I was seriously concerned. Then, around 10:30 p.m., she replied.

"I'm home. Later."

My gut and heart told me to bounce. My mind said to stay. It was like a mental tug of war life throws at you. I chose to be the rope. The next day, she called while I was still catching Z's. She was hella sorry. I told her it was scary seeing her drink like that and then lose her cool. She apologized. She knew she'd overdone the drinks, but it was her way of coping with her pain. I suggested we chill away from each other for a week, get our heads straight, and then figure things out. It was bound to happen. No relationship stays in the honeymoon phase forever. I knew tension was bound to roll in at some point. That's a thing for a lot of folks, not just in my crew. They're all stuck in that honeymoon-phase mindset, but their moves don't line up with their mental game. It's like their heads are playing one track while the real world's bumping something completely different. We needed some breathing space, not just for her but for yours truly. I had to break this mess down to the nitty-gritty. Especially knowing that those deep connections living rent-free inside her were overshadowing everything I'd ever done for her, both physically and figuratively. As the week wound down, I caved and headed to her crib. I chopped it up with my sister about her, and she threw an invite to Paulette. It was a Saturday, and it seemed like smooth sailing. We all sat down for some real talk no hanky-panky, no hidden agendas, just raw honesty. We dove deep, and I dropped the bomb that my sister wanted to meet her. She was up for it, even suggested I leave my ride at her mom's house since I'd driven down. I hadn't met her moms yet, but I was hoping the day would come, so I could let her know that her daughter was in safe hands. We hit the road for the 15-minute cruise to her place, right by the city's main university. The moment we stepped in, my sister and Paulette hit it off like old pals. They tag-teamed on me, but that's just how the ladies roll, you know? It was all love. There was just one thing that gave me concern. My sister was all about that wine life, and I'd already seen Paulette go off the deep end when she hit the bottle. In the back of my mind, I had my doubts. But after a few hours, I was feeling good. They were vibing, and my sister's dog kept me entertained. That little guy might've been pushing 11, but he moved like a young pup. I needed whatever my sister was feeding him, 'cause I was still looking fly for my age, but my joints were telling a different story. 8:00 p.m. rolled around, and the yawns started creeping in.

"You ready to bounce, babe?" she asked.

"For sure. Hand over the keys."

"Why's that?"

"Well, you're feeling nice, babe. Just wanna make sure you get home safe, you know? I got your back."

I could see what was brewing in her eyes. It looked like round two of drunk drama was on the horizon, and drama was the last thing I needed.

"Why you always tryna tell me what to do?"

I shot a glance at my sister, who was staring at her like she'd just dropped a bombshell. I didn't want my sister to unleash her inner fury on Paulette, so I reached out my hand to her, telling her that I got this.

"Listen, I ain't trying to boss you around. I'm just saying, let me drive you home. Is that too much to ask? I just want to make sure you're good and get back safe."

"Fuck you, Junior."

She stormed out the door.

"What the fuck was that?," my sister said.

"Sis, I swear this mess happened last week too. I'm trying to understand what she's going through, but it's starting to get on my fucking nerves. Hold up."

I stepped outside and flung open my sister's gate, catching Paulette pulling off down the street.

"FUCK!!!"

My sister joined me outside as I stood there, steaming mad.

"This bitch really left you," she said. I was fuming.

"Yo, can you give me a lift to her mama spot? My car's parked over there. I'm sorry about all this."

"Naw, nigga. No need to apologize."

My sister and I hopped into her BMW truck and made the eight- or nine-minute drive to Paulette's mama crib. When we pulled up, Paulette was still in her car.

"You want me to wait?"

"Naw, sis. I'm getting in my car and heading home. Plus, I need you to chill. I don't want you whoopin the whole Kansas City down on her."

"Junior, please, whatever you do, don't get physical with her. Just ignore the bitch."

"Come on, you know me better than that. We don't lay hands on women."

"Don't even talk to her. Just go home."

"I will."

"Love you."

"Love you too, sis."

I hopped out and watched my sister drive off. I made sure to tell her to chill, 'cause I knew her, and I didn't want her throwing down with anyone messing with her baby bro. My ex-wife had the good sense to keep her distance because she knew a beating was coming her way if she crossed paths with my sis. I didn't even wanna imagine what she would do to Paulette. I walked over to my car and swung the door open.

"JUNIOR!!!," Paulette yelled out.

I acted like I didn't hear that mess.

"JUNIOR!!!," she screamed again, hanging out of the car.

Against my better judgment, I got out and walked up to her car.

"What you want?"

She looked like she was out of it, just staring at me. Then, she hung her head.

"Nothing."

"Alright, I'm out," I said, heading back to my car.

"JUNIOR!!!"

"WE AIN'T GOT NOTHING TO TALK ABOUT, PAULETTE!!! GOOD-NIGHT!!!"

I didn't care anymore. This was two weeks in a row my night got wrecked. I didn't wave goodbye or anything. I just hooked up my bluetooth, peeled out, and hit the road for the 30-minute drive home. I needed some good tunes to

95

chill out. As I approached the first traffic light, which seemed to be stuck on red forever, a text popped up on my phone. It had two words: 'SINGLE-AFRAID.'

I thought, "Well, that's it." Almost four months of pouring my heart out had led to this. She'd finally crumbled under the pressure. It was over. No more worries. I'd already been divorced once from an unappreciative partner, and I wasn't about to deal with another one who saw drama as the norm. Who knows, maybe the spirits inside her were throwing a wild party, with Blueface performing 'Thotiana Bustdown.' As the light finally turned green, I switched the music to some classic Texas tracks and sped through the city streets. Junior, the nice guy, was gone. It was back to Junior, the savage, like my older brother. I no longer gave a fuck. I was at that age where I was ready to settle down with one woman. But after this drama, there was no way I was going to subject myself to that kind of trauma. The longer I drove, the calmer I felt. Music did wonders for my soul. And, eventually, I could smell Crown Royal in the car. I didn't have any liquor, but I knew only one person who could down that stuff like water. That was my pops. Somehow, I felt his spirit riding shotgun, trying to calm his baby boy down, and he succeeded. I started a conversation with him for the rest of the drive home. Our relationship hadn't always been perfect, but the old man had been there for me. Plus, he never pushed me to be something I didn't want to be. After a solid ten minutes, the scent vanished, and he dipped to his chill spot for all eternity. It's wild how expressing yourself with no one physically responding can soothe the soul. I was good now. My old man's vibe had me sure of one thing: "Never take BS, especially from an ungrateful someone. If folks show you who they are the first time, believe it." My heart may be big, but my mind's bigger, and it knew the call I had to make. It was time to distance myself from this drama queen. As I approached the crib, she started blowing up my phone. I let it ring, ain't nobody ruining my night any more than she already had. No way, captain. By the time I hit my driveway, she'd called three more times, and I ignored every single one. Inside, I jumped in the shower, brushed my teeth, and slipped under the covers. You know I had to have that fan on; I can't sleep without it. I dozed off, knowing I was finally free from the stress of someone else's messed-up life. Morning came, and I did my epic stretch, yelling like I'd just escaped a cave after a week. Life was smooth right now. I got up, handled my business in the bathroom, and stepped outside. Birds were singing a bit louder today. Maybe they'd found some action or just had a buffet in the ground. This feeling, it was really nice. I decided I needed a pick-me-up, street style. So, I headed back inside, grabbed my wallet, phone, and shuffled my flip-flops to the convenience store. On the way, I noticed the graffiti artists had blessed the power station wall again. I ain't about marking up someone else's property, but I couldn't deny they did proper murals, not just wasting paint. Today, a huge George Floyd face stood beside the words "WE AIN'T FORGET." The world's a trip. When the Holocaust happened, they told us to remember, and they were right. When 9/11 hit, they told us to never forget, and they were right again. But when it's about us, they ask, "Why can't you move on?" Didn't we let enough slide? Didn't we watch our history get whitewashed? In the Bible, Jesus had bronze skin and sheep's wool hair. Today, they've got some 1960s rave guy with blue eyes everywhere. Our music, rock-n-roll, country, you name it, ain't ours anymore. Even hip-hop is getting a makeover, and we created all of that. So, yeah, I respected the art. Next to those words, there was a Black Panther mural with "WAKANDA FOREVER" underneath. If only Wakanda was real, and we could bounce from this place. I glanced at my boy Will's house. No one dared mess with his crib. That dude had a dog that was part gorilla. Try anything funny at his place, and that dog's serving you a five-course meal. I crossed the street and hit the convenience store.

"Yo, what's good?"

"What you doin' here so early, man?"

"Breakfast."

"You ain't sippin' on liquor for breakfast, right?" We both laughed.

"Nah, just some sweet tea, snickers, and sunflower seeds. I need that morning boost."

He cracked up as I grabbed my stuff. This is one cool thing about us. We'd seen each other for ages, but I never knew his name, and he didn't know mine. We just exchanged nods, shot the breeze, did the cash exchange, and kept it moving. That's how we roll sometimes. If we know your face, we're all good. With my snacks in hand, I dipped and headed home. As I crossed the street, my phone buzzed.

"Can you please contact me? I'm sorry."

My gut, my mind, and my heart all said no. Enough with fixing broken women, Junior. But being me, I kept that door slightly open for a reunion.

"What you want? You cussed me out, left me hanging, and dropped 'single and afraid' like a bomb. How am I even supposed to respond to that?" As I walked home, there was no reply. Good, I thought. Maybe she'd had time to think about her words. I kicked back on the couch, dug into my second peanut butter Snickers, and then my phone buzzed again.

"Just listen to the song." I was confused as all get-out by now. I scrolled through our chat and saw the YouTube link that I hadn't noticed. The way I felt, I figured I'd listen to it to close this chapter. I was just chillin' in the crib, soaking in the vibes, flowing through the first verse and rockin' out to the whole track. Man, I could feel I'd given out a whole lot of my energy dealing with this lady. But then, the tune hit me like a ton of bricks. You know what? There's real power in words, no doubt. Right about then, I was straight-up lost. I'd formed a tight bond with her daughter when I did spend time with her. Paulette, she'd spilled her whole heart out to me, making me her confidant. And now, she lays it on the line. She's scared to love me. She's never been down that road, don't even know what love looks like. Trying, but it's all so alien to her that the only love language she speaks is chaos. It's easier for her to push me away than let me in. Back in the day, young me would've bounced, no doubt. But now, I'm 36, 'bout to hit 37, and I'm in a whole different mental zone. This song, man, it's touching me in ways nothing ever did. I wanted to hit her up, but something was holding me back. You know the drill once bitten, twice shy. She's messed me up more times than I can count, and each time, like a total dumbass, I kept going back. Can you even imagine being compared to a child molester just to hurt someone you care about, all 'cause you've been hurt? Dealing with someone who can't control their drinking, spilling way too much info about past flings, all unasked for? Blaming her mom and everyone else for her own life mess-ups, but never owning it? Man, there's a lot that went down these last four months that folks didn't see or hear. I hid it well, but inside, I was just withering away, while hoping love conquered all. Why, oh why, was I putting myself through all this? Maybe I'm just too much of a romantic at heart. Maybe I love hard 'cause I wanna believe in the good in people, even when they do me dirty over and over. Or perhaps, I'm just a plain old dumbass. After hearing this track, I couldn't even put my feelings into words. I knew what I wanted in life: love, family, and so much more. All she wanted was some peace, but she didn't even know what that looked like. Right now, I had more questions than answers. I cued up some music, and it's like the perfect jam comes on, telling the story of what's happening. Leave it to Outkast to speak to you, even when they ain't speaking directly. Shoutout to Andre 3000.

We stepped out of the shower, sharing laughs and grins. It was kinda weird but refreshing at the same time. Wrapped in our towels, we held each other tight in a hug that spoke volumes.

"This is so different." she told me, as I planted a soft kiss on her forehead.

"Different how?"

"Only one other guy's been in my bed like this before, you know?"

"Hold up," I interrupted her. "I ain't about going back, only forward. I get it, it's gonna be a long road, but I forgive you for it all. I know you ain't out to mess with my head. You've been through a lot. I know I don't deserve to be anyone's punching bag, but if it helps you make it through the rounds, I'll take some hits."

She looked up at me, her eyes watery.

"Junior, I love you. I truly do."

"I love you too, Paulette."

"Junior?"

"Yeah, what's up?"

"Please, don't tell anyone about what just happened."

I let her go and burst out laughing. "JUNIOR, I'M SERIOUS!!!"

Paulette was on fire. But not because of the sex in that house, or sharing a bed with another dude. It was because I made her climax so hard while she was riding me that she, well, let's say things got messy. It wasn't the highlight of my sex life, but you know, things happen. This time, it was literal. I tried to comfort her, 'cause I know that's a real embarrassing moment. I even Googled 'pooping during orgasm' and found out it's way more common than folks think. But, you know, it's not the kind of thing you just put out there. I understood. Eventually, she calmed down, and now I've got the memory that the phrase "I'm gonna fuck the shit out of you" got some real meaning. As I finished drying off and she headed back to the room to get dressed, I dropped my towel and looked in the mirror at myself. "You're a bad motherfucker, man," I said, quietly enough so she wouldn't hear. The journey continues. I'm still kinda lost. Can't tell if I'm being dumb or if I'm truly going all-in for someone I see a future with. But either way, we're here, and that's all I'm focusing on. Suddenly, that Outkast track I played when I saw her text came back to me. I ran Andre's verse back in my head. I snuck out to my car later that night when she was knocked out. It was a cool breeze and gave me a surreal feeling. I sat in my passenger seat, grabbed the journal out of my glove compartment, and wrote two journal entries. One titled 'Single and Afraid.' The other was titled 'Paulette Thumper.'

Journal Entry: Single and Afraid

Today, I had an experience that moved me profoundly. It was a Saturday evening, and I found myself sitting in my dimly lit room, engulfed by the hauntingly beautiful melodies of Xavier Omar's song "Afraid." The music flowed through my ears like a river, carrying emotions and stories I had heard before but never truly comprehended until this very moment. As I listened to the soulful and poignant lyrics, I couldn't help but be transported into the shoes of a Black woman who had experienced the struggles and pains of love and life in ways that are unique to her. The way Xavier Omar's voice harmonized with the gentle strumming of the guitar, and the vulnerable, raw emotion in his words, was like a key to a world of emotions and experiences I had never fully grasped. The song tells a story of a Black woman who is afraid to love again, afraid to open her heart, afraid to trust. As Xavier Omar sang, "I still say I'm fine, but I leave my brain, Don't wanna think no more, I can't defeat my shame, Don't wanna play no more, I can't defeat this game But that phone still rings, can't delete your name," Those lines hit me like a ton of bricks. It wasn't just a song; it was a window into the heart and soul of countless Black women who have faced pain, disappointment, and heartache. I'm a Black man, and I've always thought I understood the struggles of Black women. I've listened to their stories, witnessed their strength, and tried to be a supportive friend and ally. But "Afraid" made me realize that there's a depth of pain and vulnerability that I could never fully fathom without music like this. As the song continued, I felt myself empathizing with the hurt and fear that the protagonist was expressing. It was as if a veil had been lifted, and I could see, for a moment, the world through her eyes. I saw her resilience and the weight of her past experiences that had left her scarred and broken. It's easy to underestimate the emotional burdens that Black women carry daily, navigating a world that can be hostile, judgmental, and unforgiving. This song reminded me of the importance of truly listening and empathizing, not just hearing their words, but feeling the weight of their emotions. Xavier Omar's "Afraid" served as a profound reminder that we should all take the time to understand the experiences of others, especially those whose stories and struggles may differ from our own. It's a call to compassion, to actively stepping into someone else's shoes and trying to comprehend the complexity of their journey. It's a reminder that music, art, and storytelling have the power to bridge gaps and create empathy in the most unexpected of ways. As I finished listening to the song, I felt a renewed sense of purpose and empathy. I wanted to be an ally who listens, supports, and understands the pain of Black women and all individuals who carry the weight of their unique experiences. Xavier Omar's "Afraid" will forever remain a profound and moving piece of art that reminded me of the importance of compassion, understanding, and the power of music to foster empathy.

Journal Entry: Paulette Thumper

Today, I found myself engrossed in an in-depth analysis of André Benjamin's verse on the iconic hip-hop track "The Art of Storytelling" by OutKast. The song has always been a personal favorite of mine, but it was only today that I truly appreciated the complexity and depth of André 3000's lyrical genius. As the track began with that now-familiar, soulful melody, André's voice painted a vivid picture in my mind. His storytelling prowess is second to none, and his verse on this song exemplifies his extraordinary skill in narrative hip-hop. What struck me first was André's delivery. His voice is like a warm, velvety instrument, perfectly complementing the storytelling nature of the song. His tone, inflections, and enunciation work in harmony to draw the listener in, making us eager to hear what tale he has to share. It's as if he's sitting across from you, recounting a personal story, pulling you into his world. But it's not just his delivery that makes André's verse stand out. The substance of his narrative is equally remarkable. He spins a tale of a chance encounter with an old flame on a rainy night, while cruising in his car. His use of descriptive language is exceptional, painting a vivid picture of the scene, making us feel the raindrops and smell the rain-soaked asphalt. I can't help but be transported to that moment, as if I'm right there with him. His storytelling ability shines through as he navigates the complex emotions and nostalgia of this chance meeting. André's verses are a masterclass in character development. He creates two relatable personas, himself and the old flame, and reveals their inner thoughts and emotions with such depth and authenticity. We feel the bittersweet mixture of joy and sadness that envelops him as he reconnects with this person from his past. The depth of his lyrics is astounding. He touches on themes of love, loss, and the passage of time. André's words are like a time machine, taking us back to moments in our own lives where we've experienced similar emotions, making us reflect on the bittersweet memories of our past. André Benjamin's verse in "The Art of Storytelling" is a testament to the power of hip-hop as a storytelling medium. It goes beyond simple rhymes and beats, transcending into the realm of poetry and literature. His ability to weave a compelling narrative that resonates with listeners on an emotional level is what sets him apart as one of the greatest lyricists in the genre. Today, I am reminded of the incredible impact that André 3000's verses have had on my love for hip-hop and the art of storytelling through music. Paulette, she had that Sasha Thumper vibe, you know? Dealing with a guy, and possibly, guys, who were treating her all wrong. She wanted to live life to the fullest, but past infidelity, a lack of responsibility, questionable choices, and a messy sexual history had her feeling like that girl you'd find at the back of the schoolyard. The thing is, she was still kicking, still pushing through. People say men, no matter where they're from, don't show their feelings, can't be vulnerable, or have their moments of weakness. But here I was, breaking down those stereotypes. The real question was, when would I truly recognize my worth? Big shoutout to Andre, Big Boi, Outkast, Dungeon Family, and the city of ATL, Georgia. Thanks for letting me have my moment, all through a simple twist of words.

—4—

KICK, PUSH

"How will I live? Listen here, life is still a bitch Money don't change shit, stuck in the same shit To get it all, gotta risk it all or forget it dawg A winner ain't a quitter and a quitter ain't a winner y'all"
–Nappy Roots, Good God Almighty.

Waking up on this gorgeous Monday morning in August, life's realizations hit me. For the 37th year, the universe let me open my eyes. I thought about all the crazy stuff I've managed to survive during this time. Three car wrecks, one of which should've had me six feet under. Two major surgeries that could've had me sporting the swankiest funeral in town. I mention this because as humans, we often throw grand funerals, but forget to show up when folks are above ground breathing. I reflected on the choices I've made so far - self-employment, a passion for traveling, and a tight-knit circle of influential friends. I had it all, even when it seemed like I didn't. It was precisely 6:13 a.m., as I've always been an early bird. Just like most folks worldwide, I reached for my phone, though I knew I needed to kick that habit. Technology had a vice grip on me, and I had about a million text messages. 'Happy Birthday, you morning breath monster,' read my niece's text; she was studying down at Southern. 'Hey old man, time for your prune juice and those blue pills,' teased my other niece, a junior at Fresno State. Man, why were my nieces this savage? Just as I wondered that, my nephew from St. Louis chimed in. 'Happy birthday, rusty knees. I'll whoop your old ass.' I couldn't help but laugh. I loved him, but if push came to shove, I'd have to shoot his ass. He was 6'3 with dreads, looking like a transformer a fight I'd have to settle with bullets. 'Yo, happy birthday, you ancient, buff, and bookish dude,' came my buddy Vinnie's message. He was only 5'6, but his confidence could've made him seven feet tall. His text reminded me to call him and find out how his rooftop Love Jones movie date went with that chocolate masterpiece. We may have disagreed a lot, but our friendship was unbreakable. He was sharp as a razor, and I was as straightforward as a comb struggling through dry, unruly hair without afro sheen. We were total opposites, but that's what made our bond so tight. I stretched and hopped out of my comfy bed, feeling a bit like Akeem from Coming to America, minus the women. I headed to the bathroom for my first act as a 37-year-old - a refreshing trip to the toilet. There's something liberating about peeing without worrying about someone barging in. Afterward, I scrubbed my teeth to a date with Colgate, its foam dancing on my pearly whites. Today was all about me, and I dubbed it 'no fucks mode.' I strolled outside, gazing at my truck in the driveway. As I looked back at my home, I couldn't help but feel grateful. I had transportation, shelter, food, and good health life's essentials. I'd learned not to complain about missing beans when I had a whole garden to choose from. Life breaks down sometimes, but when you've got alternatives, there's no reason to fuss. I savored the little things that many consider big a house is just bricks and wood, but a home is the comfort within. A car is just a set of wheels, but it means nothing without a meaningful destination. Clothes don't make the man; the man makes the clothes. I've seen the most confident folks in $30 outfits and the most insecure ones in $1000 suits.

"WHOA MAN!!! GET YOUR DOG!!!"

"STAY OFF MY LAWN, AND BE GLAD HE AIN'T BITE YO' ASS!!!"

I chuckled as I glanced at my neighbor, Will, and his Cane Corso, Ghost. You could tell it was a "nigga's" dog by its name taken from a character in Power. Every time Will hosted a barbecue, I'd be wary, though. Ghost might've been a big baby, but he had grown-up behaviors, especially when he was with Will's wife. I felt for the guy; his lady was all about Ghost, and vice versa. I wouldn't be surprised if Ghost paid the mortgage, and Will had an 8pm curfew with the kids. He became the first man in history to get married and become the side nigga to a four legged human. I decided to treat myself to breakfast this morning, because sometimes, solo dolo is the way to roll. I couldn't understand why some folks get jittery about doing things on their own. I got dressed and headed to a local gem a farm-to-table joint that was Black-owned and served top-notch grub. The place had an interesting name, "Boo Boo The Fool." I still never figured out what that dude looked like. When my mom asked me if she looked like "Boo Boo The Fool," I thought he was some guy she knew. Our parents sure had a way of confusing us when we were kids. I parked right in front of the place and noticed it was unusually packed for a Monday morning. Yo, the spot was crackin', man. I paused for a sec. See, where I reside at, there ain't many of us around, and these faces? Total strangers.

"Morning, how many?" she asked.

"Just me. What's the deal? I ain't never seen this many folks like us in one place, all at once."

"Some Minnesota peeps are in town for a conference, and they deep in here this morning."

"Alright, it's a family reunion then."

"You know it. When we roll deep, we're all practically kin."

She led me to a booth, right across from a table packed with like 20 folks. I already had my order ready, so I chilled and waited for the server.

"Ayo, fam!" shouted a cat at the end of the table. "You from around here?"

"Nah, but I've been posted up for a minute. What's good?"

"I feel you, man. Our folks deep in our hometown, but here? It's like we're just a sprinkle. Where we at?"

"You only gone find us deep here in the hood. Can't compare to where y'all from, huh? Minnesota, right?"

"Yeah, bro. You stumble into a Black brunch without even trying."

"I hear you. Junior."

"Darvin."

Man, that vibe was so fresh and welcoming. Seeing a bunch of our people gathered, just chilling without any drama. I missed that about my hometown back East. Last time I felt this was down in Atlanta, where the food was fire.

"Hey there, welcome to Boo Boos. What can I get you to drink?"

"I know exactly what I want. Give me some OJ. Oh, and hook me up with 'The Man by the Dog' omelet, and a side of those 'put-your-foot-in-it' grits."

"Toast or hash browns?"

"Toast, with the red jelly."

She grinned as she took my order.

"Why the smirk?"

"Red jelly over grape. But, I got you."

"You're too fly to have bad taste."

"You're too smooth to be making wack food choices. Now, the grits regular or 'the slap' style?"

"Alright, I'm down with 'the slap,' but easy on the cheese. Shrimp, bacon, green onion, and again, go light on that cheese."

"Want sugar on them?"

My face scrunched up right then and there. I was shocked. I felt disrespected. I never thought I'd flip a table, but at that moment, it crossed my mind.

"What? Can't believe you asked me that."

"Well, it's kind of my job."

"Nah, we can't disrespect the holy food that Noah and our ancestors survived on that ark with."

"Wait, you really backin' up a white dude from The Bible?"

"Everyone in The Bible was our people, sweetheart."

"So you think a brother built an ark and let two roaches, mosquitos, spiders, and stuff like that roll in? You trippin'."

She hit me with a side-eye and a laugh.

"You're one of them folks Jesus warned us about, huh?"

"And you're a man who needs some help. I'll be back with that OJ."

She smiled as she stepped away. It was a funny, low-key flirt session. I can't front; she was lookin' good an 8.5 out of 10, easily. But co-signing sugar in the grits? That dropped her rating to a solid two. It's tough seeing someone stumble in life like that, but not everyone's elite, right? I settled in, vibing to the old-school jams bumping through the speakers. Two folks at the big table got up and started two-stepping to Clarence Carter's 'Strokin'. These older cats used to talk about us and our music. Curtis was out here naming spots like 'Clap Cheek City', address 69, Spread Cheeks Avenue, zip code 304. But could you say anything to them? Hell nah.

"Here's your OJ."

"Hmm, that's a bit aggressive, ain't it?"

"You sensitive, huh?"

Oh yeah, she was definitely laying down some flirtation vibes. She kept messing around, and she was gonna end up on the list of future tenants eyeing a spot in Clap Cheek City. I sipped my OJ until the Cupid Shuffle, which was like the jam for the Black community, started bumping. There was a sweet open space in the joint, and what's funny is that almost all the Black folks got up to groove. The few non-Black peeps in the spot looked puzzled as hell. One brave soul, though, decided to jump in on our Chocolate City vibe. Let's just say, he stuck out like a sore thumb, repping Vanilla Valley in the weirdest corner of town. As soon as the tune ended, we all settled back into our seats, and the waitress brought over my grub. I got my head in the game to tackle this deliciousness. My neighbor's plate had this epic omelet overflowing with corned beef, bacon, and sausage. And don't get me started on those grits they smelled so good they could wake the dead at a funeral. Then I peeped something sly she left a little sugar pot with my order. Guess she wanted to play petty Betty this morning. Well, her tip might be feeling the sting, but I wasn't trying to start any drama. Mid-meal, she swung by.

"How's everything?"

"Dope. Everything's on point," I said, wiping my mouth. "Except you threw in some bunk cocaine with my order. I don't mess with that stuff, and neither should you."

"You're right. But, you know, if you can get someone addicted, it might be worth it, right?"

She hit me with that curveball, and I was left speechless.

"Give me a shout if you need anything," she said, walking off. These ladies out here always throwing surprises. I needed to stay cool; I didn't want to dive into another crazy situation, seeing how I was still in one. After wrapping up my meal, settling the bill, I dipped. Luckily I didn't run into her on the way out; things might've taken an unexpected turn. If she saw the tip I left, I might've ended up in a different kind of spot behind the grill. I jetted home for some chill time. This birthday was all about kicking back. I got home, hit the shower, tossed on jeans and a snug white tee. I knew I had plans later, so I got ready early. I enjoyed the morning with a Living Single marathon, watching Kyle Barker doing his thing. He was smart, smooth, a stockbroker the kind of role model we should've aimed for as kids. TV nowadays doesn't show Black men like that; they'd rather have us wearing women's clothes or playing the negative stereotype. The issue isn't masculinity; it's the lack of it. Around 11:30, Max was knee-deep in her drama on TV, and someone knocked on my door. Who in the world was dropping by unannounced? I looked through the peephole nobody there. Lesson number one for us: you better call before you roll up. I threw the door open, and from the side of the house, I heard a party horn and saw confetti going everywhere. It was Paulette and her adorable daughter, Destiny the little girl who'd captured my heart.

"HAPPY BIRTHDAY!!!," Paulette shouted, while Destiny kept showering me in confetti.

I kept it together, no tears. I gave that little girl the biggest hug. I couldn't forget about Paulette, but this little one had me hooked for a while now. She was my saving grace, no doubt. I couldn't bear to lose her.

"Happy birthday, Ju Ju."

"Thanks, Suga Duga,"

That was my nickname for her. I looked up at her mom.

"Thanks, love," I told Paulette, as she leaned in to kiss me. We headed inside, with Paulette carrying something huge she had leaned against the house. We chilled on the couch, while the little one showed off her gymnastic moves at the door.

"You know, I figured you'd be busy this morning, so I didn't trip when you didn't call."

"Yeah, I was getting things ready, hoping you weren't mad. Open your gift."

I looked at this thing, wrapped in basic brown paper. It was rectangular shaped, and I honestly had no clue as to what it was. Slowly, I tore the paper off, and the shock of my life was before my eyes.

"Wow. Yo. I can't. I'm speechless."

"It's possibly the best way I could tell you happy birthday, I love you and appreciate you, all in the same breath."

Paulette had gifted me with a 24in x 36in frame, which inside, was a giant collage of photos we had taken, sharing some of our most intimate moments together. It was taking everything in me not to cut on the waterworks. In all my years of life, no one, and I mean no one had ever given me a more thoughtful gift. We had been through some shit, but this reminded me why I felt it was worth going through that shit. Seeing this, it made me feel that her feminine side was coming back, and that all the negative energy that made her put up walls was slowly breaking down. I kissed her, and immediately went to my tool box. I hung this up on my living room wall, and it became everything to me.

"You ready?"

"Ready for what? What better could you do than what you already have?"

"I'm taking you somewhere."

"YEAH, JU JU!!! WE'RE TAKING YOU SOMEWHERE!!!"

Unbelievable. Sometimes, you just gotta go with the flow. This felt like family right here. Despite all the ups and downs, I realized I truly loved this woman. And that kid? I loved her more than I loved myself at this point. It was even better that me and her father got along fine. We had our face-to-face one night when I had to help them work out an issue about Destiny. Paulette thought it was gonna get messy, but it turned out to be respectful and cordial. He had my respect, I had his, and I made sure Destiny was in good hands whenever she was with me. I can never speak on how a baby mama-baby daddy relationship is. I can only go by what I see and experience. So far, me and homey were good, and I had no issues. We were just some regular guys, trying to handle our business, making sure the child was in the best position at all times. We stepped out of the crib, and little mama reached for the car door.

"SUGA!!!"

"Oops, my bad, Ju Ju."

"You remember the golden rule?"

"Never open a door when a man's around."

"That's right, my girl."

We sealed it with our secret handshake, and I made sure to open the door for her and her mom. Our journey was underway.

"Is this in the city?" I asked Paulette.

"I ain't spillin' the beans, you'll have to wait and see."

I just gave her a what the fuck look. She was up to something, and I had no clue what it was, but I knew it was going to be good. Twenty minutes into the ride, little mama was gazing out the window, and we were cruising east on the highway, away from the water, and into the mountains. No nerves here, I felt safe with her. We chatted for the next hour as we left the city life behind. Destiny was now in the back seat, snoring louder than a freight train. I had plenty of time to think as we rolled through those tiny mountain towns. Sometimes, Paulette and I caught each other's eyes. That look said happiness. Maybe she'd moved past some of those bad choices she made; I didn't know much about her first husband, but not many folks tie the knot at 18 and make it. She didn't talk about it much, so I let it be. Out of nowhere, a sign emerged from behind some bushes.

"You brought me all the way up to Mercury Hills?"

"Yup, you've never been here?"

"Nah. I've heard about their famous pies and all, but I only drove through once without stopping."

"Why you ain't stop?"

"Small mountain town - that's not the recipe Black folks usually cook up in the kitchen."

"Look, not everything's like 'The Hills Have Eyes."

"Well, when I see no familiar faces, I tend to steer clear."

We both shared a laugh as we cruised into Main Street, the heart of the community. Sleeping beauty in the back finally woke up, and all I could smell was fresh pastries. Despite the barbecue joint, this place was all about pie. I hopped out and stretched my creaky bones back into alignment. Before Destiny could pull a fast one on me, I opened her door.

"Thank you, JuJu," she said with enthusiasm.

"You're welcome. And if a man doesn't open your door, he's no good." Paulette playfully tapped me on the chest.

"I appreciate you, but she's seven. You think she's gonna remember that?"

"Kids forget a lot of things, but they never forget how grown-ups make them feel."

We locked eyes for a moment. I hoped this little girl remembered everything I taught her as she grew older. It was going to matter more as time went on. God forbid if I was no longer in her life, I just hoped she'd carry the lessons with her. We strolled across the street into the Mercury Hills Pie Company. The vibe and aroma in this place could make me a permanent resident. Well, almost. I spotted what I wanted right away: a couple slices of warm peach pie. The only thing better than peach pie was real peaches, and by that, I mean Black women. My ladies opted for some chocolate ice cream, but I didn't have time for the basics. Today, I was 37, and if there's one day to indulge, it's today.

"Don't go overboard. We're heading next door." I shot Paulette a look as I was about to take that first bite of pie. I halted, kind of annoyed.

"Girl, you're lucky I love you."

I put my dessert back in the bag and strutted out the door, heading a few steps over to the barbecue spot.

"HAPPY BIRTHDAY!!!"

A bunch of folks in the joint shouted as soon as I walked in. I nearly jumped, ready to rumble. You've got to stay alert up here. You never know if it's a genuine birthday greeting or a setup to have you tied to a chair later, stuffing cotton in your ears to survive. We were seated by one of the staff, and Destiny crowned me with a party hat and some blue beads she'd picked out. Normally, I wouldn't go for all that, but when kids, especially little girls, put something on you, you wear it. There's nothing that melts a grown man's heart more than a little girl he cares for. She sat next to me, coloring in one of the sheets from the coloring book they provided. I joined her, coloring my own. I caught a glimpse of her mom, and she had a smile on her face. I returned the gesture, silently letting her know, 'I've got you and your daughter, always.' After about seven minutes of bonding, the food arrived: a huge bowl of rib tips, two bowls of baked macaroni, another bowl of roasted pork, and the biggest beef rib I'd ever seen. I swear, if I smacked someone upside the head with that thing, they'd be headed straight to the hospital. It was a feast, and once we got home, Paulette was up next. As they enjoyed their light meal, they were watching me in awe, seeing me scarfing it down like there was no tomorrow. I wasn't Junior Mitchell right now; I was tapping into my inner Fred Flintstone. Morals? Not today, this was my day, and I wasn't letting anyone or anything ruin it. Growing up in the city, reaching 18 was already a blessing. Making it to 37, I'd beaten all odds set by the folks in charge. That's why I didn't flex about coming from the hood. You flex about things you'd willingly give to someone else. I didn't know anyone who wanted

114

to pass down poverty, struggle, gangs, and drugs to their kids. If they did, they were the dumbest folks around. Unfortunately, I knew quite a few. That's why I couldn't associate with that hood stuff anymore. The older I got, the more it disgusted me. I'd always have love for where I came from, but if I never saw it again, I'd be content and happy. Finishing up my meal, the entire staff came out, singing "Happy Birthday." Suga Duga was right in my face, belting it out. I took it with a smile. I knew this precious child would be my daughter one day, and notice, I didn't say stepdaughter. I said daughter because when you're with a woman, you take on everything that comes with her. There was none of that step shit over here. We left the barbecue joint and explored the shops on Main Street. At one point, we walked into a homemade jewelry store. I looked at those rings and thought about that one time I made the biggest mistake of my life. It wasn't getting married; it was marrying the wrong person. Out of all the choices, I ended up with a one-arm, one-legged llama. That didn't last long, and thank God it didn't. If only I'd listened to my best friend when she looked me in the eyes and said not to marry that witch. In all seriousness, I should've married my best friend. Now, I was thinking about it again, and this time, there were no doubts.

"Can I get that black tungsten ring in a size 10?"

Paulette shot me a look as the lady behind the counter snatched it, gave it a quick wipe, and handed it over. I slid that ring onto my finger. A perfect fit.

"I'm taking this one," I said.

"$12.50, sir," the cashier told me.

I handed over my card, and Paulette beamed at me, giving me a playful nudge in the chest.

"What's up?" I asked.

"Why'd you pick up that ring?" she wanted to know.

"So, when I'm out and about, these ladies know to keep their distance."

"You really have that much faith in me?"

"I believe in us. Big difference. So, what's your favorite gem?"

"Opal," she replied, her eyes getting a little misty.

"Alright, one day, when the time is right, that opal will symbolize something more than just a stone. This time, it's gonna be different, and I can promise you that. It'll be your first marriage. The first two, those weren't marriages. Those were impromptu infatuations. When you say I do to me, you'll know what love truly is."

We shared a moment, but I wasn't sure if she fully grasped what I'd just done. They say when someone's getting treated right in a relationship for the first time, they might try to sabotage it. Not because they don't want love, but because it feels too good to be true, and their mind can't quite process what's happening. Paulette had seen me stick around through all the BS, even the stuff I shouldn't have. She'd opened up to me about things she probably shouldn't have, especially when her mind wasn't in the right place. I'd been her punching bag and her safe haven all in one, and I'd accepted that role. We left the store and headed to a nearby convenience store. But, it turned out they were closing at five.

"Is there another store around here that's still open?" I asked.

"Nah, man. This town shuts down at five," the cashier replied.

Paulette and I decided it was best to head home. The sun hadn't set yet, but we didn't want to be stuck in this town after dark. She might not have been thinking about it, but I sure was. In some places, they'd hang you at the town square if you got left behind after dark. As we drove back toward the mountain roads, we stopped at an overlook. We stepped out of the car, and I hugged both my favorite ladies, gazing at the mountains, trees, and the beauty of nature. It didn't matter whether you thought of God as a divine masterpiece or a cosmic architect, you couldn't deny the beauty in the world. Screw all the pronoun stuff–God was God, the universe was the universe, and this moment was just perfect. This time was different. We got back in the car after a while and made the hour-long drive back to the city. Once we got back to my place, the little one needed to use the bathroom, so I let her in. While she was inside, Paulette held me back.

"Junior, my period didn't come. I have the contraception device, but I'm nervous," she admitted.

"Have you taken a test?" I asked.

"No, not yet. But I can't handle this right now, with the divorce proceedings and my financial situation. I know you've got my back, but it's just how I feel."

"Look, go get a test and let me know. If things aren't as you want them to be, take this."

I handed her $600 from my wallet.

"What's this for?"

"In case we have to consider other options. I'm not thrilled about it, but I understand. If it's not enough, I'll give you more."

"What if I'm not pregnant?"

"Just keep it. I need to make sure you and Destiny are okay. You two mean the world to me, and if my world falls apart, I go down with it."

She hugged me, tears falling onto my shirt. I wanted kids, but it had to be the right situation. Still, it didn't sit right with me. If she was indeed pregnant, it would mean making a difficult decision. We both knew what we were doing; I hadn't used protection. Being responsible was the most significant part of being an adult, and many adults wanted to dodge accountability. They'd rather point fingers at others than themselves. For a long time, Paulette had been doing that, always blaming her mother for much of what happened in her life. But slowly, after I'd interacted with her mom on numerous occasions and told Paulette how it went, she began to grow and accept that her problems were her own. She still had some growing up to do, but she was definitely better than when I'd first met her. I hugged Destiny as she returned to the door, and we did our handshake. Then, they headed off to the car, with me walking them to it and opening the doors. Consistency was key. I walked back into the house and slumped on the couch, feeling a light breeze from my open living room windows. There had only been one other time I'd come close to having a child, but it ended in a miscarriage. I hadn't told anyone except my dad, and even now, it's hard to think about on some days. Now, if Paulette was pregnant, things were about to change once again. What if she had a change of heart? I was prepared for whatever came our way. I didn't have any other plans for the day, just a night of corny Hallmark movies. People could say what they wanted, but I was comfortable in my own skin. Or, as one of my buddies once famously said, "Insecurity kills all that is beautiful, and we are beautifully constructed to be who we are." Two hours passed uneventfully until I got a knock on my door. I decided to do the usual and ignore it, even though whoever it was could clearly hear the TV through the open window. But, this person meant business. BOOM BOOM BOOM!!! Those were three thunderous knocks. Now, I was getting annoyed. It was one thing for me to ignore my door, but this was like someone trying to break it down. I got up, contemplating whether I should grab my gun, but I figured it wouldn't be that extreme. I peeked through the peephole and got the shock of my life.

"Yo, what's good, man?" I said as I opened the door.

"My dude, can I crash here for the night? Please, man?"

It was my guy Marlon, and he looked like he'd been through the wringer for a minute. I let him in, and he sat at my kitchen table, breaking down, tears streaming. Asking why he was crying would've been the obvious thing, but it didn't feel like the most pressing issue right now.

"Man, your clothes are a mess, and you've got a stench on you," I told him. "What's going on? I'm not trying to clown you, but you clearly ain't in a good place."

Marlon looked up at me, his eyes as red as a blood moon.

"Bro, I messed up. Got caught up. It's a wrap for me, man."

"What did you do?" I asked.

"My wife said she can't do it anymore. The job, the lifestyle, it's just too much. She told me not to show up at home after my Friday morning shift. I don't want anyone at work to know, but I've been crashing in my car for the past few days. Man, it's been almost a whole week."

"Wait up, hold on. You're not on call tonight, right?"

"Nah, not at all."

118

"So, what's up with the crazy schedule? I thought you adjusted your hours a while back."

"Alright, bro, for real. I'm struggling with this whole husband thing. She stood by me when I had those late-night shifts every three days, voluntary overtime, and out-of-state training every couple of weeks. She dealt with that for years. Now, I've got all the time in the world, and I don't even know how to give it to her."

I just gave my guy a nigga please look. Part of me empathized, and the other part thought knew he was really fucking up.

"Alright, man, listen up. Head to the bedroom, grab a fresh pair of boxers, throw on some basketball shorts, a tee, and freshen up. I'll cook something up for you, and we can chop it up."

"Man, you don't need to go that far. I just need to talk."

"You need more than just talk, bro. You need help, a friend, and someone to keep it real with you."

"Bro, I got this. I'm a man. I'll figure it out."

"Man, that's your ego and pride talking right now. Don't be stubborn. Go get cleaned up, and we'll deal with this."

Marlon knew I was dead serious. He got up and went to the back room to grab the stuff I'd told him. I headed back to the kitchen, took out the chicken wings from the fridge that I wasn't planning to cook until Wednesday. At the same time, I texted Marlon's wife, Alicia, letting her know he was here and that I'd get him back on track. I even shared the contact for a therapist I knew since neither she nor the kids deserved to miss an essential part of their lives. I also asked her to let me be the last resort in helping him before she called it quits. She agreed. I heated a pan of oil on the stove, got the chicken seasoned, and the leftover cabbage, mac and cheese, and half a pan of cornbread from Sunday night were still good to go. As I got lost in my culinary zone, those two minions came back, starting with the wild one.

"Hey, nigga. Fuck is you doing?"

"Fam, there's no woman here, and I really don't need your drama today."

"Man, I just came to tell you that you're wasting your time. That guy doesn't need any help."

"What do you mean?"

"Exactly what he said," the righteous one chimed in from my other shoulder.

"Listen up, man. Evil and good both understand responsibility. Evil knows it's responsible for the chaos it causes, and good knows it's responsible for the good it brings. Marlon, he's avoiding responsibility on both ends. This nigga ain't shit bruh."

"Man, you used to be all about the drama in people's lives. Breaking up families and all that."

"True, but even in our twisted world, there's a way to handle things. Evil has its ways, but they're chaotic with a mission. This nigga just bullshittin'. If you're not gonna help him, at least don't make things worse by co-signing his shit."

They disappeared, with evil once again saying the shit that I needed to hear. Sometimes, it's not about good or evil; it's just about making sense. As I started frying my special seasoned wings, Marlon walked into the kitchen, this time smelling and looking like a new man.

"Man, what deodorant did you use?"

"Oh, man, I went with the Arm and Hammer."

"Good call. If you'd used my Axe, we'd have a problem."

We both chuckled, even though I was dead ass serious.

"What's cooking, man?"

"Just frying some wings. Got some leftover cabbage, cornbread, and mac from Sunday night that you can mix with this."

"You didn't cook any meat with this on Sunday, did you?"

"Nah, there's some salt pork in the cabbage."

"Got it."

"Now, tell me the truth, man."

Marlon sat down.

"What are you getting at, man?"

I grabbed a can of mango nectar from the fridge, joined him at the table, and took a sip.

"I know you're fucking around, man. This ain't about your work schedule or recovering from a crazy routine. This is about you not keeping your act together."

"Bro, who are you to come at me like this?"

"I'm being a real nigga coming at you like this. If I was full of shit, I wouldn't be telling you the truth. Now tell me the truth. Evil and good might have different approaches, but they're both spelled with four letters, and they're connected in a way."

Marlon knew I wasn't playing around. I might not be a public servant, but I could still serve up a 50-piece if he pushed me. As I checked on the chicken, he broke down in tears. I cooked while he spilled the beans on his misdeeds. I was being a friend, because a true friend tells it like it is when you mess up. But after today, I wasn't sure if I could roll with him. There were two types of people my grandma warned me about: those who cheat on their partners and those who neglect their kids. I made a plate as he continued sharing his mistakes. Alicia had kicked him out, and she was on edge. Three kids, working from home, and not wanting her children to lose the man they loved was a lot to handle.

"Dude, I don't even deserve this grub, man, or your hospitality."

"Listen up, my dude. Check out this plate. Cornbread, cabbage, salt pork, mac 'n' cheese, and some crispy wings, fried to perfection. This right here, it's made with love. A classic plate of soul food, and this crispy fried chicken, it's the heart and soul of the meal. It's like that warm, homey feeling of love. My Grandma used to call it 'southern fried intimacy.' Just like I put in the effort to season and prepare this food, that's how you should approach your relationship with your wife. You've made vows, man, and you've got those kids. You've got three daughters, and you're the first role model, more importantly, man they'll look up to. If you act like an ass, they'll grow up thinking asshole men are who they should be with. You've put that woman through a lot. Just like when you

121

mess up in the kitchen, fix it. Fix what's broken. There's no other way to put it. If I weren't your friend, I'd be giving you some bullshit talk right now."

I took a bite of a wing, slathered in mild sauce, while looking at my friend, really hoping he was getting what I was saying.

"I got a question, man."

"What's on your mind?"

"Yo, man, what's the deal with mild sauce?"

I dropped my wing on the plate and let out a chuckle.

"Mild sauce is what the true ride-or-die folks use to spice up their wings. It's for the real loyal ones."

"Come on, really?"

"Absolutely. Not just for me, man, but for those ladies in your life. Think about it. Do you want them growing up with someone acting like you?"

"I'm not a bad guy."

"Never said you were. Good people can slip up too. Remember, even Jesus went off in the temple because folks were hustling in His house. He flipped all that shit over."

"You're messing with me."

"Check Matthew 21:12-13. Now, wrap it up, call your wife, and be straight up with her."

"Bro, how do I do that?"

As I walked toward the bathroom, I turned to him.

"Same way you were with those other women. Keep it real, my man. Leave your dirty shit where you left it at, and lock the door when you go out. I've got business to handle."

I stepped into the bathroom, put my phone on YouTube, and enjoyed a peaceful moment. A good shit always capped off a great day. While relaxing to Usher's 'U Don't Have to Call,' my mischievous side paid me a visit.

"Man, your bathroom smells like trouble."

"Well, what were you expecting?"

"Not that, man. Not even hell stinks that bad. But hey, good job, even I wouldn't go that far with the chaos."

The angel on my shoulder spoke up.

"Didn't expect to hear you say something so meaningful." The devil glanced at me.

"If that nigga got a woman, she's probably fucking someone else. Even his wings are tiny. I doubt he's got much going on down there."

I couldn't help but burst into laughter. Those two were cracking me up, especially the devil in timberlands. I finished up and returned to the living room, where Marlon was outside talking to his wife. I continued with my Hallmark movie marathon. I might not have been a saint throughout my life, but I knew the importance of growth and what it took to be a man. Family always came first, and you don't mess with that. Bringing unnecessary drama into your home was a major no-no.

"Yo, man, I appreciate it."

Marlon came in and we gave each other a fist bump before he headed home for that much-needed heart-to-heart with his wife.

"AYE BRO!!!," I hollered at him from the front door as he walked to his car.

"What's good?"

"Remember what I told you."

"Yeah, yeah. This love stuff is like fried intimate chicken, or some shit like that."

I couldn't help but laugh. My man had a point. I strolled back inside and enjoyed the rest of my night. The following day, I swung by to pick up Paulette and her daughter so we could have a family day of sorts. Suga Duga's school didn't start for another week and a half, so I cherished this time. We headed to the city's biggest park, loaded with museums, a duck pond, a botanical garden you name it. It was the perfect spot to relax and find some peace. Walking hand in hand with my two favorite ladies, with the seven-year-old boss in the middle, was a beautiful feeling. There's too much drama and division in our families on

TV. I knew better, but people had already made up their minds. As we strolled towards the giant fountain the park's centerpiece I couldn't help but notice the reactions. Some folks smiled, while others seemed surprised. Can a Black couple just be happy and harmonious without it being a spectacle? Then, I spotted another brother in the same situation as me, with his daughter in the middle and him and his lady on either side. As we passed each other, we exchanged that universal head nod. But this time, it meant more. It was like he was saying,

"Do your thing, Black man. We need more of us out here." I gave a nod to my brother, feeling a surge of pride. We reached the fountain, where Destiny was putting on a show with her flips and whatnot. Meanwhile, Paulette and I stood close, sharing affectionate moments, the kind that make you feel whole again. Those walls I'd put up, thanks to her and sometimes life, suddenly felt like they were taking hits from a wrecking ball. Patience, man, patience. I'd truly learned its real meaning. This moment, it meant the world to me. I might not have been to space, but with her, I had the sun, the moon, the planets, and galaxies. After wrapping up there, we strolled across a bridge, entering a serene, even more peaceful stretch filled with trees and cacti. The selfie we snapped was legendary, although it couldn't quite compete with the giant framed photo of us back in my living room. We still had plenty of the day left, and our growling stomachs led us out of the park. Baby Simone Biles had her heart set on pizza, and you know how it goes with kids they usually get what they want. We drove close to the ocean, hoping to stumble upon a hidden gem. Paulette's Google came to the rescue, and we found a hidden gem of a spot. It was like if Baskin Robbins and a pizza joint hooked up and had a foodie love child. This place wasn't just about the basics; it had nearly 31 flavors of Italian magic. I reverted to my inner kid, ordering us all personal pan pizzas because, let's be real, I wasn't about to share. Now, fellas, let's talk about enforcing those ten relationship commandments.

Ten Relationship Commandments

1. No food-sharing allowed. If you wanted it, you should've grabbed it yourself. Keep your hands off my plate.

2. Stay in your lane on the bed. Mind your manners, or you'll catch a swift kick to your side.

3. There's a two-t-shirt and hoop shorts limit. Quit raiding our stuff. I want to hit the court, and now we can't find a thing because you're sporting our gear in the grocery store's aisle six.

4. Save irrelevant conversations for after the game. Sheika and her hubby's drama can't trump the Cowboys vs. Eagles on Sunday Night Football.

5. The dog can't claim dominance over my cheeks just because he's a mama's boy. I'll toss his behind out in the rain.

6. Adjusting our nuts is standard procedure. Don't tell us to stop. We don't complain when you scratchin' yo titty meat.

7. Shopping for your man isn't an excuse to blow the budget on yourself. How'd I end up with six pairs of socks while you got two new pairs of heels, and a U-haul from Bath and Body Works?

8. Bathwater should be just right, not scalding. We want our nuts clean, not cooked well-done. So, keep it under 85 degrees on couples' bath nights.

9. If you say you don't want to talk about it, we're leaving it alone when we ask what's wrong. Don't have us waking up in the middle of the night with you staring at us, saying we need to talk. I'm asleep. Save it for the morning.

10. "It doesn't matter" means just that. If I bring home Chick-fil-A, and you say you don't eat it, then, guess what? It doesn't matter. Eat it or go hungry. We don't give a shit.

With our bellies full, we made our way back to the park. In this part of the city, it was one vast playground for all kinds of activities. It used to be an old, massive prison, but now it was a place for everyone to enjoy. It's incredible what can happen when someone's got a brilliant idea. We sat at a table, cherishing the time together, while Destiny kept a tally of squirrels she spotted. That's what mattered most to me. Growing up, I knew what it was like to be an unhappy kid, feeling unloved, unappreciated, unliked, and invisible. It warmed my heart to see this little girl feeling none of those things. She wolfed down her meal because she had bigger missions at the monkey bars and slides pretty much everything that the playground had to offer. I was at peace, but the look in Paulette's eyes raised some concern.

"You okay, babe?"

"Junior, I'm running low on funds. My savings are drying up, and that asshole put me in a bind. I appreciate everything you've done, but I need a more permanent plan for her future. I can't keep living like this."

"What's on your mind?"

"Honestly?"

"Yeah, no games. Lay it on me."

"I'm thinking about enlisting in the military."

Man, those words hit deep. In a short time, I fell hard for this woman and her daughter. I've been there through thick and thin. I've seen how military life goes down, with many of my family members in the mix. Deployments, separations from family, and the constant uncertainty it's a whole lifestyle shift. I had a lot of thoughts swirling in my head, but one thing's crystal clear. When you love someone, you do what's best for both of you, even if it ain't your favorite choice.

"Well, check this out. My grandma used to drop wisdom on me. She said, no matter how far a dog wanders from home, it always finds its way back to the folks who care for it."

"Junior, enough with the down-home sayings, you're fucking me up. Speak English, please."

I couldn't help but chuckle.

"Long story short, no matter what, I've got your back. I love you. I love your kid. I can't change what happened with that loser, and I hope he's catching some karma in prison. For now, let's figure out what comes next. And in the meantime, you got Zelle?"

"Why's that?"

"I'm sending you three stacks."

"I can't accept that."

"Yes, you can. You're just not used to someone caring about you that much."

Paulette started tearing up. These weren't fake tears; these were the real deal, like, 'Why's this guy so deep in my corner?' tears.

"WHY ARE YOU STILL HERE???!!!"

"Whoa, whoa. Chill, love."

"I'm sorry. It's just no one's ever done something like this for me. I don't get why you love me so much. I'm a lot to handle, and right now, it's a messy situation. Seriously, Junior, ask yourself why you want this. I'm broken. I'm no good for you, my daughter or myself."

"Remember when you asked me if I was sure if I wanted this that second time you were at my place?"

"You mean the night you fucked me and turned me into jello?"

We both cracked up at that.

"Yeah, that night. You asked me then, and what did I say?"

"You said you were sure and not running away."

"I meant every word. I get why you got upset when I had doubts that one time and suggested we call it quits because I felt overwhelmed. You've had enough people break their promises to you. I didn't want to join that club. So, I took responsibility and made sure my actions matched my words. I love you. And that little girl doing flips on the monkey bars, scaring me half to death right now I'll never let her down. I love her, and I love you."

"I love you too."

We shared a kiss and turned our attention to Destiny. Even though her mom wasn't too worried, I was a bundle of nerves. I didn't want that little one falling and cracking her head open. I knew she had dreams of becoming the next Gabby Douglas or Simone Biles, but ghetto gymnastics ain't the move. As she eased my worries, and eventually took a slide, another dad came by with his daughters.

"Good to see, man," I told him.

"Thanks, bro. Which one's yours?" Right then, Suga Duga screamed as she whooshed down the slide.

"The one making all that noise halfway across the block." He got a kick out of that.

"Take it easy, brother. Black dads matter, and you're doing it right."

"Likewise."

He went on his way, and Paulette shot me a smile.

"You're really loving this, huh?"

"Absolutely. You're my future, she's my daughter and I'm loving every bit of it."

We held hands and let Destiny play to her heart's content. At one point, I had to climb up that massive jungle gym and chase her around, just like she demanded. I even had to give the stink-eye to some little dude who tried to show her a rock he'd found. That kid better keep it moving. Go chat with the other apple juice drinkers; my Suga Duga was off-limits. Afterward, I dropped them off at home. As I stepped out of the car, Destiny gave me the most epic hug and we did our secret handshake.

"I LOVE YOU JUJU!!!"

"I LOVE YOU TOO, SUGA DUGA!!!"

Paulette watched as I let go and rushed to the door.

"Thank you."

"You got it. Let me send you that cash."

I whipped out my phone and sent her the three stacks through Zelle. I never really understood why people trusted Cash App.

"I owe you."

"Pay me back on our wedding day. I love you."

"I love you too."

We locked lips, and she headed inside the house. I made sure they got in safely and rolled out. The moment I got away from their place, I found the nearest parking lot and pulled in. Right then and there, I let it all out. Hearing that little girl say she loved me made me realize I was doing the right thing. For the longest time, I was in a mental tug-of-war. They weren't kidding when they said kids bring out the best and worst in you. Destiny wasn't bringing out my best she was uncovering my vulnerability. I couldn't afford to mess this up or let things go south, because losing her meant losing a part of myself. I sat in that parking lot for a solid half-hour, contemplating everything. The mind can be your greatest ally and your fiercest enemy. It can make you feel like you can conquer the world one moment and have you second-guessing every move you've ever made the next. I took a deep breath. There was a lot on my plate right now. I gathered myself and headed home, getting ready for the next steps I had to take. The next few weeks were a whirlwind, with many moving pieces. Most of it revolved around helping Paulette get into the military. She picked the Navy, but there was a catch. They wouldn't accept her unless she gave up custody of her daughter to her baby daddy. I had no issues with him, but I'd heard plenty of stories about him from her. I stayed out of it. I was there to listen and provide support. Not to judge or interfere, or say that she was lying, but some women thrive on drama to build their own narrative. Some guys might be jerks, but not all of them. I'd seen that from my own brother. His ex-wife was a drama queen. She despised him because he focused on his kids and not her. She disliked me just because we shared the same blood. It is what it is. I wasn't getting caught up in that mess. I accompanied her to the recruiting office a few times just to show my support. Those military folks tried to throw shade, and I had to remind them that I wasn't just another dude. Uncle Sam didn't mean jack to me, and they were about to get fucked up, or end up with their significant other fucked by one of my homies.

Whichever came first. After I laid it out straight to the big shot to cut out all the nonsense the first time, they pretty much left me be. Paulette caught a breather from everything and came over to the crib to chill for a bit one day. We did our regular antics. Kicking it on the couch, watching some random show, and taking snaps of our feet side by side, checking out the size difference.

"What's that?"

"What are you pointing at?"

"That," she gestured to the decor on my living room table.

"Ah, that's some obsidian my buddy brought back from a trip to Arkansas. He says it's supposed to ward off bad vibes or something."

"You know that's witchcraft stuff, right?"

"Ummm."

"Yeah, it goes against The Bible."

"Paulette, don't start with that."

"I'm not starting anything. I'm just telling you like it is."

"Alright, let's just enjoy our time and relax."

"You know what, I gotta bounce. I can't be part of this."

"Are you serious?"

"Yeah, Junior. I can't risk my soul. I'm out."

At that point, I could've said a lot before she split. But I kept my cool. Obsidian was supposed to repel negativity, and now her drama was out of my house, so it obviously worked. I didn't know where she was headed. As long as she wasn't here with her drama, I was cool with it. I looked up at that massive picture collage of us. Why was I still dealing with this? Her random outbursts were really getting on my nerves. I swear, she was more than just broken. She was all over the place. I shook it off because I wasn't going to let her ruin my day. I kept watching TV on this beautiful weekend when those two characters showed up on my shoulder.

"What y'all want?"

"Chill out, Junior. Breathe. She's still going through a lot. Remember that."

"Oh, come on. Junior, you're dealing with a woman who's got more toxic vibes than an infected pussy. My man, let her go before you pick up some of that negativity."

"Her past doesn't matter," I told him.

"It's not just the hundred-something guys she's been with. It's the bad decisions, the lack of accountability, the anger fits, the trouble, and all that nonsense."

"Damn, man," I told that wicked dude.

"Look, it's one thing to want chaos. It's another to see a guy getting dragged by a woman whose aliases are manipulation and self-centeredness. Come on, man, you're better than this. Do what you know you should before you end up messed up, like that soft guy on your other shoulder."

Both of them disappeared, but evil's words hung in the air. Screw it, it was time for a nap. I figured I'd get a solid two hours in and then hit the store later. A good grocery run would set me right. I crashed on the couch under the fan. When I woke up exactly two hours later, the first thing I did was check my phone and logged onto the book. I saw Paulette had posted a video, and it had a million people in the comments. I listened, and with each passing minute, I got angrier and angrier. This woman was acting all holy and righteous on that blue app. Talking about how she'd encountered someone with a demon and had to kick them to the curb because they were messing with stones. I scrolled through the comments and saw a bunch of folks falling for her bullshit. Oh, someone blessed her with three grand, she claimed. Funny how she didn't mention it was me. Oh, I'm a demon, and you're all holy now? Tell them how you've been with me the whole time, even while you were legally married. Oh, she conveniently left out the part about adultery. Oh, now we all need to be cleansed, huh? I guess all the people who fucked you before me were like cleaning products. If I needed any more signs to dump this woman, this was it. She was full of it right now. Tell them how you wished death on your kid's dad? Oh, that's so biblical. Tell them about you sucking my dick in downtown parking lots. Oh, now fornication is a holy act. Your drunk nights, talking bad about your own mother, all that stuff. Tell them that. Tell them how you talked trash about "your friend" who introduced us, yet wanna post that he's your best friend later. This was why I could care less about church or so-called church folks. Dealing with her was one thing. But now, she was taking cheap shots, after all I'd done for her. Yeah, fuck you. I got up and snatched that frame off my living room wall. I took my time to take it apart because I wasn't mad enough to ruin a perfectly good frame. Once I had it all separated, I snatched the picture out and looked at it one last time.

"I love you, Destiny, and this has nothing to do with you," I said out loud. I tore that thing into a million pieces. The more I tore it, the angrier I got. I felt like I was tearing myself apart. All I'd given this woman, and she didn't appreciate a thing, all while living in her own world. I broke down crying, kneeling on my living room floor. I wasn't mad at her. I was mad at myself for letting someone so lost, mischievous, and manipulative get to me. I wondered if this woman loved anyone other than herself. As I got myself together and started picking up the shreds of paper all over the floor, one piece stood out. Amid all the torn bits, the picture of her daughter wearing one of my hats was perfectly intact. I sat on my couch, clutching the picture like it was a lifeline. This relationship had taken so much from me, but it gave me one thing: a deep sense of love. One person loved me under her terms, and the other, unconditionally, knowing JuJu would always have her back. When she needed help with her homework, and tears flowed at her grandma's house, it was JuJu who uplifted her. JuJu helped her understand that everything was a process. Getting the wrong answer wasn't a reason to get frustrated; it was a reason to reevaluate and see how smart she really was. When her mom was overwhelmed and needed sleep, JuJu took her to the park. JuJu watched over her like a hawk, not to harm her but to protect her fully. Paulette's situation made me wary of any guy around her who wasn't her biological dad. Lastly, I thought back to when we once hung out at my sister's house, watching Disney movies together. No fear in her eyes, no worry, and no negativity in her spirit. This little girl had complete trust in me, and I was ready to go all-in for her, 'cause I loved her like no other. Even when her mom had a moment and asked me to step back, I was down with it. Destiny didn't quite get why I did it, but I'd do whatever it took to let them both know they were in a safe zone. Cool as a cucumber, I set her picture on my living room table, grabbed my keys, and hopped in the ride. Zooming down the highway at 80, cruising until traffic turned into a total roadblock. It was beyond annoying that this same stretch of freeway had been under construction for, like, two decades. It's like they fixed a tiny bit of road each year. After a 20-minute ride turned into a frustrating 45-minute crawl, I finally hit my exit on Baltimore Drive. Different from the bustling city, this route led to a beautiful suburb, where the beach was absolutely breathtaking and relaxing. Slowly, I drove through the winding hills of this beachfront neighborhood, checking out the houses that, even though they were close together, still brought a sense of calm. Rolling down the main strip, I let the wind blow through the windows. It felt like it was talking to me. I was half-expecting those two dudes to pop up on my shoulders at any minute, but surprise, they left me be. I guess even good and bad vibes can agree to keep their distance. I pulled into the parking lot off the main road, cut the engine, and sat there for a moment, soaking in everything that went down. I was foolish to keep giving this woman chances, but my heart was too big to just walk away. Yeah, I saw the red flags, but that little girl, plus everything her mom went through, messed with my judgment. I stepped out, staring at the sand and the cliffs. Mother Earth was something else, and she was a queen of all colors. I strolled through the sand and along the beach, taking in all the families having a blast. It hit me deep. Back in the day, a woman I loved went through a miscarriage. My parents never really had a stable relationship. The one that got away, well, she got messed up marrying the dude I warned her about. My love life was basically a no-show. It felt like every time I got close to something real, it got snatched away because of stuff beyond my control. Or maybe, it was more like my lack of control. A buddy once asked a deep question: What's more disrespectful, calling a woman a bitch or a bitch a woman? I threw in another one: What's more disrespectful, loving someone who doesn't love you back or not loving yourself enough to walk away? The answer? Shamefully, I had to admit I was guilty of the latter. I planted myself under a massive cliff. I was just Junior Rashad Mitchell today, son of a funeral home director, lost in his own world. I gazed at the ocean, thinking about all I'd been through. Even though I believed I was doing the right thing, it all went wrong. I learned the difference between love and infatuation. I saw the gap between a woman's tears and a con artist's tears. I realized that I was the clown, not the ringmaster. I lost track of time sitting there, and when I finally noticed the sun setting, I glanced at my watch. It was almost eight o'clock. More than four hours had flown by. I got up, stretched like I just rolled out of bed, and the sun's farewell chat hit me. I had to wrap up this chapter and step into a new scene. I had no idea why, but Puerto Vallarta was calling me. I made my way back to the parking lot. Most families were gone by then. Even wilder, I couldn't spot another person with Black skin around. Maybe being the needle in a haystack was a good thing. I opened the car door, hung one leg out, and enjoyed the remaining light. Grabbing my phone, I hit the travel site, and luck was on my side. I snagged a deal five nights in Puerto Vallarta for $285. Not all-inclusive, but I didn't care. It was time for a fresh start, a new beginning, and all that jazz. I thought about calling Paulette, but nah, she'd kill my vibe. Checking my Alaska app, I saw I had enough points for a round-trip flight. Alaska and Delta were my go-to airlines. You'd never catch me on those budget carriers like Spirit, Frontier, and Allegiant. People pay $19 for a ticket just to have the devil in the cockpit. I flew Spirit once, years back, and I swear I thought I was heading into a mountainside. Legroom was tighter than a closed door. Plane smelled like an old car with sunflower seeds all over the floor and some weed left in the ashtray. Worst part? They lost my luggage. No way I'm flying with them again, not even if they gave me a free ticket to Heaven. Everything was booked, and I drove home in a much better mood. Paulette was in the rearview mirror, and all I wished for was Destiny's mental well-being. No kid should have to deal with different folks coming in and out of their lives. A week breezed by, and now I found myself at the airport. No contact with Paulette, and I was fine with that. For the first time in forever, I felt at peace. I had elite status, so I got on the plane first. Honestly, it didn't matter; Alaska's legroom is so good that you're comfy wherever you sit. Just as I settled in, my phone lit up. 'Hey. I hope you're doing alright. I love you.' I thought about ignoring it. She'd put me through enough pain and drama. But not responding wasn't my style. 'I'm good. On my way to Mexico for a week. I hope you're well. Love you too.' Why, oh why? Why did I end with "love you?" I knew why because the petty nigga I aspired to be, well, it wasn't really in my nature. I switched off my phone and decided to let go of my worries, including anything to do with Paulette or life's daily grind. For the next week, I planned to just kick back, relax, and throw any moral concerns out the window. I glanced up and saw a stunning sister serving as one of the flight attendants. She was definitely going to rack up some serious air miles with that level of beauty. I felt a sense of freedom in my mind, even though my heart had its own agenda. I mumbled my usual pre-flight prayers and settled in for the journey to paradise. Just when I thought I was in for a smooth ride, two dudes slid into the seats next to me. Dang, I thought I'd have this one in the bag. As we took off, I threw on my headphones and queued up John Wick on my phone. I couldn't help but wonder if they ever thought about making a brother the lead in that flick. I mean, we wouldn't go all John Wick for a little dog and an average car. A Black John Wick? He'd be rolling in a classic Box Chevy, on some serious rims, with a pitbull named Bacardi. If you messed with that ride or his pup, well, you were in for a world of trouble. But, amidst all the action, it struck me that this was some real "white people" stuff. Dude practically started World War III over a pup. I guess the lesson here was that you never really know what's valuable to someone, so you best leave their stuff alone if it ain't your business. I didn't make it through the whole movie; I knocked out halfway. When I woke up, I heard those magic words: "We're starting our final descent into Puerto Vallarta." Bliss and nostalgia filled my senses. The only downside, in my book, was going through customs. And as expected, as soon as I grabbed my bags and hit the customs checkpoint, they were all over me. They popped my bag open and acted like I was the next El Chapo.

"CBD?"

"Nah, vitamins."

I mean, this cat went through all eight vitamin bottles, opening them up and giving them a sniff. Thank goodness he didn't dig into my joints. It felt like an eternity, but I finally made it through. Outside, I called an Uber from the outdoor counter.

"Hola?" I said,

"Hey, um, The Grand Bliss at Nuevo Vallarta."

"Vidanta. Bueno."

"No, Grand Bliss."

This was getting frustrating, and I could almost feel myself headed to some cartel hideout for a ransom. So I tried a slower approach. That's when he turned around in the car.

"I know where you're headed, man. Trust me. I make this drive at least three times a week. I got you. No worries. You're from the coast. I see the hat."

"Yeah, Southern."

"Good," he replied.

The way he said "good," I just knew he was connected with something deeper, like the Surenos, because he said it way too smoothly. I leaned back, stayed quiet, and enjoyed the ride. Puerto Vallarta seemed like any other place. There's always some news about Mexico being a no-nonsense zone. But, for now, I was at peace. About 20 minutes later, we left the main road and hit a massive brick wall with "VIDANTA" in bold white letters. We stopped at the gate, and he lowered the back window.

"Name."

"Junior Mitchell."

After some scrolling on her pad, she found it.

"Mr. Mitchell. Five nights at the Grand Bliss. Enjoy your stay."

The driver pulled away and drove down the road for another 30 seconds until we reached a spot with a ton of cars.

"This is it. You're all set, man. Hope I didn't spook you."

"Naw, man. A bit thrown off, but not scared."

Who was I kidding? I was scared almost to the point where I thought I'd break a sweat. I handed him a $20 bill for good measure, just to stay on his good side.

"De nada. If you need a ride anywhere while you're here, here's my card. Juan."

"Yo, Junior."

"What's good? Nice to meet you, fam. Enjoy your stay. There's a whole vibe with a lot of hynas here."

I was a bit lost, and my expression gave it away.

"Beautiful ladies everywhere. Enjoy the scenery," he said, grinning.

We hopped out of the car, and he took my bags. An attendant swooped in to collect my info, grabbed my bags, and handed me a ticket. Turns out, I had to hop on a small van to get to my resort. This was shaping up to be an adventure. The drive to the main lobby was short, but the vibes around here were crystal clear: it's all about having a good time, and nothing else matters. I glanced at my phone like a rookie one last time before stepping inside. Deep down, I still had that burning question: Did she love me or just the idea of me? But, honestly, that wasn't even a real question. I was just overthinking things at this point. It wasn't healthy, and I knew it. I shook it off and strolled inside. The Grand Bliss interior was straight-up lit. From the aroma, the décor, to the hotel staff's smiles, everything was on point. I checked in and got a ticket for a free margarita. I knew this night was about to be one for the books. I swung by the bar and got my drink, making sure I didn't spill a drop. As I rode the elevator up to the sixth floor, I took my first sip. Damn, this was stronger than a heavyweight champ's right hook. Stepping out of the elevator and heading to my room, I was met with pure luxury. I had a killer ocean view, an oversized hot tub, and a TV that popped out from the wall. Two king-sized beds sealed the deal. Yeah, this was definitely paradise. I finished my drink, and it hit me pretty hard. Next thing I knew, I was handling business in the bathroom. Then, I heard three knocks at the door. Damn, I thought. The bellhops would show up just as I was handling my business on Mexican soil. So, I did what anyone would do. I pulled my pants up and answered the door. Once that was done, I went right back to my business. Luckily, I ain't have one shit stain on my boxers. I was one lucky guy. After I freshened up, I planned to have an amazing dinner on the oceanfront. The first night was always chill on any vacation. I never went all out on the first day. I had gotten in after four, and I'd be crazy to try to have day five vibes on day one. I was clean and feeling good. I threw on my hoop shorts, a white tee that fit just right, and headed out. Walking behind the hotel, it felt like I'd entered a jungle in a flash. I followed the signs leading to the oceanfront, hoping no wild creatures would pop out and make me their main course. On my way, I spotted tons of spider webs in the trees. I wasn't down with that. Me and spiders? We weren't friends. I didn't like them, and they didn't like me because I always had a size 15 ready for them when I saw them. But this was Mexico. I knew these were some rugged cartel spiders. American spiders were child's play compared to these.

Finally, I made it through the trees and stepped out onto the open sand. I paused to take in the stunning view. At that moment, I felt free and at peace. Paulette had left her mark on me, and my love for her wouldn't let me move on. However, the sun felt like a divine message, telling me to let it all go. I grinned and made my way to the restaurant, Balche. The name meant a fermented drink from a tree's bark. If they named it after a drink, you know it's a top-notch spot. A stunning Latina waitress welcomed me and got me seated. Night one was about treating myself right. I checked out the menu, and knew exactly what I wanted.

"Hey, what can I get you to drink?"

"I'm ready for everything. I'll take the Octopus Pot and the seafood special over rice. And for the drink, just some water."

It was a smart move not to have a drink. That margarita was no joke, and I didn't want to feel woozy on an empty stomach. Plus, after seeing how Paulette acted with liquor, alcohol had become a major turn-off. If she didn't do anything else, she definitely made me pause on excessive drinking. I patiently waited for my grub, soaking in the ocean sounds and people's chatter around me. It seemed like I was the only one bringing some flavor to this place. I was surrounded by well-off retirees, and that was cool. As long as they didn't bother me, we were all good. My octopus dish came out quickly since it was an appetizer. It looked amazing. The octopus, with crispy tortillas, fresh avocado, and that pickled onion and cabbage mix, was pure elegance and flavor. I tackled it like a pro, wrapping everything in a tortilla and savoring each bite. Before long, my main course arrived. It was a bomb seafood sauté in a killer garlic, chili pepper, and mushroom sauce, drenched over some mouthwatering au gratin rice. I knew I'd be sleeping like a champ tonight. It took me a solid half-hour to crush that plate, and the sun was still high in the sky. With my belly full, I had no complaints. I settled the bill, just 50 bucks in good ol' American cash, and strolled around the neighboring resorts. There were 11 resorts in total, and the further I walked, the more I realized how vast this place was. But you know what? Screw it. After hitting up the third spot, I did a 180 and headed back to my own resort. I wanted to explore everything, but not all in one night. I took in the ocean view, and the tranquility of the place was just what I needed. By the time I made it back to my room, it was only 7:30. I flipped on the TV and landed on

"Colombiana," featuring the stunning Zoe Saldana. That mix of Dominican and Puerto Rican? It was like a match made in heaven, a fusion of flavors that just worked. Black was Black, and we're all the same at the core; it's just where the boat dropped us off that was different. About halfway through the movie, I saw my facetime was blowing up it was Paulette. I was in a good mood, so I figured we could have a grown-up chat. No hard feelings on my side, right? And, indeed, we did. We hashed out our feelings and emotions, and everything seemed copacetic. Life has taught me that it's not always perfect, but two imperfect souls can make something beautiful. She dropped some big news too she'd joined the Navy and was shipping out in November.

"You know I love you."

"I love you too, Paulette. Are you good?"

"Yeah, but I've got something to say."

"Not another pregnancy scare, is it?"

We both had a good laugh over that one.

"Nah, nothing like that. But, um, I've gotta end things between us for good."

I stared at my phone, completely taken aback.

"What are you talking about?"

"I had a talk with the Man upstairs, and He told me you're not my future husband."

And just like that, my world turned upside down. I guess she felt like she was calling the shots now, finally in control after living a life where she hadn't been. Who breaks up with someone while they're on vacation? At least she could've been woman enough to do it in person. I tried to keep the conversation going, but she didn't have much to say, aside from

"I'm sorry" and

"What do you want me to do?" Eventually, my heart couldn't take it anymore, so I hung up. Man, this flip-flopping holy act was really starting to grind my gears. God told her to do it? Okay, whatever. Did God tell her for most of her life to ignore everyone who didn't tell her what she wanted to hear? Did God tell her to get romantically involved with a woman at some point? I guess God told her that marriage wasn't her strong suit, considering it would be divorce number two. Did God tell her it was cool to associate with a guy who raped her when she was younger, all while saying it was no big deal? Did God say it was okay to be sly with her supposed best friend? I knew him personally, and I had to call her out for talking trash about someone I considered a close friend. I knew it was just a matter of time before he found out how conniving she was. Did God greenlight infidelity overall? Not just with me, but still. At this point, she wasn't a woman, she was a confused, bruised, and battered bitch, and my anger reached its boiling point. I switched off the TV, still in shock. I didn't have a problem with anyone except for criminals and Patriots fans. Now she'd made the list. This was the result of opening your heart to someone who couldn't recognize love if it smacked them in the face. I was torn. It was over. After a nine-hour first date, financial help to make sure her and her kid were fed, assistance in getting into the military, a roof over her head when she felt like she had nowhere else to go after all I'd done. I took all the hits, compared to that short, dark, worthless ex of hers, who was getting pounded in jail. After all I did, she locked me out of her life for good and threw away the key. I was hurt, sad, and furious all at once. I left my room immediately and made my way back to the pool bar, open until eleven. I didn't know what else to do except drink. I know it wasn't the best idea, but it was the only thing that could numb the pain, even if just for a little while. I knocked back four Long Islands, and my head was spinning. I sat at the bar, feeling low. I'd been through heartbreak before, but when you commit to someone who doesn't love themselves, and you endure all the chaos that comes with it, it cuts deep. I was foolish, and now I could see it clearly. I was naive. I allowed a master manipulator to pull the strings on me to the max. Amidst teary eyes and some pretty dark thoughts, I seriously contemplated doing harm to someone, or something. Deep down, I knew I wouldn't go down that road. The joint closed up shop, and I got the boot to clear out so they could tidy things up. I somehow made it back to my hotel room, stumbling all the way. As I approached my door, I could feel the nausea building up. Once inside, it was like someone was knocking on the door of my stomach. I made a beeline for the bathroom and threw up everything I ate for a solid seven minutes straight. After that, I just slumped down by the edge of the hot tub, tears streaming down.

"FUCK YOU, PAULETTE JEFFERSON!!! YOU UNGRATEFUL, COLD HEARTED BITCH!!!"

I screamed it out loud, full of raw emotion. Honestly, this mess was on me. As messed up as she was, she did ask me if I was down for this. I practically turned into a sucker for someone who was far from whole. I should've heeded her warning. Now, I was the one they'd remember as the person who couldn't help falling for someone with issues. I just sat there, by the hot tub's edge, for what seemed like forever. Sleep wasn't even on my radar—just thoughts of wrecking stuff. There's an old saying from historian Jean Rostand that I started thinking about:

"Kill a man, and you're a murderer. Kill millions, and you're a conqueror. Kill everyone, and you're a god." For my spiritual self, she slowly killed me, torturing me until there was nothing left. She became a conqueror by taking away every part of who I was. She became a god because I'd no longer be just another face in the crowd. I was unrecognizable. Nice work, Paulette. You got what you wanted. You drained me to recharge yourself. Maybe people were onto something. Maybe there's some truth to the idea that intimacy can swap energies. She unloaded all her broken pieces onto me. I handed her the reins to my life. Now, she was the one calling the shots, and I was the one shattered. Sad that, after all this time, I realized I'd been sticking my dick inside of a haunted house, having hundreds of depressed spirits attached to me. I pulled out my wallet and, for the last time, gazed at a photo of me and Destiny. I kept saying sorry a million times for not being there for her, for not being able to lift her up. The toughest part about breakups, you know, is the kids. I saw her as my own daughter. I had enough courtesy for her real father to make sure she was safe whenever she was with me.

"Goodbye, Destiny," I whispered to the pic, gave it a kiss, and tucked it back into my wallet. Funny how that kid was named Destiny, and the destination I hit was a brick wall, with demons laughing at me. I guess it's true what they say: Sometimes, the devil can disguise itself as your deepest desires. Even crazier, the devil was the one telling me to stay away from her. Shit is wild.

Journal Entry: The Demise of "US"

It's been a rough few days, and I find myself compelled to put pen to paper, to sort through the emotional whirlwind that has been my life. The wound is fresh, and the pain is still vivid, so I hope that this journal entry will serve as a catharsis, a place to gather my thoughts, and perhaps a record of how I felt when the love of my life ended our relationship over a cold, digital screen. I met her when life was just beginning to bloom, like a spring flower emerging from the winter's slumber. She was a burst of color and warmth in my world, and every moment spent with her felt like sunshine after a storm. Our love story was a collection of unforgettable moments - laughter, shared dreams, and whispered secrets. She became my confidante, my greatest ally, and the keeper of my heart. But love, as beautiful as it is, can be a turbulent voyage. We navigated the storms together, hand in hand, finding solace in each other's presence. It wasn't always easy, but it was always worth it. Then came the day when I received the call that left me in a haze of disbelief. She wanted to talk, she said, and it had to be over FaceTime. I knew, as anyone in love would, that something was amiss. As the screen blinked to life, I saw her face, and her eyes bore a weight I could barely comprehend. She broke the news that she could no longer be with me, that our paths had diverged, and it was time to let go. The words seemed to hang in the air, suspended in time, refusing to land and form a reality I could accept. It felt surreal, as though I was watching a scene from a movie, not my own life. Tears welled up in my eyes, and I felt a pain so profound, it was as if a piece of my soul had been torn away. The distance created by FaceTime only amplified the emptiness I was feeling. I wanted to hold her, to see her eyes up close, to beg for an explanation or a second chance. But the pixels on the screen were all I had. In the aftermath, I turned to glasses of Long Islands, seeking solace in the amber liquid. It dulled the edges of the pain, at least temporarily, and I found myself in a haze of melancholy, trying to grasp the enormity of the loss. I replayed our shared memories, our smiles, and the warmth of her laughter, and I couldn't help but question what went wrong. Love, they say, is a bittersweet journey. It has the power to lift you to unimaginable heights, but it can also send you plummeting to the depths of despair. Today, I'm left trying to make sense of it all, holding onto the memories that once brought so much joy and praying that, one day, the pain will subside. Until then, I'll keep this journal close, a companion to help me navigate the turbulent seas of heartbreak and healing. As Wale said about breakups: Breaking up is hard, to move along, it's even harder.

— 5 —

THERAPY

"A child that grew accustomed, jumping up when I scraped my knee
Cause if I cried about it, He'd surely tell me not to be weak Daddy
issues, hid my emotions, never expressed myself Men should never
show feelings, being sensitive never helped"
–Kendrick Lamar, Father Time

"Thanks for kickin' it with me, much appreciated."

The real question was: Why did I even agree to this? I didn't even wanna see her no more. Paulette had just four days left before she shipped off to Navy boot camp. Whether she had an epiphany or regrets for her actions, honestly, I didn't give a damn anymore. But I knew what it's like to leave everything behind, man. So, when she hit me up for this meet, I said, "Yeah," even though my gut was telling me not to. I've never served a day in my life, but my cousin, who did, dropped some wisdom on me I won't forget. He said, "If someone is joining the military after 30, it means life's been a real mess, and they are desperate to get it together." I can't even picture being in my 30s, getting hollered at by folks who still smell like similac. But right now, I had bigger things to worry about.

"You're welcome." I said it flat, sippin' my water, struggling not to just bounce from the table.

"Umm... this spot's pretty dope, ain't it?"

145

"Yeah, it's cool. Never knew it was here. How'd you find it?" She could tell I was there physically but not emotionally. For the first time in this whole journey, it seemed like she finally realized how messed up she'd been. The guy who'd put up with her drama all this time, he'd hit his limit.

"Some friends put me on to it. Honestly, I'm just glad you're here." The server came back, and we ordered some grub. Me, when I saw octopus on the menu, I knew it was on. Seafood is my forever love, like Ed Reed and interceptions.

"Well, I figured you're about to start a new chapter. I could be all salty and hold grudges that would only hurt me. But I'm letting go of that. Just wishin' you the best."

I flashed a little smirk at her. She put her head down and let out a laugh. That's when she knew she'd really fucked up. Someone who's spent their life pointing fingers can't really understand taking responsibility. It's a foreign concept to them.

"I regret breaking up with you."

My mind was blown. I wasn't expecting that at all. That was a bold move. My head was spinning a hundred different ways. I was in the twilight zone, for real. This was wild.

"No worries, we don't gotta dive into all that. Let's just enjoy tonight for what it is. You ready?"

"I think I am. But I'm scared."

"I get it. It's like a fresh start."

"Nah, it's somethin' else."

"What's that?"

"So, there's this dude who works at the boot camp place. Back in the day..."

"Paulette, is this another 'I hooked up with a guy and now I'm embarrassed' story? 'Cause if it is, I really don't need the details."

"I'm sorry. I just... I don't know. I wanted to keep it real with you before someone else spilled the beans. When I was young, there were two guys. He was there."

"So they ran a train on you?"

"Yea," she said, lowering her head in shame.

"Paulette, stop. Seriously, I hope you can move past all this. No one who cares about you wants to hear your old hookup stories. If it bugs you that much, to the point where you feel you gotta do this, please get some therapy. This is why I was upset with you before. I'm sayin' this out of love. Nobody wants, or needs, that info."

"I get it. My bad."

We just locked eyes, man, and what she saw, I can't say. What I saw was a woman who'd been through the wringer, leading up to this moment. I'd never had a woman straight up tell me she'd been around the block. Even though I was tryna not to care, deep down, I did. Our food came, and I made sure to keep the conversation on her future, not her past. Soon enough, the vibe shifted, thanks to the card game she brought, with random questions. For a sec, I was taken back to our first date, that April 17th night. We were free, with no worries. Regardless of our ups and downs, I couldn't forget the good times we had shared. I still had those selfies from that night on my phone. I'd glance at 'em when I was down, but they'd been buried in memory since our last meeting.

"You ready to bounce?" I asked her.

"Yeah, thanks for this, again."

I paid the tab upfront, and we hit the road. As we peeled out of the parking lot and cruised through the downtown streets, I played Erykah Badu's 'Love of My Life,' tryna remind her of the good times from our first meet-up. I guess that did the trick 'cause once we hit the Italian section downtown, I was ten times more focused than usual. Her mouth was working its magic as the city lights shimmered off the buildings. As she kept going, feelings I wanted to forget started to resurface. I never thought a guy could be fuming even in moments of pleasure, but there I was, seething like crazy. One last rendezvous with her, just for old times sake. After that, I'd finally be done with her. I eased up as I approached a stop sign, and then, bam, I couldn't hold it anymore. With a few

147

more flicks of her tongue, I released it all. This time, it was a release of all the pain and turmoil she'd put me through. If "swimmers" could talk, I hoped they'd be bidding adieu to the chaos right then. She looked up, cracked the window, and spat out.

"Wow, you had quite the load tonight."

All I could manage was a smirk. Revenge wasn't my thing; I wasn't a spiteful dude. But tonight, it felt oddly satisfying. I hoped the next person she messed with could always smell me on her breath. We kept cruising until I pulled up in front of her mom's crib. She sat there for a minute, looking kinda down.

"Can I ask you something, Junior?"

"Shoot."

"Why'd you stick around?"

"I'd pondered the same question on many nights. The honest truth? I shouldn't have. But, I guess love makes you do some wild stuff."

Unfortunately, she didn't know the first thing about real love. It sounded good, and it was partly true. I didn't want to spill the beans about Destiny and the fear of letting her down. I didn't want to reveal the bond I'd built with her mom, or the fear of losing the woman who had lent me an ear when her daughter was giving me hell. It was complicated. Love was like 20 percent of it, and the other 80 percent? Well, chalk it up to plain old foolishness.

"Will you be there when I head off to boot camp?"

"You write, I'll write back. I got your back." She flashed a smile, and that was that. I walked her to the door; our hug felt like an eternity.

"Take care," I told her.

I walked back to my ride, glanced back, and saw her still at the door, waving. As much as I wanted to peel out and tell her to kick rocks, I couldn't. I needed to make sure she got inside safely. There are plenty of things to be mad about in this world, but one thing I know for sure: we've got to protect our women. Even something as simple as walking her to the door could spark a change for the next person. I didn't know where her life was headed next, and, honestly, I didn't care all that much. But one thing was non-negotiable - protection. I'd always have love for her, just from a distance - a long, long distance. The night before her departure, we had a marathon facetime chat. It's crazy how someone can consider you their safe haven in times of need yet see you as a stormy sea when all you've done is give them what they needed. One thing she shared stuck with me. Paulette, eyes filled with tears, admitted that the only reason she didn't commit suicide during those tumultuous times in her life was because of me. Despite all the lies and manipulation, I believed her. I'd lost friends to that dark place before. I never thought anyone would play around with talk of taking their own life. But in that moment, it took me back to a grim space I'd once escaped. Now, I was revisiting that haunting place. I'd lost my little brother to that same darkness years ago. I'll never forget the call I got when his roommate, another friend of mine, found him, lifeless with a pistol nearby. Imagine starting a beautiful Monday morning, ready for work, and suddenly your world shatters. It was a painful period in my life, one that led me to steer clear of therapists, family, and friends. I put down the pen, my trusty companion. One night, I loaded my pistol, held it to my temple, and closed my eyes. I imagined how life would be without me. The only difference between a garden and a graveyard? It's the seed you choose to plant. Those were the words of a poet named Rudy Francisco. I never understood what kind of seed my brother had been. His tombstone spoke a language I couldn't decipher. Maybe that's why I stuck with her through it all, despite the destruction. It was all coming full circle now. I carried her pain, her scars, her emotions. I let her hurtful ways batter me just so I could see her whole again. It's a process that no one should endure, but sometimes, love outweighs common sense. We talked on the phone for three hours until she decided to rest up, gearing up for the next chapter in her life. I was sticking around, this time as a support, not a punching bag. I felt no need to attach emotions to it. A crutch is just a tool to help you stay upright. This relationship between us now, had no vibes, no soul, nothing. I told myself, "This might be the only way to dodge the hurt." Time would reveal the truth. Paulette's boot camp stint went off without a hitch. During her nine-week absence, I received 16 letters from her. Each one got a response with a touch of emotion, my first mistake. The emotions were still there, stuck to me like glue. Once boot camp was over, she headed off to her journalism school on the East Coast, a surprise in the military world, as I thought everyone there either slung guns, typed code, painted floors, or bought Dodge Chargers at 33% interest. My cousin had some mysterious boatswain mate gig, but he'd just say it's like playing God on Earth, making sure things don't go haywire when the big guy takes a nap. I didn't grasp that, but he was a character, so I let it be. We talked almost every night, me trying to keep her motivated in every way possible. Then one night, it all hit me like a freight train. I'm not sure what went down in her school, but she ranted about folks always underestimating a Black woman. I got it; I know our ladies face extra struggles in this world. When you're Black in America, you gotta work twice as hard, prove yourself twice as much. I simply asked her, "Is it really them looking down on you, or is it your emotions talking?" She lost it on me and hung up. I didn't mean to be harsh; I was coming from a place of love and understanding. I asked her to think about it, but she had her mind made up. Again, she hit me with "you're deceptive," "you're manipulative," and more. Why was I putting up with this? We didn't talk for about three days after that. I knew I had to do something. So, I reached out to her mom and asked for a sit-down on a Saturday night, seeking wisdom from someone who knew their child best. On the Saturday she agreed for me to come over, I kicked things off with a solid workout at the gym near my place. Saturday workouts had a chill vibe. Plus, on weekends, there was this curvy short-haired lady always working out. You could tell she was dedicated. We followed different schedules during the week, so Saturdays were our non-verbal connection day. We'd pretend not to check each other out, but occasionally, she'd give me a sly smirk with a hint of a smile. I played it cool most of the time, but I'm sure she caught on. She'd walk by, silently saying, "Yeah, I know." I mean, I'd think, "I'd love to spend time with you all day, every day," but I'd keep that to myself. I was just a regular guy, and our interactions were simple. What I'd really said in my head was something like, "This thick beauty right here could get all of this dick." I worked out for two hours that morning and treated myself to my favorite of eggs benedict and hash browns. My usual spot was packed, but I wasn't a snob, so I hit the bar, which was wide open. I sat down, beat from my workout, with empty seats on both sides. I was in my zone, and although there were some attractive folks around, I wasn't thinking about romance at this point. My focus was purely on food; my body was exhausted from the workout.

"How you doing, man? What can I start you off with?"

"Water. I'll take the crab and crawfish benedict, with an extra three strips of applewood-smoked bacon, and that'll be it."

"You're a regular, huh?"

"Yeah, I'm a creature of habit."

"Got it, man. I'll get that going for you."

Life's a lot simpler when you know what you want. The server brought me water, and I zoned out. Then, someone asked, "How you doing?" My head was down, and I was wondering why this person was checking up on me again when he'd just seen me. That's until I realized he was a she. I glanced over to my right, and I was greeted with one of the most beautiful sights I'd ever seen.

"Huh," I said.

She let out a chuckle.

"I asked, 'How's it going?' and 'Is this spot taken?'"

"I'm holding it down, I mean, 'They're posted up,' 'Girl, have a seat.' My bad, for real. Sit down woman." Man, I was cringing hard at this point. She pulled out a chair at the bar. Then reality came back to me, "My apologies. Can you get up real quick?"

"Excuse me?"

"I apologize, you already sat down, but I didn't pull your chair out like a gentleman should. Can I have a re-do and do you the honors?"

A sly grin crept across her face.

151

"Where you from? 'Cause you definitely stand out from the usual crowd here," she asks.

"Etiquette Boulevard."

"Hmmm. Maybe I'll enjoy ridin' down that street sometime."

Her smile shone like a supernova as she nodded. We started over, and I pulled out her chair.

"Thanks for this. I appreciate it," she says.

"I appreciate you. What's your name?"

"Shani. You?"

"Junior."

We shook hands, with a solid grip, and locked eyes.

"You've got a lot on your mind it looks like."

"Nah, I just came from the gym. A little worn out, no biggie. Sorry if I'm not smelling like a bouquet, but a brother was starving."

"No worries. Let me guess. Heartbreak is weighing on you, making you ponder all sorts of moves. You want her out, but you also want her in. Ego and pride battling the sensible choice, and you're too proud to admit it."

"You think you got me figured out?"

"I know a heartbroken man when I see one."

Shani came with the heat, like she's my grandma schooling me.

"Hey there, can I get you something to eat?" the waiter butts in. Shani eyeballed the waiter, then me.

"I'll take the Harvest omelet, protein pancakes, and a fresh-squeezed OJ. That's all." She flashed a smile my way.

"Gotcha," the bartender acknowledged as he headed off.

"Seems like you're into the healthy vibe."

"What you put in your body tells me a lot."

"So, if I said I'm ordering eggs benedict with crab and crawfish, a side of avocado, and some hash browns, what would that tell you?"

Shani sipped her water, raising her eyebrows.

152

"It tells me you're complicated."

"You got it."

"Think so?"

"Absolutely, you got it."

"So if I've got it, what's stopping you from getting it?"

We locked eyes, deep in thought, just as the bartender brought my plate and silverware. She had definitely thrown me for a loop with that one.

"Alright, time for some eggs benedict and hash browns. You know, for us complicated brothers. It's healthy enough for me."

"But are you healthy enough for yourself? I'll be right back; gotta hit the ladies' room. Mind pulling my chair out, or am I about to remind you of a favor you didn't get props for?"

I didn't know what was going on, but I pulled out her chair and my mind was blown once again. She smiled, got up, and strolled off. She had me hooked at this point. Plus, let's be real, she's got some great curves, so it's worth the watch. I looked at the bartender, and he just shrugged.

"Looks like you found the right one, bro," he said, dropping off her food. Her plate looked different to me, not in the food sense, but in the people sense. She had her act together, and I was out here trying to clean up my act. She came back, and I was on my feet, pulling out her chair.

"Consistency is key. Thank you."

"Manners maketh man?"

"Alright, Kingsman. Who you vibin' with? Eggsy, Merlin, or Harry?"

"Man, I'm definitely Harry, no doubt."

"Harry was never about that broken vibe. Eggsy, bro."

She took a sip of her OJ and let out a laugh. I knew I'd met my match for sure. We kept our meal flowin', trading jokes and jabs just like old friends. But when the check dropped, that's when my jaw hit the floor.

"What you doing?"

"I'm 'bout to handle my own tab."

"Nah, nah, I got this."

"I can't let a lady front my bill, I'm sorry."

"You've held it down enough. It's time for some payback. Bartender, take my card. Both our meals, and make it a cool $20 tip. Thank you."

She locked eyes with me, and I glanced at the bartender as he took her card.

"Yo, why you doin' all this?"

"Doing what?"

"Being this mad generous to me, and we hardly know each other. You show up, sit next to me, droppin' all this wisdom. Don't get me wrong, I'm diggin' the convo. It's deep and refreshing. But covering my breakfast and all that? Nah, I ain't feeling worthy of it."

"That's the thing. You think you ain't deserving of nothing. Is that why you stuck around, dealing with someone who didn't deserve your love, care, and effort?"

I went quiet.

"Plus, peep this: care stands for Compassion, Affection, Reverence, and Effort. Real talk."

That shit right there took me over the edge. The bartender slid her card back, and she got up.

"Shani, how in the good hell did you pull all this outta me?" She chuckled.

"I'm a certified therapist, rockin' a Master's degree from Hampton. The real HU. Trust me, I had the Black experience even before I hit those books. I'm reppin' Detroit, Eastside, Warren and Chalmers. When you grow up 'round folks dealing with struggles, it makes you wanna uplift 'em when they need it. Let's step outside."

My mind was blown. Outside, I found out she lived just a couple blocks from me, and I ain't talkin' Black-blocks, meaning five miles away neighbors; she's two blocks down from me, literally. We agreed to clean up and meet at her place by noon. As the shower water washed over me at the house, tears fell. I started to see more than just a dude with baggage. I saw a whole community

154

with unhealed wounds we've been brushing aside. I once heard a poet named Kalvin from Dallas drop some deep lines. He said,

"Keep our family biz to ourselves. Don't heal. Mend your own scars. Tackle your emotions. Piece together the parts of your life you'd rather forget. Keep our family skeletons locked up in the closet. That way, folks won't peep the chaos inside." Those words hit close to home, man. I was taking on a hefty load of our community's struggles, and I had to confront all the mess I'd been avoiding. Was I truly healed, or was I hiding in isolation to dodge any triggers? That was the $64,000 question, no doubt. I finished up, got a sharp shave not 'cause I expected anything, but when you're heading out to meet a lady, you wanna look fly. I cruised down the street to her crib. I knocked on the door of this swanky house in our chill neighborhood. She opened the door, rockin' a wife beater, tight jeans, a glammed-up belt, and those natural curls flowing past her shoulders.

"Yo, what's up?," I said, trying not to make it obvious that I was observing her bomb ass curves.

"I'm looking different outside my sweats and tee, right?"

"Nah, you just bringin' some extra fire."

She stepped back.

"Check you out, Mr. Debonair. Let's bounce, we'll take my ride."

"Wait up, is it cool if I roll in my whip?"

"You tryna keep yourself distant to avoid triggers, huh?"

How she read my thoughts like that, I had no clue.

"Where we heading to?" I asked, walking towards her car.

"You think a 5'3", 115-pound Panamanian girl's gonna snatch over six feet of man and do him harm?"

"Good point."

I hopped in her ride, no clue what the day had in store. And just like that, Eminem's vibes filled the car.

"Wait a sec, I can't boss you around about what tunes you bump in your ride. But tell me this, have you ever heard any Black person say, crank up some Em

155

in my car?"

"Nah, I ain't about following the crowd, I'm about staying true to myself, you feel me?"

I threw up my hands and she flashed a grin. As she vibed out to "The Real Slim Shady," I couldn't help but wonder just how much Eminem's voice I could take. After about 20 minutes of driving, we pulled up in front of a gym.

"We're here."

"The gym?"

"It's above the gym. Now, sit tight and don't move until I give the green light."

Honestly, I had no clue what she meant, so I just chilled. She came around and popped my door open.

"But why, though? I thought I was the one who was supposed to open doors."

"Yeah, but I'm doing this for you. C'mon."

I was kinda puzzled by all this attention. Why was she making me feel so special? Checking out the building, I spotted a set of stairs on the side leading up to a bunch of windows. Clearly, there were office spaces above the gym. I followed her up the stairs, trying not to be too obvious about admiring her ass.

"After you," she said.

Inside, the vibes took over. Plush couches, a classy oak desk, and some smooth background tunes. It felt more like a spa than an office space.

"Have a seat," she said.

I checked out the walls, noticing her degrees, family photos, and some dope ass paintings.

"What's that piece?" I asked.

"Oh, that's 'Critical Race Theory' by Jonathan Harris. He's reppin' the D, where all the greats are from, so it had to be on the wall."

"Yeah, that's some cool shit."

She settled into her chair and stretched.

"So, why'd you bring me here?"

156

"It's a safe space. First and foremost, I want you to feel safe. Plus, you need a friend right now. A real one."

"But you barely know me."

"I know enough. Have you ever been to therapy?"

"Once upon a time, yeah. But now, I've got peeps to chat with when I'm going through stuff. Paying professionals? Nah, doesn't make sense to me anymore."

"Why's that?"

"Why pay someone else to listen to my problems? Seems like a waste of money, in my humble opinion. I can chat up folks for free and get the same results."

"What makes you think that, though?"

"Talking is free."

"Nothing in life is truly free."

"What do you mean?"

"Talking, it costs time. Just like everything in life has its price. It takes me time to choose the right outfit to look my best. I saw you and thought, 'Hey, he's cute,' so I decided to show my true self. That decision costs me time.

Bringing you here, it cost me gas, and my emotions got the better of me when that slowpoke on the road tested my patience. Talking to you at the restaurant? Well, it took a toll on my sanity 'cause I was on a high, and you seemed like you were hitting a new low. Nothing's free in this world. Every action comes with a cost. You gotta ask yourself, 'Is it a worthwhile investment?'"

"Am I?"

"That's a question you need to ask yourself." I paused again, taking a moment to gather my thoughts and find the right words to continue our conversation.

"So, am I here for a therapy session?"

"Nah, you're here for a safe space where Shani can connect with you. You down for some Mario Kart?"

"Absolutely. Are you up for the challenge?"

"I got a '64 stashed behind this desk. It's nothing to hook it up and get it in."

"I don't believe you got a '64 in here."

That's when she pulled it out and placed it on her desk.

"Thought I was bluffing?"

"Alright, it's on."

She set it up, and I pulled a chair over, checking out that massive 65-inch screen she had mounted on the wall. Right away, she picked Princess Peach, and I went with Toadstool. It was clear she was just like me, into those speedy characters rather than the heavyweights like Koopa, Wario, or Donkey Kong.

"What level are we starting on?"

"Rainbow Road."

"You're going for the toughest track in the game, huh?"

"What, you can't handle it? You've got this game in your office, and you're telling me you can't handle it?"

"I can handle a lot, especially when the challenge is need I say...big." She flashed me a smile, but she better slow down on the flirting before she ends up with a Koopa shell right in her pink palace. We were both on the edge of our seats, waiting for the countdown. Three... two... one... and we were off. As I sped out of the gate with a turbo boost, I thought to myself,

"This is gonna be a cakewalk." But then, she pulled a fast one on me. I hadn't played Mario Kart in forever. She hit a jump from the top of the rainbow, landing perfectly on another part of the track, cutting off about half the course.

"HA!!!" she yelled triumphantly. "This is a walk in the park." I was so pissed that I didn't even realize I hit a block, bounced off the track, and bit the dust. By the time the ghost got me back on the track, she was already finishing up lap one. This was more embarrassing than Appalachian State beating Michigan at the Big House in '07 or Patrick serenading Kat on the football field in "10 Things I Hate About You." After she won the race, she gloated and did a little victory dance. I looked at her in disbelief. How did I let her beat me?

"Want a rematch?"

"Nah, I'm good. Just an off day for me."

"Okay, Mr. YouTube. You're not off yet. Write a journal entry about this ass whoopin' in Mario Kart."

"Excuse me," I said, with a puzzled expression.

"Oh, you didn't think I was paying attention when we were chatting in the restaurant. You told me your pen name, your work, your artistry, and I even listened to some of your stuff in the car. You love writing in your journal. Your oh so precious journal."

"Damn, you caught all that?"

"It happens. Now, do you need my laptop or pen and paper? This is your second challenge of the day."

"And what's that?"

"You've got 10 minutes to whip up a journal entry about Mario Kart. So, laptop or pen and paper? Your call."

Man, she was really on top of things. She opened her laptop as I settled into the chair, still not quite sure.

"Google Drive or Word?"

"Huh?"

"Nigga stop playing with me. You heard me."

"Google."

"Let's get to it," she said, rising as I moved around her desk to take a seat.

"Can I ask you something?"

"Sure."

"Why do you want me to do this?"

"You'd be surprised what you can pull off when you put your mind to it. Your 10 minutes start now."

I thrive on a challenge, but I was constantly trying to wrap my head around what she was really up to. In those initial 30 seconds, I didn't even type a word; I just sat there, lost in thought.

"You know what's funny? You can dive into a game just for fun, but when it comes to doing something for a woman who's asking out of love, after spending who knows how long doing it for the wrong reasons, based on false hope, now, it's a problem. I bet if you had to dive into some pussy, it wouldn't be a problem."

That statement hit me hard. I couldn't help but feel a surge of emotions, but I suddenly got what she was getting at. Without missing a beat, I found my groove.

Journal Entry: Mario's Greatest Race

Today, I found myself pondering the popular game Mario Kart and its curious ability to reflect some of the issues we face in the world today. While it may seem like a lighthearted racing game at first glance, there are intriguing parallels worth exploring. First and foremost, Mario Kart features a diverse cast of characters, each with their unique abilities and attributes. Looking at this diversity, it reminds me of the value of inclusivity and representation in our society. In an age where diversity and inclusion are vital topics, Mario Kart presents us with characters from various backgrounds, representing different species, shapes, and sizes, all coming together to race on equal footing. However, there are some aspects that merit deeper consideration. Donkey Kong and Bowser, both prominent and DARK characters in the game, are often depicted as strong but slower racers. It's essential to be cautious about making direct comparisons between character attributes in video games and real-world stereotypes. While it's essential to be aware of potential misrepresentations in the media, we should remember that game characters are primarily products of fantasy, not meant to reinforce harmful stereotypes. Similarly, we can examine the character Princess Toadstool, who is often pursued by the male characters in the game. While it's true that this aspect of the game can be seen as reinforcing traditional gender dynamics, it's essential to recognize that games are evolving and offering more diverse and empowered female characters over time. We should use such observations as opportunities to advocate for more progressive and equitable portrayals in gaming. Another interesting point to consider is the Rainbow Road track, widely known as one of the most challenging in the game. Rainbow Road's vibrant, chaotic design can remind us of the struggles the LGBTQ+ community faces. The beauty of rainbows, an emblem of diversity and unity, contrasts with the challenges and persecution that many individuals from the LGBTQ+ community endure. This track serves as a symbolic reminder that even in the face of adversity, beauty and unity can be found. In the end, I am struck by how video games like Mario Kart can, unintentionally or not, reflect aspects of our existence. As we examine these reflections, it is important to foster discussions about the real-world issues they may bring to light. Moreover, it reminds us of the potential for change and growth.

I was all wrapped up, peeping my words on the screen, extra time on my hands. She was chilling in the corner, absorbed in her phone, barely noticing me.

"You good?" she asked.

"Yeah, it's a wrap. Now, can you break down the why for this?"

"Read it out, and I got you."

"HEY, COULD YOU EXPLAIN WHY WE'RE DOING THIS CRAZY SHIT??!!!"

I had to check myself there, 'cause I ain't about bringing heat to a lady or making her feel uneasy. But she just stayed cool, no reaction to my words or my vibe.

"That's the first real passion I've seen from you today. The first time it feels like you're keeping it 100. Forget the fucking words. Let me show you something."

She cruised over to a big cabinet and pulled out an hourglass. I'm thinking, who keeps an hourglass on deck, you know? She came back, and flipped it upside down in front of me.

"Yo' peep this, right? You know what it is, no need to break it down. This sand? It's you. Down below? That's her. Up top? It's shrinking by the second. You're letting this woman drain you. That's what happens when folks leech your energy. We're just like this sand. Sand might not seem like a big deal to most, but when you hit the beach, you chill in the sand. Kids build castles, bury each other the whole deal. The Sahara Desert? One of the planet's biggest deserts, not the biggest, but it's up there. All sand. And at night, critters pop up from that sand. Glass, man. Beautiful glass, with the illest designs, all made from sand that's been cooked. Even the Ancient Egyptians, the folks from Kemet, whatever you wanna call 'em, used sand when they put up those pyramids. What I'm saying is this: you're the sand. You can either shape yourself into something beautiful and become more than you ever thought, or you can give yourself away to someone else, let them run the show. Junior, it's your call."

She perched on the edge of the desk, and my mind bounced from my first date with Paulette to this moment in some random therapist's office. I had one last question for her.

"How do I shake her off?"

"You don't. None of us can just ditch the good or bad stuff that's happened. That's the deal with people. That's why I do what I do. You can't erase the experience, but you can live beyond it. Those people, they'll stick around. Just find a mental and physical space where they ain't running the show. When you're unfazed by that person, you're good. The best way to clap back is by living a better life, trust me. Karma has its ways, dealing with folks like her, and it can deal with you too, 'cause you're still holding on to her energy."

She snatched the remote, cutting the TV off.

"My card's right there on the table. Grab it when you bounce. The door locks itself, so call me when you're heading to the whip. I'll be waiting, vibing to some tunes."

She headed for the door, popped it open, then turned around.

"Oh, by the way," she said, grinning. "You're looking fly. You're good enough to fuck. I'd fuck you six ways to Sunday, and put a mouth on you that would make a hurricane jealous. But nobody wants a broken man in their life, let alone inside of them. Keep that in mind. Who you vibe with is who you become. Think about it."

"So why you even throw out that offer and take it back in the same breath?"

"I'm a woman before I'm a therapist. I gotta keep it real to make you come back. So ask yourself, do you wanna roll with the drama and go home stressed, still stuck in the same mess? Or you wanna link up with someone who'll help you

heal, go home happy and whole, knowing there's a callback in the cards? Once
again, I'll be posted up in the car when you're ready to roll." She slammed that
door shut, and I took a moment to really digest what she'd just dropped on me
in this tranquil space. For a good 15 minutes, I marinated in her words. Then,
bam! It hit me like a ton of bricks. The chat with her mom couldn't be just any
old conversation tonight; it needed to be a soul-purging session about all things
Paulette. Before we headed home, we hit up this curry joint near Shani's office.
Fun fact Paulette was the one who put me onto this spot, but I never understood
those folks who said you shouldn't eat where your ex introduced you. Good grub
is good grub, right? Besides, this was a chance to make some fresh memories.
We both ordered curry, keeping the spice on the low-low. The first time I tried
Thai curry, I had asked for a "3" on the spice scale. Turned out that "3" was more
like a "10." My mouth was on fire, my soul was screaming, and my stomach felt
like it was doing gymnastics. I barely made it through four bites that night before
I tapped out. I swear, I almost wanted to dial 911, but my pride wouldn't let me
be that dude who called an ambulance over some spicy food. We got our grub to
go and bounced.

"Hey, can we hit the beach? I need to clear my head."

"You wanna see something, or are you trying to escape from 'her' thoughts?"

It was eerie how Shani kept reading my mind, but I wasn't mad about it.
So, we drove down to the beach where me and Paulette had our very first date.
Weirdly enough, our usual parking spot was vacant, which felt like either a wild
coincidence or the universe telling me to face my past before I embarked on a
fresh journey, minus the drama. I went with it. Shani parked, and we strolled
over to the 7-Eleven. The curry was for later; I needed some sweet tea and a bag
of popcorn. As we approached, we spotted a naked white guy making a quick exit.
We did a 180 faster than you could say "police report." Who needed that drama?
It would've been just my luck naked white dude by the beach, and I'd be the prime
suspect in the "stolen clothes" case. No, thanks. We hit the sidewalk, parallel to
the sand. In the distance, we caught sight of a heated argument between a Black

bike patrolman and two white dudes. You could hear their yelling from a mile away.

"Oh, they're about to throw down," Shani said.

I looked back and saw one of the white guys all up in the officer's face. In my head, I was like, "C'mon, swing, dude!" And, swing he did, but it was the white guy who landed the first punch. The Black officer took a step back, threw his hat in the air, Bobby Shmurda style. It was on. I couldn't believe what I was witnessing. The whole beach seemed to be thinking the same thing. Out of the blue, five more white folks appeared and jumped in, ganging up on the officer. No way, I sprinted as fast as I could, Shani right there beside me. This nonsense wasn't flying on our watch. In my peripheral vision, I saw all the Black people coming from the beach. It looked like today was

"fuck around and find out" day, and we were about to serve up some righteous ass-kicking. As I closed in, I saw another brother vault the seawall.

"WHAT'S UP, FOE!!!"

He started throwing punches. Shani even delivered a clothesline to a lady trying to join the brawl. I tackled one of the white dudes, wrestled him down, and started throwing punches. When I turned around to see who else wanted a piece, it was like Wakanda had decided to crash the party. Anyone without melanin in their skin was fair game. The police sirens wailed in the distance, but we didn't give a damn. One of those folks stumbled, and I sidestepped one of my fellow warriors to clock him.

"THAT'S FOR TRAYVON, NIGGA!!!"

Then, another brother pushed me aside, eager to get in some stomps. At this point, it was like 30 against six, and it was game on. You could tell we meant business when folks came sprinting out of the water, having just been swimming, to join the fray. The cops rolled in just as one of the OGs snagged a beach chair, folded it up, and served one of those Mick Foley-style chair shots to a fool. All we were missing was Jim Ross screaming,

"GOOD GOD ALMIGHTY!!! GOOD GOD ALMIGHTY!!! IT KILLED

164

HIM!!!" The police swarm came, and man, it was like a scene out of a movie. They pushed us back, and whoever made that call, they knew the Cracker Barrel Clan and Crew had jumped one of ours. I was dead certain we were all headed to the slammer. But, I guess God was on our side today. The whole scene was pure chaos, like my last relationship, to be honest. But then it hit me. I realized that God put me here not to relive some magical moment with Paulette, but to witness chaos and remind me I ain't got no time for that in my life. Still, it was some wild chaos, and I couldn't remember the last time I saw us all come together like this up close and personal. I mean, it's like Oakland storming police stations after Oscar Grant got murdered by the cops, Tulsa beating the colonizers in South Tulsa until the military stepped in, Nat Turner, The Haitian Revolt, Black Panthers - we got a history of raising hell. And yeah, we're all our ancestors' legacy. To say otherwise disrespects them and shows you got no respect at all. If I could name this craziness, I'd call it the

"Nigga Please Brawl," with a hefty dose of mayhem on the side. If you thought you was just gone get one of ours without us jumping in, nigga please. As things finally calmed down, we checked on each other.

"Hey, man. You good? I saw you sprinting ahead of everyone."

"Yeah, man. Couldn't let that slide. Junior."

"Slim."

"Yo, dude. Did you really throw down with a camera hanging 'round your neck?"

"Skills, my friend, skills. You'd be surprised what can go down when you turn up. Plus, I couldn't risk putting this down, someone might've snatched it."

"Damn, you're slick like a can of oil, for real."

"Shit. You down for a few pics?"

"I ain't dressed for a photo shoot bruh."

"Nah, you're in your authentic self."

That statement hit me deep, deeper than he knew. I struck a few poses as he called all the folks in the area. Just like that, we gathered, dapped each other up, and posed for those pictures. For a moment, even if it never happened again, we were a family. For the next hour, I found myself relaxed, chatting, and just enjoying the roller coaster called life. But I knew the inevitable was coming. Shani took me home late in the afternoon. First things first, I hit the shower. After spreading some Malcolm X wisdom by the sand, via hands, I had to get fresh. No matter what life throws at you, a funky smell ain't cool. I dried off, wrapped that towel around my waist, and brought the fan into the bathroom. I sat down in the dark on the toilet, the air drying gave me goosebumps all over my skin. I was in complete darkness, contemplating Shani's words, thinking about how a random restaurant visit brought me here. I had to get my head straight before I hit Paulette mama's place. Then, like they were summoned by the universe, those two voices popped up on my shoulders.

"Junior, you know what needs to be done. This is closing the chapter." I looked left because I knew the demon time was coming, and he was about to say some crazy stuff.

"I mean, my nigga, I'm a little petty. I might mess with her homegirl or something. She's probably spilled the beans to her friends, talking about what a good man you are while leaving out her own flaws."

"Nah, man. I've been down that road. I ain't trying to go there again."

"Well, listen, soft and soapy. Handle your business tonight, and whatever comes next, roll with it. If one of her homegirls wants to give you the pussy, go for it."

"That's just asking for trouble."

"Hey, hoe with a halo, I wasn't talking to you."

"BOTH OF Y'ALL, BOUNCE!!!"

Just like that, they were outta there. I sat there for about 20 minutes in total, got up, and put on my gear. I gathered all the letters she sent me from boot camp, with no need to reread them. I recalled enough of what she said.

"I can't wait to create more memories with you in the city."

"I'm trying my hardest to come back to you, and only you."

166

"I'm sorry for leaving you in Mexico."

"I wanna swallow more of your kids."

All those words were fluff and nonsense. I didn't need to relive that. I bagged up the card game she left and, lastly, her red-framed stylish glasses, the ones I wore on our first date, I packed those up too. This was the end of the line. No traces of that woman lingered in my crib. I hit up her mom, told her I was rolling through, and asked if she needed anything. She replied with a "Nah," but she was looking forward to my visit. I wasn't showing up empty-handed, though. I swung by the store and copped a load of Lunchables 'cause I knew Destiny was chilling with her, and she's all about those snacks. I may have no longer had a connection with her mom, but that little one, she had my heart, and I'd do whatever it took for her, even if it meant giving all of myself. That's how much I loved that little girl. The store run was smooth, and I hit the freeway southbound. When I pulled up to her place, I took a deep breath. No beef with her, but I didn't wanna drop my baggage on her. It was time to face it. I stepped out with bags in hand and rang that doorbell.

"You know I must dig you, 'cause it's usually bedtime by now. How you doing, baby?"

"I'm good, mama." We hugged, and it felt good. We strolled over to the dining table, both happy to see each other.

"What's all that?" she asked, pointing at the bags.

"Well, this right here's a stash of Lunchables for Suga Duga. I know she's all about 'em, so I wanted to ease your load."

"Baby, you really didn't have to."

"That's my heart. No-brainer for me."

"True, she's got that magic. That's my grandbaby."

Before I unveiled the second bag, I took a deep breath.

"This bag here, it's all the stuff Paulette left at my place, along with all the letters she penned. I love you, and I love your daughter. But I gotta love her from a distance now. I tried all I could to make it work, and I know I ain't perfect.

There were things I could've done better. I'm just worn out. The pain, the hits I took, it's all too much. I ain't trying to cast her as the enemy, but it felt like she was more of my enemy than my love."

Phew, I laid it all out. Now, I was waiting for her response. To my surprise, she cracked a laugh. I was left totally baffled.

"Baby, believe me, I ain't laughing at you. I'm just gonna stash all this stuff in the spare room for when she returns. Let me drop some truth on you, and I want you to remember this. Thank you for what you did for my daughter. I can't thank you enough, and I'm forever grateful that you were in her life, helping her get back on track. I never liked that short, stuttering fuck she married, but that's water under the bridge. I want you to enjoy your life. Don't let what my daughter did hold you back. I love my child, but I know my child. And honestly, Paulette needs to grow up. It's that simple. Paulette needs to grow up."

I thought, well, damn. That wasn't what I expected, but it was good to know that me and her moms were cool no matter what. I hugged her, and she told me again to live my life. If her daughter's actions weren't holding her back, why should I let them hold me back? I've always been resilient, but I hadn't loved someone like I loved Paulette, even with all of her history. It takes a lot to admit when you're wrong, mixed up, good, bad, smart, dumb, all of that. The first step to self-improvement is looking in the mirror and being real with yourself. At that moment, I was honest with myself. I allowed it and accepted what came with it. Her mom and I shared a meal, talked for another hour, and I grabbed some candy from her stash before saying goodbye.

"Remember," she told me at the door, "Your life doesn't stop. I'll always be here for you. Love you, baby."

With a grin stretching as wide as a landmark bridge, I returned the love. I walked to my car, finally feeling free. Sitting in the car, I felt the urge to spill everything to Shani, but it was late on a Saturday night. I didn't want to disturb her, but I took the risk and called her.

"Hey."

"Shani, it's Junior. Thanks for today. I just dropped everything off at her mom's place. I'm done."

"How are you feeling?"

"I don't know. I've never had my freedom snatched away. I feel like a caged bird set free. If that makes any sense."

"Well, I'm glad you took that step, even if it was tough."

"Yeah, it was. But meeting you made it possible. I know it's late, but I just wanted to say thank you. Thank you so much. Without you, I wouldn't be where I am tonight. But I'll let you go. I know it's late."

"It's not even nine yet."

"I know, but I'm just going to go home to unwind. Enjoy my newfound freedom that you inspired. Maybe pour a glass of wine."

"Well, why not have breakfast instead?"

"At nine at night? Nah, I ain't feeling breakfast."

"Hold up, hear me out. Why not start your day right with a morning grub session, chillin' with me?"

"Sounds cool, for real. Where and what time do you wanna meet up tomorrow?" She let out a laugh.

"You ain't catching what I'm throwin'. Look, I've got some wine here at the house. Swing by, let's celebrate your newfound self. And tomorrow, I'll whip up some breakfast magic."

Oh snap. This was totally unexpected. I didn't wanna come off like some player or a guy taking advantage, but hey, when there's grass in the infield, you play ball. I hit the road like a bat outta hell, excited to see what was in store. Come Sunday morning, we were just laying there, deep in thought and sharing happy vibes.

"You good?" I asked her.

She rolled over and flashed a grin.

"Yeah, I'm good. I'm just...wow. I didn't see this coming. Maybe I should whoop you in some Mario Kart more often."

I had to laugh and throw a little comeback her way.

"Hey, I had to get my payback for that L, right?" We both cracked up, and the good times kept flowing.

"So, where do we go from here?" I asked.

"I'm hittin' the kitchen, and you're headin' home."

"Dang, kicking me to the curb like that?"

"Yep, pretty much. You got your therapy, some pussy, getting some breakfast, and then you're on your way."

"Dang, you're cold."

"I'm a woman before I'm a therapist. I've got my needs too. You've stepped up your game, and you took a major step last night, so I couldn't resist the urge to give you some. You've still got some work to do, though. But, just so you know, you're worth a callback. So, can you make me nut a few more times before I whip up some grub? I need jelly legs again."

"Depends on what's cookin' for breakfast."

"Well, after last night's action, you've got French toast in the works. And if you top last night, there'll be some L.A.-sized pancakes on the menu." I was down for it, and those pancakes hit the spot. I left her place, feeling like a mix between Eddie from Boomerang and Darius from Love Jones. No matter how you slice it, I was in a better place than when I started. Deep down, I only had one thing on my mind–Junior Mitchell. This was a whole new level of amazing. And to think it all began when she invited me upstairs to her therapy office just for a chat. We talked alright, and that conversation was pure gold. Love Jones ain't have shit on what I had just experienced. Just then, my phone buzzed with a text. It was Shani. 'You found yourself. Stay on the path, and know I'm here to support you. P.S. You've got me googling how to make eggs benedict, LOL. My back's feeling better. Thanks, LOL.' I didn't even reply. I just strolled into the bathroom, dropped my pants, looked down, and couldn't help but smile. You're a bad motherfucker, I told myself.

170

Journal Entry: Shani, the cure for my illness.

Today was unlike any other day I've experienced recently. I found myself at a crossroads in life, reeling from the emotional wreckage of a broken relationship, and little did I know that an unexpected encounter with a therapist named Shani would be the turning point in my healing journey. It started as a seemingly random occurrence at a cozy restaurant. I was nursing my simple glass of water, trying to find solace in solitude when she walked in. Shani, with an aura of calm and understanding, introduced herself as a therapist. There was something about her presence, a serene confidence, that put me at ease immediately. We exchanged pleasantries, and before I knew it, I was pouring my heart out, sharing the pain and confusion I felt after the breakup. Shani was an empathetic listener, gently guiding our conversation toward the underlying issues that had contributed to the end of my relationship. It was as though she had a knack for peeling back the layers of my emotional turmoil, revealing the deepest wounds that I had been trying to bury. As the day unfolded, Shani stayed by my side, patiently offering guidance and support. We explored my feelings, insecurities, and past experiences that had led me to this point. Her insights were like a beacon in the darkness, and her words resonated with me on a profound level. It was clear that she had a gift for helping people heal, and I was fortunate to have crossed paths with her. As the sun dipped below the horizon, Shani and I found ourselves drawn to each other in a way that went beyond the realm of therapy. There was a magnetic connection between us that transcended words. The transition from emotional healing to an intimate connection felt organic, like a natural progression of the day we had spent together. As I emptied the last shattered pieces of my soul to my past love's mother, I eagerly confided in Shani, thanking her for giving me a strength that I thought was dormant forever. An invite followed from her, offering a deeper level connection between us. Our night of passion and bliss was filled with an intensity that can only be born from a deep emotional connection. It was as if the physical intimacy became an extension of the emotional healing process we had embarked upon earlier. In Shani's arms, I felt a sense of catharsis and renewal, a reassurance that life could be beautiful even after heartbreak. As I lie here now, reflecting on this extraordinary day, I am filled with gratitude for the serendipity that led me to Shani. Our encounter was a reminder that sometimes, the universe has a way of sending the right people into our lives when we need them the most. Shani, the therapist who became so much more, has left an indelible mark on my heart and my healing journey. Today was the day I met Shani, and it was also the day I took the first step towards healing and finding love again.

— 6 —

DEUCES

"See, breaking up is hard, to move along is even harder, It's over, she
got colder, now can't locate where her heart is And I'm just being
honest, se we not even talking My mind won't let you go, shit even
considered stalking"
Wale–The Break Up Song

It had been a minute since Paulette bounced. Try as I might, I couldn't help but miss her. The love I had for her was just too deep, you feel me? It wasn't even a choice my soul wouldn't let me forget her. I kept thinking about those letters I dropped off at her mom's crib. Each one hit my heart like a hurricane and caused all kinds of chaos. Love's supposed to be simple, but sometimes it's just a puzzle, you dig? Sometimes I thought her comeback was for real, that life would circle us back, and she'd be the one rocking my last name. I wanted to be her superhero, helping her leave behind all that hurt and drama. But on the flip side, I couldn't ignore that feeling like I was just a punching bag, too blind to see she was using me as a sparring partner. She didn't wanna face her real demons, all that baggage from before her ex did some messed-up stuff. She wanted to pretend, taking one-minute breaks between rounds. She'd been through hell and back, constantly taking return trips. She'd been hurt and taken advantage of, and it felt like she couldn't escape it. Two failed marriages one when she was just 18, marrying some dude who would've sold her into slavery two centuries back. The other, you already know, the man who did the unspeakable to a teenager. I still couldn't shake that horror. People say it doesn't take five years to know if someone's the one, but I guess that's what you get when you rush in three months before saying, "I do." You ain't meeting the real person; you're meeting their representative. And man, she'd always throw "YOU'RE JUST LIKE HIM" at me when she was mad. It cut deep and pissed me off. All the other bullshit she would spew to me. Why would you tell the dude who's holding you down and trying to heal you, negative shit that you know would make him look at you differently? No matter how much I'd had to drink, I knew there were some things you just don't say. But for some reason, I kept trying to rebuild this shipwreck that'd been at the bottom of the ocean for ages. The Titanic had nothing on Paulette's mess. She blamed everyone for her messed-up life, even a mom who sacrificed everything to keep her from seeing her dad's abusive side. When you're stuck in that emotional bind, you can't see the good in people. I became her journal, deciphering her twisted stories. It was like a broken record, and I couldn't turn the volume down. In turn, she had my own journal looking at me sideways. I know the emotions I filled it with, had it ready to separate with myself. Now, she's all into that military life, on the East Coast in Norfolk, Virginia. Who knew what she was doing. Maybe she was getting the desperate help she needed. Maybe she was now torturing another man, who had not yet experienced her blockbuster movie- 'Fucked up and Frail.' Maybe, just maybe, she was reciprocating the love equally to someone else. When people settle into new environments, sometimes, they become what they always wanted to be, emerging from under the skeleton pile of dirty ass clothes they slept under for years, in their own closet. I was torn between my heart and my head, and I knew I couldn't wallow in sorrow forever. I tried therapy after that encounter with Shani, and it helped, along with the occasional meet up we agreed upon, where she reminded me of what a woman is, in and out of the bedroom. But those therapy sessions also dragged me back into all that darkness. So, I bailed after just two months of mental work. I was scanning the web on this bright morning, searching for an escape. My spirit was on a mission, not to check out but to toss that trapped part of me overboard and let the happier me take over. He'd been down for too long, too dumb to let go of the misery. Then, I discovered a trip into the other side of the mirror. A twenty-eight day cruise. I didn't mind going on vacation and leaving home for a couple of weeks. But twenty-eight days seemed like some military-style mission, and that wasn't really my scene. Cruise ships and warships are two different ball games, and with no disrespect to the military, I wasn't sure about being on the water that long. But, home is where the heart's at, and nothing beats that kind of peace. So, I decided to move my heart to the Pacific Ocean for an extended period of time. I was going to hop aboard a Carnival cruise, set to sail on February 3rd, but let me tell you, it cost a pretty penny. They called it the Round Robin Cruise hitting up Hawaii, Central America, South America, and even making a pit stop in San Francisco, all in just a month. I had to put things in perspective. Water's got that whole baptism thing going on, right? So, maybe this was my rebirth, even if it meant dropping a cool $2,600 for an ocean-view cabin. But water, man, it's also seen some dark times for Black folks. Imagine that vast ocean, where countless ancestors we'll never know about went through unimaginable struggles and ended up in a country that made hell look like paradise. I dialed the number on the screen and waited, though 'impatiently' would be a better word. Why do we rely on robots for everything these days? It was driving me nuts. Press one for this, press five for that. After hammering a number six times, they finally told me to hang tight for the next available rep. Then came the elevator music from hell, with those random messages about the company that nobody cares about. I was 20 minutes deep, and still waiting. By then, I'd scrubbed a sinkful of dishes and polished my stove. I mean, even Jesus would've gotten tired of waiting for the disciples to show up by now. Finally, a woman named Grace picked up the phone. 'Amazing Grace,' as the song goes, 'how sweet the sound,' because if I had to endure one more minute of that funeral remix music, I might've gone full ham sandwich with a side of fries. What I thought was gonna be a quick 10-minute chat turned into an hour-long convo. Turns out, Grace was not just a travel agent, but a certified holistic therapist. In case you're not hip to it, holistic therapy tackles your mind, body, and spirit all at once. And let me tell you, there's no such thing as random. I don't believe in luck, just the Most High putting my ear in the right place at the right time. We somehow got into this deep chat about my old relationship, my broken self, and the stuff I'd buried beneath tattooed skin. She asked me how I was doing, and it's crazy how those four words can open up a Pandora's box of emotions. As I unpacked the history of my relationship with Paulette, she hit me with a game-changing question: What made me absorb all the shattered pieces of a woman who saw herself as a broken mirror? Her words hit me like a ton of bricks. I was stuck, trapped by my choices that I sometimes pretended I hadn't made. As much as she had her messed-up ways, I had to own up to accepting them and walking down a road to hell. Fire kept burning me from a distance, time and time again. I hadn't seen a therapist in a minute, but this was the push I needed to get back on track. Us Black brothers need it more than ever. See, many of us were raised to be tough, told that we don't shed tears, that showing emotion equals weakness. But that's a bunch of lies. The tough niggas were in the ground. It's why the suicide rate for Black men is off the charts, and why we're splitting from our queens at an alarming rate. We were taught how to escalate conflict, not how to resolve it. That mess has torn apart our community, leaving our mental health like barren soil trying to grow a thriving plant. I cried multiple times during our talk, and my tears turned my living room into a river. If these walls could talk, they would've heard it all, and made Kendrick jealous. Grace even left her desk for some privacy, stepped outside, and started going deep into my soul. Then, the therapist vibe faded, and out came the strong Black woman from North Tulsa.

"I want you to remember one thing if you don't remember anything else from this conversation. You build-a-bear. You don't build-a-bitch." At that moment, the air left my lungs. My soul got sucked out by words that weren't toxic or filled with nonsense. There was so much I'd let her do to me under the false pretense of love. I realized it was love for me, but for her, it was a game, with a little illusion

176

of love mixed in. She had her wins, but the L was on the table now, especially with her being separated from her daughter. I was back to being me, Junior. At the end of the convo, she hooked me up with that cruise for $2,000 and even upgraded me to a suite with a killer view of the entertainment area. And they say Black women fell off? Nah, fam, when I was at my lowest, a Black woman was the one who lifted me up, even if a few had let me down. One person can't define a whole group. Now, I get the power of words, because Grace just granted me that. Grace. Cruise day came, and it was packed to the brim. Waiting in lines? Man, I couldn't stand it. I was that person who'd be in line for one minute, but got pissed because it felt like an eternity. On the bright side, there were a ton of fine ladies in this joint. But let me tell you, the sisters were outnumbered, and I've got nothing but love for chocolate. Ain't no disrespect to anyone else, but I just can't front dating outside my race feels like turning my back on my own, you know? It's just how I roll, and I ain't losing sleep over what others think. Back in my early 20s, I'd do whatever woman, of whatever race, but now, as a grown man who's seen some things, I've come to appreciate the beauty of Black women. No time for anything else. Getting through the passport check took a minute. Once it was all said and done, I handed my bags over to the ship crew, and we finally got the green light to board. Stepping onto the fourth deck of the ship, the bar welcomed me right away.

"Complimentary champagne, sir."

"I won't say no to that."

"They're serving free shots here all night on the fourth deck. Just for today. Until midnight."

"You don't need to tell me twice. I'll be here."

Honestly, it didn't take much to convince me. I was ready to dive into that brown liquor and party 'til the sun came up. This cruise was a first for me, and as I strolled through the ship, I was a bit disoriented at first. I don't know how my cousin and those navy niggas did it day in and day out. I missed the elevator a few times, just awestruck by the ship's decor. At one point, I could've sworn I was in Central Park. Eventually, I found the elevator again and headed up to the suite levels. The vibe changed up there. It smelled like success and luxury. I may not have either, but for the next month, I'd enjoy the illusion. I swiped my key card, walked in, and man, it was like a dream come true. A massive four-bedroom suite what the hell was I gonna do with all this space? I'm telling you, God was on my side. In the master bedroom, I spotted an envelope on the bed, probably a welcome card. I grabbed it and had a quick flashback to when I set up that unforgettable night for Paulette. I took a moment, closed my eyes, and pushed that memory aside. It's never easy moving on from someone you were deeply invested in, but for my sanity's sake, I had to.

"BYE FELICIA!!!"

I shouted that out, emphasizing it, and all the negative energy just bounced. I tore open the yellow envelope and found a card with a cross on it. I thought they were hitting me with some spiritual stuff, but then I opened it. My eyes lit up it was Grace who left the card with her personal number. But the message on the next page, that's what got me. 'Remember what I told you. You build-a-bear; you never build-a-bitch. Enjoy this trip and be grateful for everything you have. Amazing Grace.' Man, I was on cloud nine, no, Pluto. I held that card close, appreciating the love. It was exactly what I needed, right on time. I put the card down and took in this fantastic place. While everyone else was in 200-square-foot rooms, I was chilling in a palace on the water. Stepping into the master bathroom, there was a marble jacuzzi that could fit a small army. I could probably fit one of those thick, members of the 175 and up club girls my brother loved in there, and still have room to spare. Don't sleep on the big girls; they've got some good, moist pussy. That's what my brother always said, and it made me laugh. I walked back out and marveled at every corner of the place the kitchen, the extra guest rooms, the living room with a massive flatscreen. It was all on point. I didn't feel like I deserved it, but clearly, the universe had a different opinion. I kicked back and relaxed. My bags made it to the room after a bit, and once I knew my outfits were safe, I headed up to the 16th floor. In the elevator, I took in the scene, people-watching as everyone was buzzing with excitement. Who could blame them? We were on this amazing ship, ready to go wild for a whole month. I initially hesitated about the length of the cruise, but after seeing my digs, that doubt vanished. I finally hit the buffet and was hit with some incredible smells. Prime rib was the special meal tonight, and I wasn't even thinking about the ribs. I wanted to see the prime, melanin yams. I loaded up my plates, not caring about the gym tomorrow tonight was a "fuck it" night. Portions, calories, all that it could wait. On one plate, I had two lobster tails and enough crab legs to feed the ocean. On the other, a perfect medium-rare prime rib with garlic mashed potatoes, drowning in a special black pepper gravy made with beef broth. It was a feast, and I was gonna savor every bite. Man, I was hoping this grub wouldn't hit me with the

"itis" 'cause I had big plans to hit the clubs later tonight. I put my joints down and grabbed my go-to drink, a mix of beet juice, cranberry, and a hint of green tea. I know beets aren't everybody's flava, and sipping it straight is next to impossible, but trust me, mixed with cranberry, it's off the charts. Plus, you already know the extra benefits in the bedroom wink, wink. I kicked back at a table, enjoying every mouthful. No empty or lonely vibes here. I felt like this was my fresh start, even though I could never truly forget about what went down with Paulette. Life takes a different turn when you're older, and the same old antics that used to thrill you in your twenties, and even early thirties, just don't cut it anymore. Some things just don't add up to the person you've become. After crushing a glorious, bottomless plate of goodness, I headed back to my spot. Lucky me, there was an aquatic dance show at 7:30, and I had a front-row seat from the balcony of my suite. I was all set to keep it classy. The perks of having the government suite included a complimentary bottle of wine. So, I would be sipping on this wine called Bodkin Wines, which had that magic sparkle. The founder, Chris Christensen, a California native, deserved a medal for that Sauvignon Blanc. It added that extra something to the whole experience. Not to mention, he was Black, and Black owned is always crack, 'cause Black don't crack. I knew I was in for a great night. I mean, this was my therapy time. I needed to embrace the moment, especially considering what I'd been through. I raised my glass, closed my eyes, and grinned. This one was for me and every other person who'd faced their share of hardships but didn't know how to let it out. I took a deep, satisfying sip, and man, that wine had some kick. As I looked out at the sea breeze and the crowd below, I couldn't help but wonder about the performers. They were doing amazing stuff, making it look like they were dancing on water. It was like magic. I knew I could barely make a splash in the pool, so I wasn't about to dive into anything like that. The acts told different stories, but I couldn't help but think about what those performers might be going through in their personal lives. What if the guy flying through the air had just lost a loved one? What if the women on the water were battling their own demons or facing criticism for their choices? There's a lot more behind the scenes than you'd think. People don't often stop to consider that stuff, but once you've been through some rough patches and had to put on a brave face for the world, you start to understand why folks wear masks. When they go home at night, they take off the happy mask and face their own struggles. As the night wrapped up, I thought about hitting the clubs and dancing the night away. But my mindset had shifted. I had a whole month ahead of me, and I decided to use this first night for some real soul-searching. I went back to my suite, closed the curtains, turned off the TV, and left the light on at the oversized work desk. I pulled out my laptop, ready to dive deep into some personal therapy. I hadn't cracked it open yet, I just glided my hand over it. See, usually, I'm all about writing. But tonight, I aimed to breathe life into my feelings, words that flip the script on societal rules. I tell folks, writers? We're people who share our vibes with unofficial therapists who lend an ear for free. It's a different kind of therapy, no cash involved, just emotions on the line. I popped the laptop, hopped on the Wi-Fi, slid into Google Drive, and began conjuring that magic.

I didn't have my journal, so this would suffice for the next month.

Journal Entry: The Masks We Wear

Today, I find myself contemplating the curious phenomenon of humans donning metaphorical masks to obscure their true selves. It's a behavior we all engage in to varying degrees, driven by a deep-seated desire for acceptance and belonging. We often disguise our authentic selves with the intention of fitting in, conforming to societal norms, or meeting the expectations of those around us. In our relentless quest for social approval, it's as if we've collectively embraced a masquerade ball of life, each of us wearing masks woven from our insecurities, fears, and societal pressures. We adorn these masks, often unconsciously, but their weight becomes increasingly burdensome as we perpetuate the facade. The allure of acceptance is undeniable. We yearn for connection, understanding, and love, and sometimes the easiest path to these desires appears to be the one where we suppress our genuine selves. It's ironic that in striving to be accepted, we may, in fact, alienate ourselves from the very thing we seek true, authentic connections. Over time, these imaginary masks become second nature, and we may lose sight of who we truly are. Our identities blend with the roles we play, the expectations we meet, and the personas we project. We risk becoming mere actors in the grand play of life, disconnected from our core essence. The detriment of this masquerade is that it leads to internal conflict and a pervasive sense of emptiness. We become detached from our innermost thoughts, emotions, and desires. We hide our vulnerabilities and unique qualities, further distancing ourselves from the profound, genuine connections we long for. In the process, we may even forget who we are, what we truly value, and what makes our hearts sing. It is only when we summon the courage to remove these masks, unveiling our true selves, that we can begin to form the meaningful connections we crave. Authenticity is a bridge to profound relationships, as it allows us to connect with others on a deeper, more genuine level. When we are open about our fears, desires, and quirks, we invite others to do the same, forging bonds based on trust, empathy, and mutual understanding. In a world where acceptance seems contingent on conformity, the act of peeling back the layers and embracing our authentic selves is an act of bravery. It's a testament to our strength and a profound step towards inner peace and genuine connection. Let us not forget that our uniqueness is our greatest asset, and it is through authenticity that we unlock the true potential of human connection and growth. So, as I reflect upon the masks we wear in the name of acceptance, I am reminded of the importance of shedding those illusions, revealing the raw, imperfect, beautiful soul that lies beneath. Only then can we find our tribe, our truest connections, and the inner peace that comes from living as our authentic selves.

Putting pen to paper, or in this case, digital thoughts to unhuman screens, there's something soul-soothing about it. Writing feels like a rare lunar eclipse in my spirit, a daily spectacle rather than a once-in-a-blue-moon event. It's my secret sanctuary, where solitude and creativity collide. After I jotted down my thoughts, It was time to call it a night. Remember, Rome wasn't constructed in a day, and neither is my inner transformation. My mind still holds on to that attachment, kind of like climbing out of a dusty mine, where most of the dirt's shaken off, but some grime lingers. It's all good, though; I'm cleansing myself one verse at a time. With the lights out, I headed into the master bedroom, with a bed the size of Shaquille O'Neal himself, and snuggled in. Then, I hopped right back out, realizing I'm missing a crucial piece for my zen mode a fan. No fan was here, so I settled for the next best thing: firing up YouTube with 10 hours of soothing fan noises to whisk me away into dreamland. I nestle into bed, eager for rest, despite that massive room-rattling fart. Man, that was one epic, never-ending fart, smelling like crab legs dipped in garlic butter gone through a garbage disposal. This was going to be a long night. Morning arrived with the sound of an unexpected call, and I was sure it was a dream. Who the heck had my suite number? I tried to drown it out by burying my head under multiple pillows, but it was no use. I rolled over, irritated, and checked the time 6:47 in the morning. I've always been an early riser, but this was different. Everything on this cruise seemed to operate around the clock, including the weight room. I needed every bit of sleep I could get. Answering the call, I heard an eerie voice on the other end.

"Stop thinking about her. Don't think about her. When you fall, just know I'll be there to catch you in my arms. Trust me. You won't mind falling into this."

"Who the fuck is this?"

"Your redemption. I'll see you."

They hung up. I stared at the phone, wondering who was playing a horror movie prank at sea. It was bizarre, and the voice sounded like something out of a horror flick a woman with a voice-box-like distortion. Maybe she was as groggy as I was in the early morning. I shrugged it off, thinking it was a dream and lay there for another 10 minutes. But the phone didn't ring again, so I figured it was someone onboard trying to mess with me. Around seven, I got up, still annoyed but wide awake. It wasn't such a bad thing, though, because round two of that lobster from last night was ready to make its exit. Nothing beats starting the day better than a good morning trip to the bathroom. Afterward, I scrolled through my laptop, checking out random YouTube clips. That's when I stumbled upon Love Jones, with Darius delivering that iconic poetry piece to Nina. You know the one where he wants to be the blues in her left thigh and the funk in her right. I couldn't get enough of that movie. It's got some killer lines, like, "I just wanna come up and talk." Pure boss moves, right? Yeah, man. Yo, we all know we've been itching for a deep conversation from someone before, right? I mean, who can blame the guy? Did you all peep Nina, or the 'urgent like a motherfucker' line at the end? That's the scene that took the movie to uncharted heights, for real. We all know no sister would stand out in the rain, messing up her hair for a brother. But in the heat of the moment, it was the perfect send-off to a perfect love story. I used to think Paulette was gonna be my Nina, but she turned out to be more like D'wana from Next Friday, you feel me? Mentally unstable and all that. After handling my business and taking a shower, I planned out my moves for the day. Most of it was about living for myself, not just existing for someone who hasn't even lived yet. I air dried my nuts and got dressed in my gym gear, stepping out into an elevator that smelled like all sorts of shady stuff - tax fraud, greed, and rich folks' antics. I made my way through this colossal boat and was blown away by how many people were on board. I peeped the bookworms reading their papers and sipping Starbucks in the oversized internet cafe section. As I strolled further, I saw folks ziplining from one end of the ship to who-knows-where through this massive opening in the middle of the boat. Got me thinking, should I give it a shot? I mean, life's too short to miss out on the excitement, right? But then, I had to remember my skin color. I wasn't afraid of thrilling stuff; it was the fear of it going south when my Black ass tried it. Knowing my luck, I'd be halfway through the zipline when the whole thing snaps, and I'd plummet down to the fourth deck. Nah, fam, I was good on that shit. I hit the gym, and the moment I walked in, two fine ladies welcomed me. I'm all about supporting the sisters, but these Latina chicas were on point. They handed me a towel and showed me they had a whole spa right there. They offered me some post-gym pampering, and I couldn't help but smile, telling them I'd think about it. Truth be told, I already knew I was gonna hit that spa once I was done. The gym was spacious with all the equipment a brotha could ask for, and there were some melanin queens tightening up their Black bodies. I didn't see any rings, so I figured they were making sure they were looking fly for whoever they might meet on this cruise. I threw on my headphones and got to work for the next hour and a half. After that, I made a beeline for the spa. A hot shower, followed by a two-hour session that felt like heaven - hot stone massage, some sizzling oils, manicure, pedicure, facial treatment, you name it. They even took care of my nose hairs. I felt reborn, man. Mind, body, and soul had been treated to some top-notch TLC. I still pondered how some men saw self care as "gay." Actually, I knew why they viewed it as that. But hey, their insecurity is their own issue to resolve, not mines. I floated back to my suite, and as I opened the door, I spotted another complimentary bottle of wine in the kitchen. These folks were on point with their service, no doubt. I hadn't finished the first bottle, but I'd downed more than half on the first night, so this came right on time. And there was a small envelope next to the bottle. Kinda odd, but a nice card goes a long way to make you feel good. It might not make the wine taste better, but it sure adds a touch of human decency. I cracked it open and started reading:

> 'I know what you're thinking. This ain't from the ship; it's from me. Save it; we'll enjoy it when the time's right. Wine always pairs well with dinner and, of course, dessert after. Just don't get too hooked on the food, lol.'

Now, I was lowkey freaked out. A stalker on this cruise? With thousands of people on board, anyone could be the one. I started thinking about that movie 'A Thin Line Between Love and Hate.' Knowing my luck, it'd be a crazy broad named Brandy. Ah, man. I didn't need this right now. This trip was supposed to help me forget about everything, not have me worrying about getting tied up to a bedpost, torched, and thrown overboard. I shook it off and took a seat on the living room couch. I wasn't gonna let anything ruin my moment. The next stop was the pool, where I could just forget about everything. You know it's gonna be lit with all the fine folks up there. I threw on my least-used hoop shorts - come on, brothers don't do fancy swim trunks. We're good with those old basketball shorts. As I stepped out of the elevator, I felt like I'd entered paradise. The first thing I saw was four stunning Dominican queens, gracefully strutting their stuff on the decks. All of 'em were at least 5'7. My boys who know me, know that my weakness is tall women, with long, sensual legs. Sure, I didn't discriminate. I'd gladly date the demon spawns that were 5'3 and under. But, give me a tall girl, and I'd have those skyscrapers of theirs knocking stars out of the sky. I knew I was in for a good day. As I walked through, shades on point, trying not to make it too obvious that I was admiring the view, I stumbled upon the ice cream machine. There was a line, so I knew it had to be working properly, not like McDonald's. When I got to the front, I scooped up a cone and chilled. To some, this raised eyebrows, but for me, it was the ladies' radar. I had no hang-ups about my manhood, unlike a lot of bruhs. Ladies appreciate a confident man. And what better way to show your confidence than strutting past them with an ice cream cone? I could care less about what the guys thought. I wasn't looking to impress them. I grabbed a chocolate cone, my flavor of choice, just like I like my women. I didn't park myself; I strolled around all three pools, including that massive one in the center of the deck. I was oozing cockiness and confidence, the dad bod god in full effect. Eventually, I spotted an empty beach chair and made myself comfortable. Four fantastic ladies with Puerto Rican roots sauntered by. Yeah, this was a clear sign trouble was lurking. I chilled there for the next couple of hours, taking dips in the pool. The water volleyball was poppin', and the bachata music had everyone groovin'. It's hard to keep your focus when a ball's whizzing over the net and there are some nice, well rounded yams all around you. That's when I met Madi, a cute Belizean with braces, and we hit it off. Initially, I had my eye on a thick Trinidadian beauty hanging out by the pool. Several fellas had tried to lure her into the water, but she wasn't budging. Oh well, no biggie. At least Madi and I hit it off, and we set up a dinner date for the Captain's dinner tonight before she went on her way. Seemed like a checkmate move; I knew I was in for some guaranteed company on this cruise. No way I was gonna be out on the water this long and not have a little fun. Back in my room, I decided to shower and catch some Z's. The shower was refreshing, but the nap? Not so much. I couldn't shake Paulette from my mind, no matter how hard I tried. I started scrolling through old text messages and photos of us, even the racy video we made at that hotel way back when. I wasn't about to put that stuff out there; that's not how a real man rolls. But I should've deleted it all a long time ago. Holding onto it was like having a toxic anchor weighing on my spirit. Love ain't easy to let go of. Even with a broken heart, you try to convince yourself it's still whole. Finally, I powered off the phone and left it alone. A good hour or two of sleep would be clutch right now. It would recharge me, and I could have dinner with a stunning melanin queen. Hopefully, we'd have a sweet dessert after. I woke up, and it was already 7:03 p.m. No need to rush out of bed; I had missed the Captain's dinner, big time. My shot at her was gone. It would be my luck that I missed out on a woman who possibly had some snapback between her legs. But no point crying over spilled milk. I just got up, brushed my teeth, and headed to the 24-hour buffet. It wasn't as crowded, so that was a plus. I grabbed my plates and got to grubbin'.

"Oh, my bad," I said.

I bumped into a beautiful melanin sculpture.

"No problem. You're good, my well groomed king." As she walked away, I couldn't help myself.

"Excuse me?"

"Yeah," she turned around, and those glossy lips sparkled like the sun over the Kemet Pyramids.

"What's your name?"

She laughed.

"You might find out. Or you might not. See you around."

She waved and strolled off. Damn, that's all I could think. She was stunning, standing about 5'8, with the perfect blend of everything - curves, natural curls, and those mesmerizing brown eyes. Seeing natural beauty in the flesh was a sight to behold. I just wish more women knew how perfect they were, without all the extra stuff the world says they need to be beautiful. I finished eating, but she was still on my mind. It hit me, her voice sounded crazy familiar. And she didn't give me her name. Now I felt like a Tevin Campbell clone; and we still don't know who he was talking about after all these years. I decided to keep it light that night. We were docking in Hawaii tomorrow for two days. No need to overdo it; I knew the food in Honolulu would be top-notch. I needed space in my stomach for that. I savored a prime rib and decided I'd hit up the hip-hop club later. Back in my suite, I opted for a laid-back look a snug black graphic tee, fitted jeans, and some black forces. You know what people think when they see black forces; they usually back off. I wasn't looking for trouble, but I wasn't taking any either. I figured folks would mind their own business when they saw these on my feet. I brushed my teeth, popped that wintergreen gum in my mouth, and headed downstairs. As I approached, the beats were already thumping, and I was like,

"Damn, it's lit!" But hey, I had to remind myself I was on a cruise ship, not some club in Chi-town where the party doesn't start till midnight. People on this ship were grown, you know? At 11 or 12, they were either catching some Z's or trying to get cozy with someone special. I walked into the place with Rich Homie Quan "Walk Thru" blaring through the speakers. It was fire! I strolled through like I owned the joint, and it was packed but just the right kinda packed, not too crowded, and definitely ready to get the party going. I took a quick scan of the room; you know, once you've seen one firm backside, you've seen 'em all. Fellas, in a club, you don't holla. Every lady thinks she's the main attraction, so don't be that guy. Keep it cool, stay chill, let them come to you. Trust me, it's a solid play. I made a beeline for the bar to get my evening elixir. "Crown and Coke, please," I told the bartender. But I had to watch this mix; some bartenders pour 90% alcohol, and I wasn't trying to get sloshed, just a nice buzz. I needed that perfect balance. She nailed it, and I sipped it down, on point. I paid up, dropped her a $20 tip, and moved on. I leaned against the wall, bobbing my head to the rhythm. "Wipe Me Down" hit the speakers, the unofficial Black national anthem. While the crowd was throwing down on the dance floor, I stayed smooth, side to side, drink in the air. Right now, I was in my zone, and nothing could mess with my vibe. Club tonight, Hawaii tomorrow. I vibed through the next few tracks, occasionally interrupted by DJ Moe's wild shoutouts. When Juvenile's "Slow Motion" dropped, I was instantly transported back to the younger days. That slow grind on the dance floor? Man, those were the days! I was grooving, singing along, and sipping my drink. Then, out of the blue, a hand reached over my shoulder like something out of a horror flick. I jumped to the opposite side, spilling a bit of my drink in the process.

"Oops, my bad. Didn't know you were that jumpy."

It was her, the girl I'd seen at the buffet.

"You again, huh? Are you finally gonna drop that name?"

"I might," she said, grabbing my hand. "But first, we dance."

As she pulled me onto the dance floor, I took that final sip of Crown before setting it down on a passing table. I liked a good dance, but I paid for that drink, and I was gonna enjoy it. The opening beats of Beyonce's "Drunk in Love" filled the air, and whoever DJ Moe was, he was on fire.

"HEY, HOLD UP REAL QUICK!!! SOME OF Y'ALL NIGGAS LEANIN' ON THE WALL WITH ALL THIS ASS IN HERE!!! GET Y'ALL LAME ASS OFF THAT SHIT, GRAB ONE OF THESE HOES AND GO TO WORK!!! LET'S GO!!! DJ MOE!!! BAMA BITCH!!!"

I cracked up, this nigga was wild. He started the song again, and shawty pressed her tall frame against mine, and I wrapped my arms around her. Let me tell you, her ass was softer than grandma's Sunday biscuits. Not those project chick biscuits, mind you those things are hard as bricks. She could do it all: suck dick, gangbang on the whole world, and rock a nappy hair game, but proper cooking was not in her skill set. We moved to the song, and a feeling washed over me. I hadn't been this truly intimate with a woman since Paulette. It was hard to forget someone you loved, even when they showed they weren't worth much. But I managed to let go and have the time of my life. It felt like the song went on forever, and it was just the two of us on the dance floor, like nobody else existed. As I got lost in the moment and the music ended, my phone buzzed. She turned around, wrapped her arms around my neck, and looked me dead in the eyes.

"Let me grab a drink. Then, we can head up to your suite. Don't worry; I just wanna talk. Is that cool?"

"No doubt," I said.

And then she did something totally unexpected. She grabbed my face and kissed me on the forehead before walking away, looking back and smiling. That backside was swaying in those jeans, like two planets that had just collided in space. Even crazier, as she reached the bar, I thought to myself, she just hit me with the Love Jones line. How in the world did she become Darius, and I, Nina? That wasn't supposed to go down like that. I whipped out my phone and peeped the email notification. I was smack-dab in the middle of nowhere, out in the ocean, so who was hitting me up. It was a message from Paulette. No subject, just a whole lotta text. I skimmed through it real quick, eyes moving fast as ever, and then I hit the words that hit me like a ton of bricks.

'That first date, man, you feel me? It wasn't shit to me.'

My heart took a nosedive right then and there. My whole body was buzzing with that adrenaline rush. It shot past my gut, swirled 'round my lungs, took a left at my emotions, and went straight for my feelings. WHY? Why was she playing me like this? More importantly, why didn't I cut my losses when I saw them waving red flags? Ditching me at my sister's place was one thing, but this? It felt like she ran me over, reversed right back, and ran me over again just for good measure. I was the ultimate fool. Some OG once dropped wisdom on me, saying women are like sponges. When they wanna soak you up, they're dripping. The moment you're no longer on their radar, they're dry as a bone, like they never even came out the wrapper. It hit me then she played the game perfectly. I wasn't the one she wanted to be with; I was the one she let inside for stability while she got back on her feet. No love for me, not even a clue about recognizing a decent man if he slapped her in the face. She wasn't interested in that at all; it was all about numero uno, herself. I hit the button to black out my phone screen and pocketed it.

"Everything cool?"

I turned to see shawty, noticing the frustration written all over my face.

"Look, I don't know what you saw on that phone, but c'mon, let's roll." She handed me a shot glass.

"What's this?"

"Just a little toast. Right now, we're sipping this. In a few, we can savor each other."

The look in her eyes was like, "Shut up and vibe with me." We toasted, downed those shots, and before I could even catch my breath, she locked lips with me. Soft and safe that's what her lips were. Not even knowing her name didn't matter anymore. I grabbed her hand, and we bounced from the club up to the room. It all started as we stepped into the suite kissing, groping, and shedding clothes. As we fell onto the master bed, half-naked, me on top of her, I hit pause. Propped myself up on both arms and stared at her.

"What's up?," she asked.

"What's your name?," I asked in a low, monotone voice.

She flipped the script, now on top of me, me looking up at the most perfect pair of breasts I'd ever seen. She snatched my hands and pressed them against her chest.

"Amazing Grace. You feel me? Sorry, when you hit me up to book that reservation and we talked about your situation, my corporate America voice took over."

My eyes popped wide. This was her the one who booked my trip, upgrading every aspect of it. I couldn't believe it. She leaned in, her face inches from mine, and dropped a line that's etched in my memory.

"When I'm done with you, I'm gonna make sure every ounce of that ungrateful bitch is out of you. Now, fuck me like you just met me, and you never wanna see me again."

Who talks like that? But it didn't even matter, 'cause the next few hours were like a marathon of us doing our thing. Correction, we experienced something deep. Sleep? What's that? They say people who vibe with you on all levels are the real deal. It ain't about all of them being the one for a relationship, and the same goes for guys. But they know how to heal us. This wasn't just an encounter with Grace; her touch reminded me that I'm a good man who made a bad call and didn't know when to let go. She knew when to slow it down, her whispers getting me to open up about my flaws. Her embrace was like a soothing balm. She wasn't using me for some action; she was using herself for my recovery. Now, I get what real connection means. With Paulette, I thought the sex was good, but with Grace, I realized it was only good 'cause of the trauma. A lot feels good after you've been put through the wringer. In our sessions, she let me take charge when I needed it, showing she was a grown woman. The next morning well,

191

actually, it was more like the next afternoon I cracked my eyes open, the light coming through the curtains. She was up, sporting one of those bathrobes, tray and plates in hand.

"Good morning," she said, her natural curls gleaming.

"You really whipped up some breakfast, for sure."

"Yeah, I made cheese omelets. I mean, the way you were knocked out, it's like you needed a pick-me-up, you know?"

"Hold on, though. How'd you manage to cook on a ship loaded with restaurants everywhere?"

"I got my ways, you know? I can do things you didn't expect, you know?"

"Man, you're keeping that 'Love Jones' vibe alive, ain't you?" We both cracked up as she slid over and handed me my plate. We kicked back in total chill mode, soaking up the moment.

"I'm speechless, seriously. You came through for me."

"Nah, not really," she said. "I didn't save you. I just showed you your worth. I didn't just hear you on that phone, I really listened. I didn't just watch you on this ship, I observed you. Last night, I gave you three keys to a deep connection. Actually, grab your phone, 'cause you're gonna want to jot this down."

This situation was wild. I wasn't sure if I was dealing with a regular woman or a low-key life coach. I opened my phone's notes app, ready to get schooled in the art of recovery.

"You ready?"

"Hit me, Clair Huxtable."

She laughed, feeling the vibe.

"Alright, here's the first one: Communication through touch. See, as a woman, we've got two kinds of touch. One's all about, 'You can have your way,' and the other says, 'Here's what you need to hear.' I could've just touched your back, but we don't roll like that. I made sure my fingertips hit every spot on your spine. Your spine, that's your core, man. It's what keeps you upright and strong. You might not have noticed, but I touched each vertebra. I hit every pressure point

192

on your body with my hands. I held you in a way that said, 'Don't just fuck me,' but also, 'Make love to me and let me feel what's up with you, so I can be there.'"

At this point, I was blown away. My mind was racing, something I'd never experienced before.

"Two, let's call this the 'third eye theory.' Check it, in case you didn't know, every pyramid in Egypt had a layer of limestone underneath it. Historians talk about the bricks, but on top, they put a pyramidion covered in gold leaf to shine like the sun. So, when I looked into your eyes, whether you were on top or the other way around, it was speaking to your soul. I could see the pain, the choices, even the not-so-great ones, just by peeping into your eyes. It's like I saw your light without even going all the way."

At this point, I was thinking of putting the plate down and showing my appreciation again.

"Three. The afterglow. Let me ask you something, do you remember what went down last night in this bed?"

"I mean, yeah, I ain't that messed up."

"Nah, my man. Do you really remember?"

"What are you talking about?"

I was seriously puzzled. Then she hit me with some deep insight.

"Alright, you got a scar on your jaw, a tattoo of a black fist, the remnants of a cut above your right eye. Your nails are all trimmed up, except that pinky one, looks like you've been nibbling on it. And there's that one tooth in your perfect smile that's slightly out of line. That's what I mean."

I pushed the plate aside for a second.

"You really analyzed me."

"Damn right. You gotta pay attention, my man. Between rounds, I thought about everything. How'd all that happen? Where'd it come from? I looked at your physical self just as much as I got into your head. That's what someone who truly cares does. They dig into every part of you. By the way, did you notice I licked that scar on your right knee before I came back up and took your soul with my mouth?"

I was completely mind-blown in the best way.

"Nah, I didn't catch that."

"That's the beauty of this talk. I need you to really understand who you're vibing with, who you're investing your time in. It ain't just about the physical. Sex is an investment, and too many relationships end up in the red because people don't do their due diligence. That's why we have more single parents than marriages. So, was your ex-married?"

"She's on her way to divorce number two."

"She got kids?"

"One."

"Is she still with the baby daddy?"

"Nah."

"Yo, do I even need to spell it out? Investments, fam. I did my homework from the moment we chopped it up on the phone, peeped your career moves, and checked your vibe on this cruise. I willingly dropped my most precious gift in your hands. Now, whether we'll link up after this month-long ride, who knows? Will you put in the effort? I can't predict that. But here's the deal–I saw you as an investment. If things go left, I'm ready to own that and be accountable for my choices. What I do know is I put my chips on you with a purpose. And if things crash and burn, it's on me, no doubt. But, believe me, I see the potential here. Next time, peep the market before you jump in. 'Cause for real, you threw your stakes into a shaky scene, and she's probably wreaking havoc on someone else's plans, wherever the fuck she is. Now, writer, let's wrap this meal and hit that bedroom again for a different kind of vibe. We've had that infatuation session. Now I'm craving some deeper knowledge, where we uncover Grace and why I'm out here being so damn amazing."

"So you won't me to write my best story inside of you?"

"Nah. You did that repeatedly last night. I wanna be the notebook that you rip all the pages out of. Basically, don't be nice. You're used to being a nice guy, even with sex. I give you permission to rag doll my ass. Just don't spit on me, and we're all good."

I was speechless. This woman had me on the Stratosphere level, and I ain't talking 'bout that shitty Vegas hotel. We ate, kept the convo flowing, and then she pulled me back in. Her lips were like a whirlwind, her warmth like tropical currents, and the chemistry was like Brady to Moss on the field, but in the bedroom. We wrapped it up, cleaned up, and she bounced, getting ready for her adventures in Hawaii, reminding me that we got a whole month of this, but giving me free reign when I'm out and about in these places. As I packed my bags to step off this cruise for a few days, the urge to spill some more of my writings was itching me something fierce. We'd already docked, and it was time to rock that mic tonight. But first, there was something heavy on my mind. I grabbed my phone and started typing. This time, it wasn't a journal entry. This was my secret sauce. Poetry. Welcome, to the other aspect of me.

The Break Up Poem:

The pros and cons of dating a poet, you can become the sweetest smelling flower with visuals told thru words, or, you can be that withering ass rose that I throw on top of the casket before the dirt is added, see I was once in love, I remember our first date, we started with tacos, which automatically gave her a 10 in my book because if you wanna get me, just say let's eat Mexican food, we followed it up with ice cream, hookah, jack in the box and later, I sat my ass in the cold sand at the beach for an hour and a half, under the big dipper, I swear, with God as my witness, the next week, I licked her until her clit became unconscious, I fucked her as if all my breaths depended on it, and before all that, I made a dinner of stuffed chicken breasts, fettucine from scratch, and we discussed goals, ten months later, she would tell me that first date didn't mean shit, and I felt like shit, I wish the sperm I shot down her throat could've stayed in my dick because she had tasted my life and ambitions, and I know to men that sounds kind of strange, how can you complain about getting your dick sucked, until I remind them, that a vacuum is a powerful tool until it pulls something that breaks its insides, causing it to be dysfunctional, have you ever been inside traumatic pussy, I'm talking twice divorced pussy, kid by a nigga you call a clown, but you still let yo' vagina become the circus pussy, on occasion, I became the nigga she hated while in that pussy, yet I still tried to find the good inside of her that didn't involve her opening her legs, see I'm not perfect in any way, but when you say nine hours of my life wasn't shit, I think about the hundreds of hours I listened to you bitch, how much it hurt that your finances couldn't match your work ethic at times, how you felt God had abandoned you, and I wanted to say fuck you, but I only had good memories of that shit, I wanted to wish petty, stupid shit on you like...I hope you catch four flats in your driveway because I still cared enough to never wish that shit happened on the road, I wanted to say the hell with you, but I wish eternal damnation on no one except rapists and child molesters, funny how ya ex-husband was the latter, and here I came, super nigga, with no red cape, just all my flaws and imperfections, ready to give them away to you, because I wanted you to know all of me, and when I saw that being me was too much, I realized that the S on my chest, stood for stupid as fuck, how could I care so much to love someone so broken, did she not realize how many nights I cut my hands trying to help her piece her broken life back together again, did you know glass is actually not a solid, it is made from sand, so maybe that's why she slipped through my hands when all I did was simply try to love her, and when I found out that a crack in glass moves at 3,000 mph, I realized I would never be fast enough to her heart, no matter how fast I ran, dear ladies, men fall in love too, and get emotional, not all of us think dick first, ask who's the daddy later, some of us actually learned how to love by never seeing it at all, kudos to my dead daddy, yes, I came out of your balls, but you never had the balls to love my mother properly, to the woman who I was once in love with, again, I would say fuck you, but it would only remind me of some of the best times we ever had...

I pulled up at The Arts at Marks Garage, in Chinatown, Honolulu. It was a chill February night on the island, and it felt like a breath of fresh air amidst the nationwide deep freeze. The spot was lit, a real gem of an art gallery with a stage ready for the spotlight. I walked in, dapping up the early birds in the place. It was a cozy, tight-knit vibe for sure. Writing and speaking was my escape, and I was craving it tonight. I couldn't have asked for a better time to be here. I strolled back to the main gallery area, and that's when I spotted my boy Ant.

"Yo, Ant! What's poppin', fam?"

"Ain't nothin', Junior. Glad you could make it. Mahalo, bro."

"Yeah, glad I made it too. But, what's 'mahalo,' man?"

"Don't sweat it, bro. And by the way, it's gonna be fire to hear you spit tonight. I've peeped your stuff on YouTube. You got mad talent." I knew Anthony from back in the day, and he made the move to Hawaii a while back. While we were chopping it up, taking in the beautiful mix of folks from all over, something crazy happened. Anthony kept talking, but I zoned out hard. I was locked on the most breathtaking sight I'd ever seen. She was rocking a black top, killer blue jeans, and had freckles on her face that looked like a road map to paradise. It felt like she got the VIP invite straight from the heavens. I usually got pre-show jitters, but she gave me first-day-of-school vibes, and I was mesmerized. The open mic was coming up sooner than expected, and I found myself going first on the list. What's wild, she ended up posted up in the second row, right in the center, so my eyes had no choice but to see her while I was on that mic. Man, God had some serious jokes up His sleeves. He served me up a five-course meal on that ship, and now, He dropped a pot of honey and gold right here. Ice-cold move, Big Guy. After a solid two-hour set with some incredibly talented artists pouring their hearts out on the mic, it was a wrap. I chopped it up with a few people, but my eyes never left her. She dipped out of the spot, and I knew this was my shot. I had to let her know how stunning she was. As I stepped outside, someone tried to drop props on my words. It was cool and all, and I appreciated the love, but I was on a mission. God didn't send an angel down to Earth every day. He already did that once, and we know where that dude ended up. But this time, it was like He personally ordered her to leave me speechless with her beauty. If that was the plan, then I was about to need some serious breathing exercises because my heart had straight-up paused at the sight of her. I bolted outside, but then I hit the brakes. She was chilling on the corner, chatting it up with her friend. In my head, I ran through a list of reasons why I couldn't approach her. Maybe she heard my pain in my speech. Perhaps it was that trauma talk or the fire in my words about racism. Maybe, just maybe, I was bringing back memories she didn't want to revisit. Maybe the tattoos on my skin wrote the same chapters as the heartbreak that last dude gave her. Or maybe my voice was a bad memory she had to relive tonight. I stood there, mind racing. I couldn't find the courage to tell her how beautiful she was. She walked off into that warm Hawaiian night, and my confidence took a hike in the opposite direction. Who knew a breakup could snatch my ability to speak like that? As she faded into the distance, I thought about the greatest poem I never got to read: Her.

"Yo, man," Ant tapped me on the shoulder. "You down for hitting up the spot with us tonight?"

I glanced at him, then looked back where she'd walked off. She was gone.

"Nah, I'm good, bro. I'm gonna head back to the hotel, heat up some grub, and chill."

"Bro, the food ain't gonna vanish."

"Nah, it's not about the food. It's more like the meal that could fill me up just walked away."

Ant and his partner shot me puzzled looks.

"Do you, man. Take it easy. We'll catch up."

Man, how can I be acting like the world just ended when I rocked the stage like a boss? The way I connected with the crowd, it was like I painted masterpieces in their minds. But in my own eyes, I wasn't Picasso; I was more like a picnic. I mean, pic-a-nigga to lynch because I couldn't figure out what negative cloud was hanging over my head. I'm Junior Mitchell, the writer, but also Junior Mitchell, the dude who loves like he's never seen heartbreak before. My rental was parked way up on the rooftop, hence "The Arts Garage." The venue was this slick spot tucked at the bottom of a parking garage a pretty dope setup. I skipped the elevator, and took the stairs. My legs were gonna cuss me out later, but I needed some alone time to think. After what felt like an eternity and a serious leg workout, I finally reached the top. Funny enough, my truck was the only one parked up there. I tossed the keys on the passenger seat and let it all out. Life had seriously knocked me around. Nine hours of pouring my soul out, and that bitch acted like it was just another night. It stung. One moment I was fine, the next I felt like an empty shell. Leaving a nigga high and dry after all the love and support I'd given felt like a sucker move. Men should be able to open up and love, but I was starting to get why some of us turn cold. The hurt ran deep, like sippin' habu sake at a bar. I pounded the steering wheel a couple of times before getting out of the car. I broke down right there in the parking lot, bent over with tears streaming. Love ain't just an emotion; it's a whole way of life. Images of my old man's cheating and my mom's rebellious streak replayed like a Netflix binge on a Saturday night. What felt like hours pouring out my soul was just five minutes. They say pain can stretch time, especially when you're hurting. As the last tears fell, I stared into a starless February night. Even the ancestors seemed to turn away. I walked back to the truck, slowly piecing myself back together. Before hitting the road, I thought of Grace. I grabbed my phone and read what she'd told me to write down. Instantly, I smiled, even laughed. "Man, you're good."

No music on the ride, just the GPS set for Waikiki. I cruised through Chinatown and took in the sounds of the city. Their lives seemed to be on track. I never wanted to be like what I saw growing up, but part of me started to understand my old man's stoic ways. I hit the H1, not bothered by the 55 mph speed limit. I needed a slow pace. My only plan was to get to the hotel, hit my room, and think about how I'd wowed the crowd in the dopest yet most gut-wrenching performance of my life. My energy hadn't rubbed off on anyone, but inside, I was wrestling with self-doubt. I felt like I'd given them a watered-down version of me, even though they couldn't tell. I didn't deserve applause; I deserved to stand on that stage and let each person take a swing at me. I hoped the lady in the black top would go last, or maybe she'd just give me that look the one that said, 'You're pathetic.' I sat in the hotel parking lot, dazed and confused, but I had to pull myself together. I stepped out of the rental and walked away from the hotel, heading down the main strip in Waikiki, where all the fancy stores, hotels, and hotspots were. After about a 10-minute stroll, I stumbled upon a crowd at a street corner. Beats were bumping from the speakers, and people were vibing. As the light turned green, I got curious. This was the kind of nosy where you could check things out without worrying about trouble. I made it to the crowd and got into the mix. It was two dudes freestyling, and the crowd was all in. The longer I stayed, the more I got into it. Slowly, the last 10 months of craziness faded away, if just for a moment. As the beats switched and the crowd kept grooving, a Samoan guy locked eyes on me.

"YO YO YO!!! Yo, stop the music," he yelled, turning to the DJ.

"Yo, my man?"

"Me?"

"Yeah, you. You're the transparency God. A Y'ALL!!! IT'S THE DUDE FROM YOUTUBE WITH ALL THE VIDEOS AND DOPE WORDS!!! Mad props, my brother!" The crowd burst into applause, and I was honestly taken aback but humbled at the same time.

"Yo, you were down at Mark's tonight, right? How'd it go?"

"Man, it was all good. But I ain't no deity, my friend. I appreciate the love, though."

"Nah, brother, you're a legend in our eyes."

"You must be mixing me up with Black Chakra."

"I ain't confusing you with nobody. Check it, look around, man. You think all these folks would be keeping it low-key, not asking for the beats to be off if they didn't respect you? Trust me, there are people who don't even know you, but if we say you're a legend on this island, you're a legend."

"Thanks, man."

He laid that big Samoan hand on my shoulder, and one thing came to mind accept this love. His grip was strong enough to toss me back to the mainland, no doubt. People started coming up, shaking my hand, and patting me on the back. I had no clue who this dude was, but he clearly had major respect. Pacific Islanders, you know, they're an awesome bunch that deeply embrace their roots. If you're in their good books, you're family. They're chill folks but always a tad cautious of outsiders, and you can't blame them for that, given the history. I rolled with that crew for another 15 minutes, grooving with the crowd who were just vibing with life, being regular people. Later, not far from that corner, I peeped inside a spot with live music. This wasn't your typical smooth jazz joint. Just a bunch of comfy chairs, couches, and people chilling with drinks. There was a bar in the back, and that was my destination. A drink was calling my name. I flashed my ID to the bouncer at the door. For such a laid-back spot, they had the Hulk guarding the entrance. I had no intention of starting any drama. Islanders, man, they're born at 5'11", 280 pounds. He handed back my ID, and I stepped in. Onstage, a woman was belting out some sweet tunes, and a dude was jamming on the guitar next to her. They were covering "Killing Me Softly" by The Fugees, and it was unexpectedly incredible. I nodded to the rhythm as I ordered a Crown and Coke. Waiting for my drink, all I could see around me was pure happiness, and it started rubbing off on me. The bartender slid my drink over, and I found an empty couch. That sofa was like heaven felt like I was lounging on a pile of duck feathers. The singer smoothly transitioned from "Killing Me Softly" to "Ex-Factor," and it was some of the smoothest stuff I'd ever heard. I was in the zone. Music was working its magic, healing my soul. As usual, I pulled out my phone to check the gram, caught between listening and scrolling. It's a guilty pleasure, but that's just part of the modern human experience. I noticed a few new followers, thanks to the show. One name stood out ANDREA. All I could see was beach body perfection in her pics. Naturally, I had to click on her profile. The music became background noise. She was a beach lover, and her photos made the sky jealous of the damn sand. I got lost in her pictures. I knew she wasn't the woman in the black shirt and blue jeans. No way someone could look that stunning fully clothed. The music? Forgotten. Her photos became the most captivating melody I'd ever heard. Her captions were pure hit material without a beat. Even if the world's best beat maker added music, it wouldn't come close to her tune. She spun tales through her posts, and I could read between the lines. My phone screen got envious, seeing her reflection in my eyes. Then, I scrolled to one particular pic. A headshot, with the island's skyline in the backdrop. Just a hint of her green bathing suit. She was the ultimate tourist attraction. I read her words carefully. 'It's crazy to think, I used to want to get rid of my freckles somehow. I hated them. Now there are filters where people can have freckles just like mine. I've even been asked so many times over the years if I draw them on, which is so funny to me. It took 20-something years, but I finally love them.' She'd fallen in love with her freckles, and in that moment, I think I fell in love with her. I touched my own cheek, embracing the scar I got when I was four. I used to dislike it. My chickenpox scars were scattered in random places on my face. I used to hate them, too. Now, I thought they made me stand out, something unique. They were like extra birthmarks, each telling a piece of my journey from the sky, out of my mother's womb. I could appreciate her even more. And maybe, just maybe, I could make peace with my own regrets. What if I walked up to her and said, 'You're beautiful'? She might have said thanks. She might have simply smiled, never hearing it from a genuine place, not someone just trying to get with her. I'd never know, and that would be something I'd carry with me for the rest of my days. I stashed my phone, polished off what remained in my drink, which was mostly melted ice by now, and headed out of the joint and back onto the street. The crowd that had gathered on the corner was gone, and Waikiki had turned quiet. I still had a decent amount of gas in the tank, but I wasn't planning to drive anywhere else tonight. I swaggered back into the hotel, crashing onto the bed in the boss-level master bedroom. Flipping open IG, I delved into her pics. How did the universe let this one slip from its grasp? They say it's all perfection up there, but this right here? Proof even The Divine can trip up. She must've tumbled off a cloud, and the Big G couldn't quite make the save. So, what did He do? He decided to slow her descent right into the heart of New York City. I flipped to my notes, and there I wrote: the deepest, most intricate journal entry I'd ever penned.

Journal Entry: Freckles

Tonight, I performed on the stage, sharing my words with the world, but it was what happened off the stage that truly left an impact on me. It was a serendipitous encounter that began with a recipe and ended with a realization. As I recollect the evening, I remember finding a unique and whimsical recipe, one that claimed to detail the creation of Black women. It read: "two scoops of chocolate, a ½ stick of almond butter, two tablespoons of honey, grated cinnamon, agave nectar, black pepper, and a bunch of onion powder." It was a metaphorical and poetic start to my evening, one that only a writer like me could appreciate. And then, as fate would have it, I stumbled upon a hidden recipe, one that was not written but embodied by the girl I would later come to know. She was a Black girl with freckles, and her presence was like a revelation as I was immersed in my poetic musings. She sat in the second row, wearing a black top and tight-fitting jeans. All I could think about was how fortunate that seat cushion must have been to hold her. After I finished my performance, I mustered the courage to share my Instagram handle with the audience, and to my surprise, she followed me. Later that night, I found myself in my hotel room in Hawaii, scrolling through her beach pictures, feeling a profound connection to the sand, yearning to be as close to her as possible. But as I read the captions on her photos, I discovered that her beauty wasn't limited to her physical appearance. She had a deep love for nature and was a nurse, a truly remarkable and caring soul. Her name was a secret I was unwilling to admit she was the kind of girl I might never be good enough for. I questioned what she could see in me, a poetry guy adorned with tattoos covering my arms, chest, and back. I admit to being a little chubby, or, let's be honest, fat, while she sported a rock-hard six-pack that I could only dream of running my fingers over, writing poems on her skin with my tongue. She was a picture of perfection, whereas my life was hidden behind the lens of a camera that often concealed my struggles with depression. Did you know I filmed a deep, vulnerable video just four days after burying my sister, who tragically left this world on the same day as my best friend? It was as if I was carrying the weight of the world in my verses. She rarely wore makeup, unlike me, who wished I could cover up 99% of my writings, concealing the vulnerable parts of myself. It's not easy to share your deepest fears, every negative aspect of your life, or the emotional neglect I endured from my father, who could never utter the words "I love you" in our home. I was taken aback when I learned that she used to hate her freckles. To her, they were flaws, but to me, they were exquisite constellations in the vast night sky of her skin. I couldn't help but think, "Girl, do you realize how beautiful you are?" I bore my own imperfections, with a scar on my right jaw from childhood, spots left by chickenpox, and a stubborn tooth that refused to align itself. I had even worn braces twice in a futile attempt to correct it. If given the chance to love her, I would realign her spine to grant her the strength to conquer her worst fears. In the grand scheme of things, I should be the one labeled as the less attractive one, and maybe that's why I faltered when I saw her outside the venue. I was too frightened to say hi, to express how truly beautiful she was, for I didn't want her to see my own inadequacies. For a moment, I left the stage and returned to being just Junior, the man with confidence, the living and breathing writing god, the one with a sharp sense of style. But in that brief second, I also became Junior from the third grade, the insecure and uncertain boy who lacked the words to tell someone how beautiful they are. I wish I hadn't left without telling her she was beautiful. I regret that I couldn't find the words to express it, not because I didn't mean them, but because I was too afraid to confront her with my own insecurities. So, here I am, writing these words in my journal, to her and to myself, confessing my admiration and acknowledging my shortcomings.

Sincerely,
Her biggest fan and dream lover
PS: I'm sorry I can only marry you in my dreams.

I felt liberated, man. From heartbreak to awakenings. I've been through the healing, the hurting, and back to healing. Met this therapist who really worked her magic, and then, I got some therapy of my own. Amazing Grace, her pleasure symphony was something else, you know? And at that point, I had a clear image of the kind of woman I was searching for. Character was king, but this lady was the whole package, a masterpiece in my eyes. I could only imagine the conversations we'd share. So, I took a shot and slid into her DMs.

'Hey, I'm Junior. I'm not the dude you saw on stage, not the fire or the fury behind my words. I'm just a regular guy. My bad for not telling you how beautiful you are when I had the chance. Forgive me for that slip-up. I don't know if you're into artists, tough types, or sweet souls, but I hope you appreciate genuine compliments. Even if I never see you again, know that you've been the most incredible poem I've ever read, but never penned.' I plugged my phone in, stripped down, threw on some basketball shorts, and caught some Z's. I must've been out cold for hours. I was like a washed-up fighter who dared to challenge Mike Tyson. When I woke up the next morning, I went through my usual routine. First thing I saw was a text from Paulette's mom, which was unexpected.

'Remember what I told you. Live your life. My daughter has some growing up to do. One day, she'll look back and realize she let something special slip away. The grass might seem greener on the other side, but it can't compare to a lush forest teeming with life. Love you, son!'

That message really touched my soul. Then, I checked Instagram. There was that familiar red dot. My heart was racing when I clicked on it. It was a message from Andrea. I was nervous, no lie. I guess I didn't want to believe she'd actually replied. But there it was.

'Thanks for your sweet words. How about dinner tonight?'

My grin was as wide as the Brooklyn Bridge when I replied.

"Nah, not dinner. I want to give you an experience that goes way beyond food. So, when I'm not around, you won't be able to look at the sand, the moon, the night sky, or even take a breath without thinking of me." I waited until I saw that brown heart emoji pop up on my message. Junior was back, Paulette was ancient history, and Andrea was my dream come true. Then came her next message.

'Be well-rested. I want you to share a marathon of words with me tonight.'

All I could do was smile. Damn, I should write a book about this wild journey. Picture a woman tearing a page out of a hundred-page diary, and a man exposing the ninety-nine that were left. Yeah, I'm definitely writing that book. The world needs to hear a man be vulnerable, admitting his wins, losses, flaws, shortcomings, all of it. But for now, Andrea was all I could think about, and, yeah, breakfast? Pancakes. Yeah, pancakes. They sound pretty damn satisfying right now."

SEVEN LETTERS OF LOVE AND HEALING

Journal Entry: Letter to my Dearest Self,

I want to take a moment to write a love letter to you, the most important person in my life. I want to express the deepest and most sincere feelings of forgiveness, compassion, and love that I have for you. First and foremost, I want to forgive you for staying in a relationship that was not beneficial for your spiritual, physical, emotional, and mental growth. I know that you did the best you could with the knowledge and understanding you had at the time. You stayed because you believed in the power of love, and that is a beautiful and courageous thing. It's okay to have made mistakes, to have been blind to certain truths, and to have needed time to see the reality of the situation. I want to remind you that your journey of self-discovery and growth is ongoing. Every experience, even the ones that didn't serve your highest good, has been a stepping stone on the path to becoming the person you are today. Your capacity for learning and growth is a testament to your strength and resilience. You are deserving of love, both from yourself and from others. I love you for your capacity to love, even in challenging circumstances. It's important to remember that your heart is pure and your intentions were always rooted in love and the desire for a deep connection. I also want to celebrate your courage to recognize the need for change and growth. You took a step in the right direction by leaving a situation that was holding you back, and that takes incredible strength. You deserve to be proud of yourself for that. Please know that

I forgive you, wholly and completely, for any perceived mistakes or shortcomings. You are not defined by your past actions but by the love and compassion you carry within you. The journey to self-love and self-acceptance is ongoing, and I am committed to supporting you every step of the way. So, my dearest self, I want to end this love letter by saying that I love you unconditionally, and I will continue to forgive, cherish, and nurture you. Your spiritual, physical, emotional, and mental growth is a beautiful work in progress, and I am here to love and support you as you continue to evolve into the amazing person you are meant to be.

With all my love,
Junior Mitchell

Journal Entry: A letter to an evil good.

Paulette, I hope this letter finds you well. I've spent a lot of time reflecting on our relationship, the happiness we once shared, and the pain it ultimately caused. It's not easy for me to find the words to say what I need to, but I believe it's time to address the feelings that have been haunting me. Our time together has been a rollercoaster of emotions, and I've experienced the highest of highs and the lowest of lows. While we once shared beautiful moments and dreams of a future together, I can't ignore the fact that our relationship became something deeply toxic and painful. You played with my feelings, broke my heart, and it took me a long time to realize just how much you hurt me. The pain I felt made me question my self-worth and what I deserved in a relationship. It made me understand what I should never accept again in matters of love. I've learned that love should be kind, supportive, and genuine, not destructive and manipulative. Despite the anguish I've experienced, I want to thank you for showing me these valuable lessons. In the midst of our darkest moments, I've learned to appreciate the importance of self-respect, self-love, and healthy boundaries. Your actions have forced me to grow and become a stronger, more resilient person. For that, I am grateful. As I write this, I want to let go of any lingering resentment or anger and wish you well with the rest of your life. I hope you find happiness, inner peace, and fulfillment in the future. It's my sincere hope that you never have to experience the pain you inflicted on me and that you can one day look back on your actions and grow from them as well. I also hope, for the sake of your daughter, that you find the healing you need. It's my wish that she doesn't grow up and become a duplicate of the person I've experienced in our relationship. May she witness a healthier and more loving example of love in her life. This letter marks the end of our chapter together, and I am ready to move forward and heal. I hope you can find the same peace and healing in your life. May we both learn from our experiences and use them to build healthier and more loving relationships in the future. Take care, Paulette, and farewell.

Sincerely,
Junior

Journal Entry: A letter to Black Men.

I hope this letter finds you in good health and high spirits. I write to you today with the utmost respect, empathy, and a sincere desire to uplift your spirits and share some thoughts that I believe are crucial in your journey towards self-discovery and personal growth. Life, as we know it, can be a challenging and complex journey, especially for Black men who often face unique struggles and societal pressures. In our pursuit of happiness and success, we sometimes find ourselves attached to people, places, or circumstances that do not contribute positively to our well-being. It's important to understand that it's okay to let go, to release the weights that hold us back. First and foremost, I want you to know that you are deserving of love, respect, and a fulfilling life. You are not defined by your circumstances, and you have the power to change your narrative. If there are relationships in your life that drain your energy, belittle your aspirations, or make you feel less than you truly are, it's perfectly okay to distance yourself from them. You should surround yourself with people who uplift and inspire you, who see the potential within you and support your growth. Similarly, there may be places or environments that no longer serve your best interests. Be it a toxic workplace, a neighborhood that perpetuates negative stereotypes, or any other circumstance that hinders your progress, you have the power to change your situation. Do not be afraid to seek new opportunities or create a better environment for yourself. I also want to stress the importance of mental health. As strong Black men, you may feel societal expectations to bear your burdens silently. But it's essential to understand that seeking therapy or counseling is not a sign of weakness; it's a sign of courage and self-awareness. Speaking with a therapist can provide you with tools to navigate life's challenges, process trauma, and develop strategies for personal growth. It's a vital step towards becoming the strong, resilient individuals our society needs. Remember, letting go and seeking help are signs of strength, not weakness. You have a unique power within you, a strength that comes from resilience, determination, and the wisdom passed down through generations. It's this strength that will help you overcome obstacles and become the role models, leaders, and pillars of your community that our society so desperately needs. Never forget that you are not alone in your journey. Reach out to your peers, mentors, and support networks. Let them be the pillars that hold you up when you need it the most. As Black men, you have the potential to shape your own destiny and positively impact the world around you. Embrace your worth, release what no longer serves you, seek help when needed, and continue to grow into the strong, resilient, and inspirational individuals that our society can look up to with pride.

With the utmost respect and encouragement,
Junior Mitchell

Journal Entry: A letter to my Beautiful Black Women,

I want to take a moment to remind you of your strength, resilience, and the profound beauty that resides within you. You are the backbone of our community, the nurturers, the inspirations, and the pillars of love and support. Your presence in our lives means more than words can express, and we, as Black men, are deeply grateful for your comfort, warmth, and love. In a world that often fails to recognize your true worth, we see your beauty in the way you carry yourself, in the wisdom that emanates from your eyes, and in the grace with which you face life's challenges. You are more than enough, just as you are. Your unique strength and beauty are a testament to the generations of powerful women who have come before you. However, there's something important we'd like to share with you. We understand that life has not always been kind, and you may have experienced painful relationships and circumstances that left scars on your heart. It's crucial to remember that those past burdens do not define you, nor do they dictate your future. We implore you not to carry the weight of that pain into new relationships. Healing is a crucial step in our journey towards love and happiness. As Black men who cherish you, we understand that unhealed trauma can inadvertently harm not only you but also the relationships you embark upon. The love we have for you is deep and genuine, but it can't fully heal your wounds. Instead, we hope to see you take the time to heal, grow, and find peace within yourself. Unresolved trauma can lead to unintentional harm, and we don't want to see you unintentionally hurting the men who love and care for you. By prioritizing your own healing, you empower yourself and those around you to build stronger, healthier, and more loving relationships. You deserve to be with someone who sees the beautiful, whole person you are, not just a vessel for your unhealed pain. In conclusion, never forget the immense strength and beauty you carry within you. You are loved, cherished, and admired for who you are, and we are here to support you in your journey towards healing. Your well-being is essential to us, and we encourage you to take the time you need to heal and rediscover the full extent of your radiant spirit.

With love and appreciation,
Junior

Journal Entry: To my Beloved Black Men and Black Women.

I write to you today with a heart full of love, hope, and a deep concern for the state of our community. We are a people who have endured immense hardship and persevered through generations of adversity, and yet, it pains me to see the divide that has grown between us. The bickering, the division, the debates over roles, status, and importance have done more harm than good. It's time to remember why we need each other, and why we must come together as one. Our families have been fractured, our bonds strained, and the world watches in disbelief as we seem to inflict our own self-destruction. We have become experts at tearing each other down, but it's time to rebuild and uplift one another. The unity that lies within our community is a strength unparalleled, but we must recognize it and harness it. Black love, the love that we share among ourselves, is a powerful force. It's like a plate of soul food, comforting, and deeply satisfying. When we authentically love one another, we fill our lives with warmth and understanding. We are the source of strength for each other, and when we stand united, the world cannot help but be in awe of our resilience and excellence. Let us not allow the candle of Black love to burn out. Embrace it, protect it, and keep it alive in your hearts. The struggles we face, the battles we fight, and the dreams we hold, they are all shared experiences. When we support each other, we create a solid foundation upon which we can build a better future. Our ancestors fought tirelessly for our freedom, and our love for one another is the key to unlocking that freedom's full potential. In a world where our differences are often used to divide us, let us stand side by side, celebrating our unique qualities, but recognizing that those differences only make us stronger together. We must remember that we are not in competition with each other; instead, we are collaborators in the grand story of our people. Together, we can achieve greatness, lift our children to new heights, and inspire the generations to come. Our community's future is in our hands, and it's time to heal the wounds, restore the bonds, and forge a path forward filled with unity, resilience, and unwavering love for one another. So, my brothers and sisters, let us concentrate on what truly matters loving one another authentically, holding each other up when we are at our best, and most importantly, when we are at our lowest. Together, we are an unstoppable force, and Black love is our guiding light. Let it shine brightly, illuminating the path towards a brighter and more prosperous future.

With love and unwavering hope,
Junior

Journal Entry: Dear Transparency.

I hope this letter finds you well, though I know you are always present, silently waiting for those who dare to embrace your power. Today, I wish to extend my heartfelt gratitude to you for the remarkable influence you've had on my life. You have bestowed upon me the courage to share a story that many would, and indeed have, shied away from. Transparency, you've been my guiding light, my silent confidant, and my source of strength. In a world often shrouded in shadows and secrets, you stood as a beacon of truth and authenticity. It wasn't easy to be transparent, to peel back the layers of my experiences and emotions, to reveal the vulnerabilities that lay hidden beneath. Yet, your unwavering presence urged me forward, pushing me to confront my past and speak my truth. Through the act of being transparent, I have not only come to terms with what once haunted me but have also found liberation. The burden of silence that I once carried has been lifted, replaced by the freedom of expression and self-acceptance. In baring my soul, I have discovered the beauty in imperfection and the strength that can be drawn from vulnerability. As I share my story, I have seen how my transparency has the power to touch the lives of others. It serves as a reminder that we are not alone in our struggles, that our pain and triumphs are shared experiences, and that there is strength in unity. I have received countless messages from individuals who, inspired by my journey, have begun their own paths toward healing and self-discovery. It is in these moments that I recognize the true impact of transparency, the way it ripples through the lives of others, igniting hope and courage. Transparency, you have helped shape my future in ways I could never have imagined. By acknowledging the past and embracing it, I have paved the way for a brighter and more authentic tomorrow. I have learned that the power of truth is transformative and that it opens doors to new opportunities and deeper connections. I carry your lessons with me, using them to navigate the complexities of life with honesty and integrity. In closing, I want to thank you once more, Transparency, for being my constant companion and guiding force. Your influence has not only helped me find my voice but has allowed me to be a beacon of hope and inspiration for others. I am committed to carrying your torch forward, as I continue my journey towards self-discovery and encourage others to embrace their own transparency. Don't you ever leave me, us, or those that are not yet here to embark on this beautiful journey called life.

With heartfelt gratitude and unwavering respect,
Junior

Journal Entry: To Love. The greatest drink on the planet.

I wanted to take a moment to express my gratitude to you, for all that you've taught me over the years. You've been a powerful force in my life, bringing both joy and pain, but through it all, you've helped me grow and prepare for the love that awaits me in the future. Firstly, I want to thank you for the beautiful moments you've given me. The sweet memories, the warmth of a caring touch, and the laughter we've shared. You've shown me the incredible heights of happiness and how love can make life feel truly magical. These moments have filled my heart and enriched my soul, and for that, I'm endlessly grateful. But I also want to express my gratitude for the challenges you've presented, the heartaches and disappointments. Through these painful experiences, I've learned about resilience, patience, and the depth of my own emotions. I've discovered that even in the midst of heartbreak, love can endure and help us heal. You've taught me that true love is not always without its hardships, but it's these very trials that can lead to growth and transformation. You've changed the way I love people, in the literal sense. You've made me more compassionate, more understanding, and more open to the needs and desires of others. I've come to realize that love is not just about receiving, but also about giving selflessly. It's about empathy, kindness, and support. You've shown me that love is a two-way street, where both hearts connect, share, and grow together. As I look to the future, I carry the lessons you've bestowed upon me in my heart. I promise that I will never waver in my commitment to love. I will cherish the person who is designed for me, embracing her with all the wisdom you've given me. I'll be patient, understanding, and supportive, and I'll always strive to make her feel cherished and valued. I'll remember that love is a journey, and I'll be there through the ups and downs, with unwavering dedication. In conclusion, Love, I want to say thank you for everything you've brought into my life. I'm grateful for the lessons, the memories, and the strength you've given me. You've transformed me into a better person, and I am eager to share the love you've prepared me for with the woman of my future. No matter what happens, I'll hold onto you, knowing that you are a powerful force that guides us towards a more meaningful and authentic existence. Furthermore, I do recognize that in order to love my future wife properly, I must learn to love myself properly, authentically, and with the acceptance that I will fall short at times. You taught me that if I can't love myself, then I can't love her properly. Thank you, Love. How some people don't appreciate you, I will never understand.

With love and appreciation,
Junior

EPILOGUE

As we close the pages of "Southern Fried Intimacy," we find ourselves reflecting on a journey that has taken us deep into the heart of relationships, love, and connection. The stories woven throughout the book have illuminated the intricacies of human relationships, offering a unique blend of charm, wisdom, and a touch of that Southern hospitality that warms the soul. Asking people about their newfound perspectives on love after delving into these tales is akin to inviting them to sit on the porch and share the sweet tea of their thoughts. The characters in "Southern Fried Intimacy" have faced the highs and lows of love, exposing the raw and unfiltered essence of intimacy beneath the warm sun. So, dear reader, what is your new view on the aspect of love? Has the Southern charm of these stories influenced your perception of what it means to connect with others? Perhaps you now see love as a slow dance on a front porch, where the lightning bugs create a magical backdrop, or maybe it's a spicy jambalaya of passion and understanding, a blend that keeps the heart and palate satisfied. The beauty of "Southern Fried Intimacy" lies in its ability to transcend boundaries and speak to the universal language of the heart. Love, after all, knows no geographic constraints. It is a force that binds us all, transcending cultural nuances and weaving a tapestry of shared experiences. As you reflect on the stories that unfolded within these pages, take a moment to savor the flavors of love that have left an indelible mark on your soul. Has the beautiful setting added a touch of warmth to your perception of love, or have you discovered a newfound appreciation for the complexities that make each relationship unique? In the spirit of Southern hospitality, let's continue the conversation. Share your thoughts with those around you, whether it's over a plate of barbecue or a cup of sweet tea. After all, the beauty of love lies not just in the stories we read but in the conversations they spark and the connections they nurture. And so, we bid farewell to the tales of "Southern Fried Intimacy," grateful for the journey it has taken us on and eager to carry the lessons of love into our own lives. May your heart be as full as a Southern Sunday dinner, and may you continue to find joy in the sweet, slow dance of intimacy.

ABOUT THE AUTHOR

Joe McClain Jr. is a retired Navy veteran, author of 12 books, spoken word artist, and dynamic inspirational speaker. His literary works have been obtained by numerous figures in professional sports and entertainment. He is a former top 25 world ranked poet who continues to tour extensively nationally, and internationally. He has opened for platinum selling R&B/Neo Soul artists Joe, Jon. B, and Dwele. He currently resides in San Diego, California.

Made in the USA
Monee, IL
27 January 2024

52068774R00128